The Ag

RECKONING

VOLUME 1

THOMAS
ANTHONY LAY

The Age Of Reckoning

volume 1

~ A World of Naeisus Story ~

Thomas Anthony Lay

RhetAskew Publishing

United States of America

Cover Illustration
& Interior Design

This book is
dedicated to my Dad,

ANTHONY MAX LAY.

The impact you left on me
and those lucky enough
to know you is the fuel
for my inspiration.

Prologue

Wisps of smoke from a burning candle danced up the stone wall. The excited whispers and low chortles of four children brought warmth to this otherwise cold castle bedroom. Prince Areth lay in his bed beside two of his three younger sisters, a thick duvet pulled up to their necks.

"Can we have one story before we sleep, Father?"

King Areth III smiled at the three children in bed. His youngest rested on his hip, nestled in his arm. "What do you think, Anya?"

The two-year-old beamed and nodded.

"Very well, my children." He placed Anya on the bed with her siblings, then strolled to an old, chipped bookcase shunted against the far wall. With a finger along the spines, he scanned the books mumbling their titles.

"Ah-ha!" Without revealing the book's title, he turned to the children. The light from the two full moons, Bo and Dalon, glinted off his deep jade eyes as he grinned.

The children gazed at him expectantly, their faces alight with anticipation. Their father sat on the bed and opened the thick volume.

"This is a brief history of Naeisus, started over one thousand solar cycles ago by our ancestor, King Areth I. Refined, abridged, translated, and filled in by the countless kings that followed."

The children clapped, then nestled in to the prince's bed ready to hear the story.

The king cleared his throat and read. "In the beginning, the divine entity, Naeis, created and breathed life into six Yultah. He tasked them to create and preside over a small world they came to call Naeisus."

His eyes flitted between the pages of the book and his children, and a loving smile was sure to follow each time.

"These God-like beings, each having their own unique powers and tasks, had all agreed to create a utopia. It would serve as a home to the organisms they would later bring to life. First, there was Mys, the Goddess of Light. She bathed Naeisus in a radiant, warm light by creating a perfect star lost amongst the countless others. Dion, the God of Darkness, created the moons. They stabilise the rotation of the newly formed planet and add beauty to the otherwise plain, speckled blackness of the night. Tur shaped the land with his skilled hands, crafting the mountains and valleys, the canyons and the cliffs, and the mighty volcanoes.

"This God of Land created a vast difference in raised land and lowlands, which allowed the Goddess of Water, Bui, to fill the lowlands with beautiful, globe-spanning oceans. These two Yultah worked side-by-side to create a flourishing environment ready for Gol, the God of Life.

Gol filled it with his living creations. From the tallest twisting Triash trees to the smallest of organisms, life thrived and evolved in this beautiful world. Naeis marvelled at this land and blessed it with the gift of time, before the Goddess of Death, Knas, took it upon herself to care for all the souls who had come to the end of their living lives and were ready to pass over into the next life."

Evelyn, the second eldest child spoke up. "So, is that what happens when people die, Father?"

"Yes, my sweet. The great Yultah, Knas, looks after our souls, transporting them to the afterlife. We need not fear it."

Evelyn's younger sister, Eleanor folded her arms. "Well, I don't fear it! I bet Knas is a beautiful lady who looks after us like Lissy does."

The king laughed; a deep, infectious laugh. "I bet she is!" He continued, running his index finger down the page.

"Naeis forbade the Yultah to have any direct interaction with their land. Obeying the request of the Creator, they each embodied a small piece of their power into a shard. When combined, the six shards created the Yultah Crystal; anyone who possessed it would have the ability to bend the world to their will, harnessing the power of the Yultah themselves. This crystal was bestowed unto the land, only to be discovered by the purest of heart when the time was right.

"Upon its discovery, the bearer would know its purpose by gazing into its infinite beauty and listening closely to the whispers of the Yultah contained inside. "For the first millennia, each race was quite content to keep to themselves. They lived in ignorance of the other races slowly building alongside them. One by one, Man, Marusi, and Wolven developed their own hierarchy. They each created their own system to govern their kin, all differing in their own unique way, yet echoing subtle aspects of each other.

"Man developed a straightforward monarchy where initially the family most capable of leading took charge. Generation after generation, their descendants would remain sole rulers of the people. The aquatic Marusi also developed a monarchical system but chose to elect their leaders with each generation, so the families of the He'en had no more standing in society than any other citizen. The Wolven evolved from forest-dwelling hounds, and they relied on displays of strength and power to decide their leader, known as the Ulv.

"To become the Ulv, one of them would simply have to take the position by force and defend it. Strength and size won the respect and loyalty of all their people.

"The Korkrenus, however, were different. They were the only sentient race to form a society where each one had their own rightful place. They respected the land around them and saw themselves at one with the natural world as if they were guardians of Naeisus. Despite their gigantic size and incredible physical power, they were the most gentle and harmonious of the races; for this reason, the Yultah decided to bestow unto the Korkrenus, the gift of the Yultah crystal."

Prince Areth's face dropped. "The crystal is why there is so much fighting and war."

"I'm afraid that's true, my son."

"What happened to it?"

"Well, The Yultah Crystal was discovered in the Korkrenus capital city of Joktuun, revealing itself to these worthy creatures who had proven they were genuinely pure of heart. It was through this gift, and the whispers contained inside of it, that all of creation was revealed. Although the crystal itself was kept a strict secret, the truth that lay within it soon spread to the rest of Naeisus, through tales and songs. Humbled by this gift, the Korkrenus vowed never to use it. The image of the world and all things in it was surely made for a reason, and they had become the rightful guardians of this most powerful relic.

"Soon, each race began to fear the others that surrounded them. Hatred and violence started to swell, and for hundreds of solar cycles, there was war, turmoil, and hardship. During this time, a powerful and dedicated King of Man defied the Goddess Knas upon his untimely death and reclaimed his soul. This incredible act resulted in the birth of the Forsaken—a race of corrupt, undead beings, content only with power and control.

"Shortly following this defiance of the Gods, the secret of the Yultah crystal was leaked to the rest of Naeisus. Greed filled the hearts of all denizens of the world, and an assault on the Korkrenus capitol city was carried out. The attack was swift and there was no time to use the crystal for defence. Thinking quickly, with desperation in his heart, one of the Korkrenus pummelled his giant, rocky fist into a magnificent golden pillar which held the crystal. Upon destroying the pillar, he grabbed the shimmering crystal in his huge earthen hands and held it high above his head. He used his enormous thumbs and overwhelming strength to crack the crystal into its six component pieces, then handed the shards to his companions, ordering them to leave the city and scatter these shards far and wide. Three shards were violently recovered before they left the confines of the city, but three evaded discovery.

"One was taken across the sea, another was hidden in flame, and the third was kept in the last place anyone would think to look—in Joktuun itself.

"The battle soon grew until Joktuun erupted into a violent, bloody brawl. It was then discovered each shard had its own individual power. Only a fraction of the power of the completed crystal, but these powers from the captured shards were used to bring a horrible and sudden end to the battle at Joktuun.

"For many solars, shards were lost, found, stolen, sold, bought, and smuggled from race to race as blind killing and greed-fuelled wars shook Naeisus to its very foundations. The world was in utter devastation, and every leader's sole aim was to gather all six shards and own the complete Yultah Crystal. Every race was driven to be the one to possess the final power."

The eyelids of the three girls fell heavy. Anya curled up with her thumb in her mouth, fast asleep, while Evelyn and Eleanor drifted on the verge of slumber.

Prince Areth, however, sat upright with a furrowed brow. He lowered his voice, so he wouldn't disturb his sisters, but his anger still shone through. "Why does the world have to fight all the time? I remembered reading about a time when all Naeisus was allied. Why is it so hard to just become allies again?"

The king bowed his head and huffed; the weight of his duty pressed hard on his shoulders. "For the most part, it's greed. Why should one share a power when one can have it all for oneself?"

"But while everyone fights, there is no power to share. I'd rather have a share of power than none at all. Does that not make sense?"

"It makes perfect sense, my boy. Now get some sleep." He stood and clapped just loudly enough to jostle the two older girls awake, while Anya remained undisturbed. "Come girls, to your own rooms now. Evelyn, please take Anya."

"Yes, Father."

King Areth made his way to the study, his son's words echoing in his mind.

A share of power is better than none at all. Naeisus allied once again...

Chapter 1

King Areth III

King Areth III, sole ruler of the race of Man, flicked through the last few pages of *The Age of Fire and Wyrmsbane* and folded shut the thick leather-bound cover.

Shadows danced and cavorted on the cold stone walls and heavy oak bookcases. Wind ghosted inside, licking the candlelight. A quick glint caught his weathered eyes as he cast them over the heavy desk and brought them to rest on a simple, rough-cut gemstone. Candlelight reflected off his gold signet ring and illuminated the brilliant white gemstone. It appeared to absorb this light and radiate warmth in a gentle haze.

He reached for the Mys shard, rotating it, studying every uneven facet in detail and formulating a risky plan.

A subtle creak whispered the arrival of a large visitor.

"Sire..." Sir Victor ducked under the doorframe shoulder first to accommodate his bear-like frame and crept into the room.

"My friend, please, take a seat." The king gestured to an empty armchair. "What brings you to the study tonight?"

"It's late, but I came to remind you about the council meeting tomorrow. I know how much you love to study." Sir Victor's chocolate coloured eyes seemed drawn to the shard rolling in the king's fingers, and then to the haggard book. "Sire? You have that look on your face. What are you planning?"

The king broke into a smile. "You know me too well, Victor."

"I should think so with the countless number of missions, scouts, raids and battles we've endured together!" He chuckled.

"Indeed! How many of those were successful?"

"Almost all of them, yet again proving your capability of planning and leading."

The king placed the shard on the table and leaned forward. "So why does your face scream worry?"

"Because none of your plans have ever involved this level of research." Sir Victor also leaned forward, lowering his tone. "And never before have I seen such concern on your face."

The shard began to vibrate as a low, subtle rumble swept through Straeta, intensifying for an instant, and then subsiding.

"That, right there; something big is happening, Victor. We've all felt those tremors. They are becoming more frequent and more powerful. We need allies if we're going to figure out the source and solution. Our war will mean nothing if Naeisus is wiped clean. We're not even safe here on Mannis. If something comes forth from the

Golzhad volcano, our island offers no real protection." King Areth's eyes burned with a familiar intensity.

"What do you mean, *something*?" Sir Victor pointed at the volume. "These Wyrms you keep reading about never actually existed. For centuries people have looked for evidence of them and found nothing, not even as much as a bone fragment. They're just fairy tales written by kings of old—by your ancestors."

"Perhaps..." His gaze dropped. The chair scraped along the stone floor as he heaved himself to his feet. "We will discuss this more in tomorrow's meeting. For now, we should retire."

"Another excellent plan, Sire." Sir Victor rose from his seat, grinning, bowed, and slipped out.

On his way out, the king paused, picked another large volume titled *Royal Bloodlines of Naeisus*, and opened the book to a page he had bookmarked a few nights prior. He refreshed his memory and skimmed the information about perhaps the most famous king in history; his great ancestor, King Areth I. Much like the current king, Areth I boasted a loyal following and complete reverence.

A sketch of the ancient king, dressed in full leather battle armour, bore an uncanny resemblance to the current king, sharing the same chiselled jawline, the same thick, wavy locks, and the same strong, determined stare that penetrated the horizon and beyond. This magnificent first King Areth was the only ruler in all of Naeisus to form an alliance between all five races—an alliance responsible for dealing with the Golzhad volcano eruption so long ago.

That alliance formed a grand army led by King Areth I himself who was, by this point, no longer among the living. He was the first person to contest the Knas, Yultah of Death, and reclaim his presence among the living, thus birthing the Forsaken. Soon after Areth I's exile by his own son, Man and Forsaken grew to hate each other, eventually waging war against one another, tearing the two races apart, and truly separating them by more than just living bodies.

It was also written that less than two-hundred solars after he became King of the Forsaken, Areth I was overthrown by his own power-hungry people. They accused him of being corrupted by the pain of death and through their treachery he was handed back to Knas, experiencing true death.

King Areth III took a moment to look at the square ring wrapped around his finger. A small, lonesome diamond nestled in the top left quarter with etchings of sunbeams surrounding it, while complex swirls symbolising light and darkness respectively covered the complete right half. In his youth his mother had regaled him with the story of this ring which had been passed down his bloodline as a sign of strength and leadership.

He ran his fingers over the sketch in admiration of what his ancestor achieved.

"I will follow your footsteps, great ancestor."

The king sat back down, pondering his plan in the comfort of his padded armchair. His empty stare rested on the ruby-red wax dripping down a solitary brass candlestick.

There are definitely aspects of this plan that I'm missing; I must consult the council tomorrow. I hope I can get them all on side. If they disagree, there's not a chance, but if I can pull it off...

The council consisted of five members including himself—one to represent each of the aspects needed to run a healthy and prosperous kingdom.

The candle flickered with a greater intensity as it burned close to the base, signalling that the time to rest and recuperate had truly come. He needed rest, so he would have all of his cunning during the morning's meeting.

Heaving his lean frame out of the leather armchair, he picked up the Mys shard, blew the candle out, and edged towards the door, feeling his way along one of the rough bookcases as he went. His strong hand reached for the brass knob and pulled open the heavy oak door.

Careful not to wake the children, the king slipped out and crept along the cold stone corridor. The night engulfed him as he made his way to the master bedroom at the end of the hallway, pressing his ear against each of the three-bedroom doors as he went, listening for his children's delicate breathing. A smile crossed his face with each room he passed, growing as he moved from Areth's door, to Evelyn's, and finally to Eleanor and Anya's.

Good. My beloveds slumber peacefully for another night.

He neared his room and ran his fingertips along the cobbled wall as he went until he reached the furthest door and crept inside.

The darkness relieved its shroud as he pressed the bedroom door shut behind him, broken by a flood of moonlight pouring its way through the window. He drew the heavy curtains shut to suffocate the last remnant of light. Removing his silk evening-wear, he closed his eyes and stood in nothing but his cloth undergarments, breathing from his stomach. His hands came to rest on opposite shoulders. His fingers passed over three claw-gouged battle scars, bringing with them difficult memories which furrowed his brow.

As if frozen in time, he breathed, meditated, and prepared his mind.

* * *

A slither of morning sunlight burned onto the king's eyelids through a crack between the curtains. He kicked and flailed beneath his sheets before gasping for breath and bolting upright. Sweat dripped from his brow as his breathing settled.

Damn you, Knas. Why do you torment my dreams with visions of death and heartache?

Despite having four children, there was no queen to keep him company; despite having many proposals and requests from eager women, he simply and politely rejected them all.

He was fiercely loyal to his children, and would never risk anything to endanger them; not only were they his heirs, they were his life. Prince Areth was the eldest at twelve, and was to become King Areth IV one day, therefore he was educated more rigorously than his three younger sisters—Evelyn, Eleanor and Anya, aged ten, six, and three respectively.

King Areth heard their playful laughter outside—the perfect sound to wake up to—and smiled. He walked toward the window and drew back the heavy, crimson curtains.

Sunlight flooded his room, dispelling the darkness within. The children chased each other through the courtyard and his chest puffed. They ducked and dived around the hedges and shrubs lining the cobblestone road to Straetan Keep. He smiled to himself as little Anya struggled to keep up with her older siblings, though still giggling and squealing whenever she was the one being chased.

The children all shared the same striking red hair and deep jade eyes as most of King Areth's lineage, as well as the famous steely determination and wondrous ambition of their common bloodline.

He backed away from the window, still smiling, and scanned the sparse room looking for something to wear. An elegant four-poster bed stood dominant in the centre of his room, and at the base sat a small footlocker containing his finest weapons and armaments, most forged from Eveston steel.

An armour stand proudly displayed his fiercest battle armour, designed by the most skilled blacksmiths in Eveston. This armour had been reforged and perfected over many solar cycles and was unmatched in combat, able to repel even the mightiest slash from Wolven claws.

When coupled with the healing power of the Mys shard—which slotted snugly into a hidden compartment behind the crest on the breastplate—the wearer became almost unbeatable in a one-on-one battle.

The king picked his most regal formal wear from the grand wardrobe. A long-tailed purple jacket with gold trimmings to compliment a white shirt underneath, a pair of his most fitted black trousers, and pristine black leather boots. He ran a hairbrush through his thick, auburn locks, occasionally snagging on a knot as he smoothed his hair. A small gold crown, adorned with gems of every colour, glistened in the morning light.

At least I don't have to wear that cumbersome thing to council meetings.

He made his way down the corridor and descended the spiral staircase into the beautifully adorned downstairs hallway. "Damn it all to Knas, it's nearly midday! There's no time for breakfast," he mumbled. He marched toward a pair of giant oak doors at the end of the hallway—the front entrance of Straetan Keep. With a deep inhalation, he grabbed the brass handles and heaved the doors.

His little ones greeted him with beaming faces. They halted their play in the delight of seeing their father, and ran to him screaming. "Father! Father!"

He bent on one knee to greet them, holding them close and kissing each on the forehead. Their freshly washed hair and joyous cries made him truly happy. His heart warmed in his chest, as if ready to sing. They didn't know it, but these children gave him more strength and courage than any blade, armour, or gem ever could.

Speaking softly, the king addressed his children with the news of his meeting. "My babies listen closely." He kept his voice warm but stern. "I have to attend my usual weekly meeting now; however, this one may be different. I may have to go away for a while."

Sad faces and groans met this news, and little Anya's eyes filled with tears.

"No, come on now, I've been away before and I always return. Lissy will take care of you like always. You like staying with her, don't you?" He turned and addressed his son, "Areth, if I must go, you're in charge. I want you to attend all the meetings for me and listen and learn. Remember: Be wise; rule with your head, not with your heart."

The young prince nodded and hugged his father tight.

King Areth hugged each of them one last time before standing. "Go play, my children." He watched for a few moments more, unable to stop a wide smile from creeping up his cheeks.

Tearing his gaze away, he entered the keep and marched briskly to the meeting hall. With his jacket tail flying behind him, he approached the double doors of the royal meeting room and gripped the handles. Taking a deep breath, he pushed the doors wide. The four other members already sat around the circular table, watching him stride toward the one remaining chair.

"Your Majesty," chorused the small council.

"Good morning, fine people." He sat between Sir Victor Blackrock and Lissy Lector, clasped his hands on the table, and cleared his throat. "My good, noble men and women, may I first hear your usual updates on the affairs of the Kingdom before I bring us to the main order of today?" He twiddled his thumbs.

Head of the Royal Guard and Commander of War, Sir Victor, spoke first; his well-formed words were low and gruff, but confident. "Your Majesty, there have been a high number of Wolven sightings from outpost Markuss to the East. What is more peculiar is that there have been zero attacks; they seem to be scouting us." Sir Victor's arms waved about, animating his speech.

"And what action have you taken, my good man?"

"I have sent one battalion of kytling riders to fortify the outpost. I have also sent a battalion of horse riders to outpost Johan further south, in case of the need for immediate back-up." Sir Victor's gold-trimmed Straeten armour clinked against the table as he drew imaginary lines between invisible outposts on the table top.

"Very good, Sir Victor. The safety of our society is our number one priority. I have the utmost faith in your leadership, and I trust your decisions."

Sir Victor smiled through his bushy black beard. His chair groaned under the weight of the giant man.

The king's gaze followed the table around to the Master Technical Engineer and Overseer of the city of Eveston. "Philos, how is Eveston? And what new technologies are you working on?"

Philos replied in an airy, mystical tone—light, but somehow discomforting. He leaned forward in his chair and spread his aged, bony fingers out on the table. "Your Majesty, my research is ensuring prosperity in Eveston and indeed, all our people. Firstly, I am researching a new compound that will allow our furnaces to burn even hotter, further tempering our Eveston steel. Secondly, I am working on a new type of machine that could aid many of them simultaneously. However, I may need to borrow the Mys shard . . . with your permission of course." His eyes filled with the hope of getting his hands on the powerful relic.

"My friend, that is not possible; at least not currently, but we will speak more of that shortly."

The old alchemist's hope-filled eyes hinted of resentment as he removed his hands from the table.

"What of the explosive weapons you were working on?"

"Ah! Of course, Your Majesty. I have finished the prototype, and would request that you test them." Philos produced a small leather pouch from the pocket of his apron and dipped his hand in. He removed a small, metallic sphere and placed it carefully on the table, his eyes wide. "I call this a Fireball. Toss one into the midst of an enemy force, and it will explode violently, causing severe damage and burns. Be careful with them, you would not want one exploding close to you. I suggest throwing them from a distance."

Philos stroked the Fireball entranced by its shiny surface. He placed it back into the pouch and reluctantly handed it to the king.

"Thank you, my good man. These will be valuable weapons in times of great need. I shall let you know how well they perform." King Areth placed the pouch beside him with care.

Philos hunched over and nodded.

The king's eyes settled next on a short, stocky man with fresh, crimson cheeks and a scraggly grey beard.

"Mister Stone, your report on the resources, if you will."

William sat up and hauled his chair closer to the table, his body rippling as he jumped forwards. He rested two stubby hands on his rotund belly and chortled. "We've 'ad a very bountiful season, Yer Majesty! Our wood stockpiles are at an all-time high, and we 'ave plenty o' stone to reinforce them defences!"

"Very good! And food? As winter draws closer, we must ensure there is plenty of food."

"Aye, Sire! Food is also plentiful. -Our fishing ships 'ave hauled enough fish to feed both Straeta an' Eveston fer months! Farms are producing well, there be enough crops fer us all. In fact, Majesty, I reckon we've 'ad a better solar than we've ever 'ad!"

William leaned back in his chair and stroked his beard, grinning broadly. Although his friendly face made that smile warm and welcoming, his stained and misshapen teeth proved a distraction.

The other council members nodded with pride. "Congratulations, William!" said Lissy. Followed by, "Good show!" from Sir Victor.

The king clapped delicately before fixing his eyes on the final council member, a petite woman with flowing, golden hair. "Lissy, my dear, is the treasury in order?" His eyes softened.

"Certainly, Your Majesty; although due to the recent wars, we've lost our positive standing with the Marusi. They are no longer willing to trade with us, meaning our coffers will suffer. There is enough for now, but we must establish more trade routes soon." Lissy spoke lightly, but with such gravity the council began to mutter amongst themselves.

The king used a gesture of his hands to call for hush, but he let a smile slip out from the side of his mouth. "Thank you, Miss Lector."

Lissy's brow furrowed as she noticed he had a hand in his pocket. "Sire?"

"I have my own news to bring which will help us establish more trade routes and possibly end the wars."

Whispers invaded the room and true confusion solidified onto the faces of these, his most trusted advisors.

"Sire? End wars?" Sir Victor thumped a palm onto the table. "Hundreds of solar cycles of fighting ended just like that?"

King Areth paused, before pushing his seat backwards and standing. He circled the table, slowly passing behind each confused council member, while arranging the mess of words in his head. With hands clasped behind his back, he inhaled through his teeth.

"My great ancestor, King Areth I, once succeeded in uniting the five races of Naeisus. In doing so, he ended all conflict in the land and brought about world peace.

Sir Victor, your great ancestor, Sir Peter Wyrmslayer, the greatest swordsman who ever lived, aided him. We have been fighting these pointless wars for centuries now—for what?" He stopped pacing and looked to the members.

Silence and bewilderment befell the room, until Sir Victor raised a finger. "With respect, Sire, each race has its own reasons for fighting. For us, it's about stopping another race from gathering the shards and thus ensuring the longevity of our people. Is that not so?"

"So," countered the king. "Are the Marusi not doing the same? What about the Wolven? Nobody knows what the Korkrenus are doing, or even if they still exist!"

Again, silence and confusion clouded the room.

The king returned to his seat, and his face grew serious as his hands fidgeted. "I don't like senseless killing. I don't like suffering. And... I'm afraid." His eyes dropped with this confession.

Lissy placed a comforting hand on his shoulder. "Afraid of what?"

"The Wyrms. If they return with Naeisus in this state, life as we know it will end."

William exploded into a hearty chuckle and slammed a hand on the table in amusement. "Wyrms, Sire? There ain't no such thing as Wyrms! Those stories in them there books of yers are fantasy! Fairy tales! An' even if they was real, they're all dead now, or we'd know 'bout it. No, them so-called Wyrms was only a metaphor fer the discord in the land, methinks."

"And what if they are real, Mister Stone? The rumblings, we've all felt them!"

"Aye! Just tectonic movement, that is!"

"Even so, this state of war and unrest cannot be allowed to continue. Regardless of my ancestor's reason for uniting the world, he did it. It's my duty as King to do the same." He stopped and bowed his head, inhaling deeply through gritted teeth, then shot a look of desperation to each of the council members.

He pulled out his hand and produced the beautifully pale Mys shard, placing it on the table for all to see. Its mystical brilliance formed a faint haze around its rugged exterior, making it difficult to look at, yet almost impossible to look away from.

Philos' hands crept out to touch the shard, but Areth snatched it away.

With the trance broken, the king gave them a small smile and re-pocketed the gem. "The shards. The shards are what the fighting is all about. Their mystical powers bring promise of Utopia to whichever society possesses them, and it's not hard to see why! All of your faces filled with greedy desire. It seems these... these... rocks, are all it takes to turn a society to war. It has occurred to me that to end acts of selfishness, perhaps one needs to perform an act of selflessness."

William placed both hands on the table and leaned into the conversation, his chair groaning. "With the greatest of respect Majesty... Yer not plannin' on doing what I think, are ya?"

The king pointed at William. "If what you're thinking involves giving up the Mys—our only shard—then yes."

Sir Victor slapped his gigantic hand onto the table. "Sire! Have you gone mad? We would lose the only object that gives us any respect in this world. We would become sitting ducks, a target to be eliminated!"

"Would we, Sir Victor? By not having a shard, what reason would anyone else have for attacking us?"

"For our cities, our resources, our technology! Not to mention the Forsaken want our people to add to their own numbers."

"Valid reasons, Sir Victor, and I acknowledge all of that. Just hear my plan out, before you object."

Lissy raised a subtle hand to Sir Victor, interrupting a further objection. "Please, allow the good King to speak."

Sir Victor nodded and settled back.

"Here is what I suggest. Sir Victor and I will take a small force, and ride to the Undying Fortress to meet with Queen Lucia. I shall offer the Mys Shard in return for the allegiance of the Forsaken—"

"The Forsaken?!" interrupted Sir Victor. A sharp glare from King Areth silenced him.

"Yes, the Forsaken! They are our best chance; I have met with the Queen on several occasions, and I feel she would be more sympathetic to an alliance than would the stone-hearted Marusi. The Wolven are constantly sending scouting parties and mounting attacks on our outposts, so it has to be the Forsaken."

"What happens if they say no, Sire?" Lissy asked.

"If they say no, then my party and I shall surely be sent away, if we're lucky."

Lissy hesitated. "And if you're unlucky?"

"They will likely kill us for the shard, and the wars will continue. My life is a small price to pay for a shot at peace, even if it is just a chance."

"Alright, alright," interrupted William. "Say we go through with this plan o' yers, Majesty. Let's say the Forsaken agree to an alliance. What then?"

"The news of our alliance will spread, putting the other nations on their back foot. Our combined forces should then be able to gain the support of the others, perhaps even uniting the world once more. It's a long shot, I know, but I consider it our only chance. Is that not worth something?" With the flats of his hands on the table, the king glanced at each council member in turn.

"I need your support on this. If we don't act now, we—"

"I'm with you, Your Majesty. This world is ripe for change and your plan sounds like the beginning of that change." Philos caressed his bony hands against one another.

"Thank you, Philos. William?"

William's broad face screwed up, painted with deep thought as his hands fondled the long, wiry bristles of his beard. With a lazy shrug and reluctance in his voice, he said, "I guess I'll be keepin' things in check while yer away then, Majesty."

Excited, Areth faced Lissy and nodded for her approval. She sighed. "Your children will always be safe with me. Go . . . and don't you dare fail."

The king put a reassuring hand on Sir Victor's thick shoulder and looked him dead in the eye. "Come on, my good man. This could be the adventure you've been waiting for your entire life! You keep dreaming about your next big feat, after that astounding victory at Blackrock!"

Sir Victor growled, and defeated, he agreed. "Argh! Let's do it. Although if the Forsaken want to fight, I promise you I will show them that the pain of being dead is more than favourable to what I will bring them!"

King Areth jumped from his position, and clapped his hands together with sheer excitement. "Sir Victor, prepare a small force—no more than twenty of your finest kytling riders. I shall prepare my own kytling, see my children, and then meet you beyond the city gates as soon as possible. If we depart when the force is ready, we can make Timbrol West before sundown, and sail to Timbrol East during the night."

"Now?" The knight's eyebrows raised.

"Yes! We must make haste. There is no time to be wasted! We can rest on the voyage to Timbrol East."

William Stone chuckled. "Well, I reckon that's us done! May the light o' Mys guide his Majesty!"

With that, King Areth left the room in a hurry, muttering.

Chapter 2

The Journey

As he stroked the beaked helmet on the armour stand, King Areth contemplated the journey ahead.

Tomorrow we'll be beyond the outposts. We'll need to keep an eye out for Wolven.

He ran his fingers across every detail of the intricate crest on the shimmering gold-trimmed breastplate.

If we ride hard for the Darklands, they shouldn't follow us there.

He pressed the crest inwards and slid it to the left to reveal a perfect set of six cradles for the shards.

Then all we have to do is find the Fortress.

With care, he placed the Mys shard into one of the small cradles, resealed and admired the elegant Crest of Man. An intricate floral pattern surrounded two majestic kytlings, their backs to one another. The impeccable hand-carved detail of the large birds was perfection. Their eagle-like heads tilted to the sky, allowing their sleek feathered necks to flow into bulbous bodies. At their sides rested two rounded wings, incapable of flight but ideal for balance as they sprinted across the land on their two sturdy legs.

And after we find it, comes the matter of a peaceful and diplomatic entrance.

The king hesitated, then unclipped the armour from its mounting and slid it over his head. A shiver trickled down his spine and hairs stood on end as the cold metal brushed the back of his neck. Piece-by-piece, he donned the rest of his protective gear. His muscles engaged to support the increasing weight. Plate legs, sabatons and gauntlet-legs, slipped on with ease and pulled tight. The armour clung to him and acted as an extension to his own skin. He grabbed the helmet, laid it on the floor, and opened the weapons chest. He rifled through the selection of weapons.

Auvreal? Too heavy... Ichtheon! No, too short. Aha! Lycanire.

He lifted a decorative scabbard and drew the sleekest blade, made from the same Eveston forged steel as his armour. Lycanire sliced through the air as Areth swung a few times for good measure. A distinct *sheng* reverberated around the room. He smiled before sheathing the sword. The familiar floral pattern etched into the flat of the blade disappeared as it slid into the scabbard. Only the plaited hilt and the kytling pommel showed. He clipped it to his hip, picked up the pouch of Fireballs and his helmet, and went to bid his children farewell.

Returning to the rear of the keep, he prepared Violetwing, his favourite kytling companion. Her unique deep purple feathers shimmered in the sunlight, fading into green on the tips of the wing feathers; her unusual size and aggressive stance towards anyone who wasn't familiar with her made her a formidable mount. The king walked toward her and ruffled her neck feathers as she stooped to greet him.

"Hello girl," he whispered.

The large flightless bird chirped and raised her hooked beak to full height, towering over the king. Violetwing spread her small rounded wings and prepared for her specially designed leather saddle. She bent her knees to a height acceptable to her owner.

He threw the saddle on and secured it in place, ensuring no feathers were snagged. "Are you ready, Vi? With you leading, I'm confident this will go well, right girl?" He hauled himself into the saddle, careful not to pull the kytling off balance, and patted her neck. "Let's go."

With a gentle tap of his foot, she set off to the prearranged meeting point, beak held high.

Sir Victor waited in full armour, a troop of twenty kytling riders behind him. He spurred toward the approaching monarch, grinding his thumbs against the leather reins. "Your Majesty!" He pointed to the rose gold sky, streaked with the waning rays of dusk. "We must ride for Timbrol West at once to have any chance of making it before sundown."

"Certainly, Sir Victor. I sense apprehension in your voice; do you wish to voice any concerns?"

Sir Victor's head bowed, and he replied in an unusually quiet voice. "I'm concerned for our lives, Sire. The Forsaken are ruthless and there aren't enough of us to fight them. I've ordered Boris to bring his messenger raven, we made need to make use of it."

The king placed a reassuring hand on the brave knight's heavy pauldron. "We will not fail, my friend. Follow my lead, keep a level head, and I promise we shall be victorious!"

"I trust you, Your Majesty."

Sir Victor faced his troops. "Onwards, warriors!" He thrust his arm forwards and pointed to the horizon. Without question, all twenty riders spurred their kytlings on, following their King and commander. Away from the great walled capital city, they rode for the coastal town of Timbrol West.

The small company rode across the rolling green hills of Mannis. "If we keep this pace, we will make Timbrol West before sundown," shouted Sir Victor. He fixed his gaze on the king, noticing his shoulders bobbing, as if he were laughing. "Sire?"

King Areth's head jerked backwards and a mighty laugh erupted from inside his beaked visor.

"Sire, what's so funny?"

"Don't you see, Sir Victor?" he bellowed, loud enough for Sir Victor to hear. "This is it! This is the start of a new world. I can feel it!" He released one of his hands to gesture behind him, sweeping his arm around in one long movement. "Together, you and I, with only this handful of men, will change the course of history!"

"Either that, or be killed on sight!"

"Nonsense, Sir Victor. Change happens now!" Fuelled with adrenaline, the king released his other hand and spread his arms wide, balancing on Violetwing.

They both exploded into laughter as their kytlings sprinted merrily through the lush grass. The king cheered and raised his fist in the air as Violetwing let out an ear-piercing screech.

Filled with courage, all the men joined in and pushed their feathered mounts faster. Swifter than horses they ran, their riders breaking into glorious smiles. The sun kissed the horizon, just as the tops of the tallest buildings came into view above the lush hills ahead.

Sir Victor pointed to the structures. "There! Half of our glorious fishing and transport colony. Timbrol West! They have no idea we are coming, and there is nothing quite like a royal visit with no time to prepare!"

The city walls grew larger as the riders approached. The dock bell's ringing drifted on the wind, and a loud horn echoed across the esplanade, signalling their arrival. A giant, ironclad portcullis heaved open the gate and four armoured horsemen greeted King Areth.

A knight rode forwards and lifted his visor, the bronze trim of his Timbrol armour glistening in the sea air. "Your Majesty! Sir Victor! What brings you to this humble colony so suddenly?" The leader of the guard seemed perplexed as he scanned the company of riders, while their winded kytlings groomed their feathers.

The king lifted his visor and beamed at the familiar ageless knight. "Sir Jacob, my good man! We wish to cross to Timbrol East immediately. Do you have room for our men and kytlings?"

"Of course, Sire! I shall make the necessary arrangements at once. Although, may I ask why the urgency?"

"Ah, always the inquisitive one!" King Areth leaned close and whispered, "We are riding to the Undying Fortress to discuss diplomacy with Queen Lucia . . . but keep that to yourself." He pulled back and winked at this trusted knight, who returned an even deeper look of confusion.

"Uhh... Very well... As you wish, Sire. If you'll follow young Alex, I trust he will see to your needs. I will prepare your ship." Hooves clapped against the stone as Sir Jacob reared his horse around and rode back into the cobbled city.

Alex, one of the youngest members of the Timbrol guards, beckoned the small force to follow him. As he led them through the city toward the docks, light-hearted music and singing rang out from nearby taverns. People waved and cheered from windows at their much-loved king, with the glorious aroma of cooking fish in the air.

"Your Majesty, may I suggest a hearty meal before setting sail?" asked Alex. "You must be famished."

King Areth shouted to the troops. "What say you, men? Shall we dine?"

The men all pumped their fists and filled the air with a cacophony of cheers and hearty laughter. The king smiled and responded softly. "A hearty meal sounds just like what we need, Alex. Thank you."

Alex whistled and tapped his greave against his steed. The horse broke away from the other two guards, leading the king and his men toward Timbrol West's marvellous dining halls.

The group approached a large wooden building, hidden away behind the halls and inns that lined the main street. This was a grand structure, at least three times longer than it was wide, with huge wooden doors and animal pens to either side.

Alex smiled. "You may leave your kytlings here to feed and drink."

The group dismounted and led their kytlings into a holding pen, complete with feeding trough and water basin. The large birds cooed and settled on straw beds to rest, while the king and his men made their way into the dining hall.

The men's eyes widened at seeing the finest matching Triash wood table and chairs, with intricately carved plaits skirting the flat panelled wood. Triash wood was difficult and dangerous to get a hold of, as the only place in Naeisus where Triash trees grew, was also home to the Wolven. Nevertheless, it was a fantastically strong and pliable wood with a deep brown-red hue, much coveted

33

for its craftability. The enormous elegant dining table easily accommodated the king and his troops.

Seating himself at the very end of the table with Sir Victor, King Areth placed Alex next to him. The rest of the men piled in as they pleased and began to smack their lips in anticipation of the meal to come. Almost as soon as they took their seats, an array of cooks brought forth silver plates and cutlery, goblets and tankards, and most importantly, stone dishes of fish pie, grilled fish, fish soup and sides of breads and salads. The men cheered once again as the delectable looking food filled their nostrils with the most wonderful smells making them salivate.

Servers patrolled the table, topping up goblets and cups before they ran dry. Sir Victor dragged the back of his hand across his bushy beard, and leaned back resting his gigantic hands on his gut. "I couldn't eat another bite!"

"Finally reached your end then, Sir?" jested another soldier. "You've eaten more than the rest of us put together, I reckon!"

"I'm thrice as big as any of you little folk!" The large man pointed and swept a finger across the troops, grinning.

"Aye! That size o' yours nearly cost us the battle at Blackrock."

"How do you expect a man of my stature to hide behind a tiny rock?"

The room erupted into laughter at the memories of the glorious battle.

King Areth stood, stumbled, and rested against Sir Victor's shoulder to balance. "The look on the enemy faces when he jumped out on them was priceless!" He quickly jumped to his loyal friend's defence. "Not to mention single-handedly taking out the commander alone."

"Single-handedly? Nay, Sire, Ol' Victor is at least five men by himself; nothing single-handed about that!"

Sir Victor's hearty laugh shook the room infecting everyone, all unable to control their cheer.

The king hushed everyone with a hand gesture. "I hate to be the one to stop the party, but I do believe it's time to depart. We have a long journey ahead of us, and if we drink much more, we'll never be up in time to ride."

* * *

King Areth and his small band led their kytlings to the docks, admiring the view of the open sea beyond a forest of masts from dozens of ships harboured for the night.

A soldier, Boris, shook the shaggy blonde hair from his eyes, and breathed in the salty sea air. With a grin he whispered to his kytling, "Beyond that water is a new world of open land for you, girl!" The sapphire kytling cawed and shuffled her feet.

Alex pointed to one of the smaller transport ships in the harbour, currently under inspection by Sir Jacob.

The ship looked no different from the others that bobbed alongside it. The pointed bow and a flat stern bracketed a large hull, designed for the transportation and protection of passengers. The bigger ones, crafted from sturdy oak, shipped wood and coal, farmed or mined from the resource-rich areas of mainland Naeisus, from Timbrol East across the reach to Timbrol West.

"Your Majesty, the ship is prepared, complete with bedding and supplies. The captain will make haste and take us safely to Timbrol East. The seas are calm and the air is without wind, but we should still be there before sunrise. I will journey with you and see you off at the far end."

The king rested his hand on Sir Jacob's shoulder and gave him a sincere thank you, before riding up the docking ramp and inside the ship.

The company boarded the ship and led their kytlings to the lower decks, where some roamed free and others slept on the large bedded area at the stern.

Armour clinking, King Areth settled Violetwing on the lower decks with the other kytlings, before returning to the upper deck. He removed his cumbersome armour, and bedded down among his best men. The gentle bobbing of the vessel and hissing of the waves against the hull lulled the men into a deep, fulfilling sleep.

A clanging bell, signalling the approach to Timbrol East's harbour, woke the sleeping soldiers as dawn began to light the sky. The men scrambled to redress themselves, equip their armour, and ready their favourite weapons.

The king led the men to the lower decks where the kytlings, already awake and happily devouring raw meat, were ready to saddle up and ride out.

When the ship docked, Sir Jacob led the troops on to the wooden pier and through the streets of Timbrol East. This city was almost identical to its twin across the water, save for heavier fortifications, due to the danger of attack from enemies on the mainland.

With no time to stop, the company rode beyond the thick walls and out onto the esplanade toward the four outposts that kept watch over the land beyond Mannis. These outposts served as the best early warning signal Timbrol East would get in case of an attack.

After a morning's ride, the group passed outpost Johann but kept pace. The early afternoon light grew dim as thick clouds blotted the sun. The great Fortress of the Forsaken was still another two-and-a-half day's ride at best.

When they spotted a small oasis among some trees, the king decided to stop for a quick break. He raised his hand and beckoned the group to stop. "Our kytlings need refreshment, they have been riding hard and making good ground."

Sir Victor nodded in agreement and dismounted his crimson kytling. "Men! We break here." A wave of nodding heads agreed to the rest, and the troops followed suit.

Hopping off their birds, they unloaded casks and hampers of food.

The flock of kytlings scrambled to the water's edge and bowed their heads low to drink. Some squawked and squabbled for the best spot to drink, occasionally nipping at the others with needle-sharp hooked beaks. Kytlings shared a special bond with their riders and served not only as steed and companion, but also as weapons; their beaks and talons almost matched the strength of a Wolven's claws, and they tore through flesh like a sword through water,

Eventually the birds settled down, refreshing themselves in preparation for the next stint. A dazzling array of rippling colours spread across the water's edge as they bowed their heads to drink and then raised them again to swallow.

King Areth and Sir Victor chatted and laughed to themselves, reminiscing over old times before agreeing to move on. The kytlings finished drinking and began to shuffle and caw, nudging their riders playfully.

Sir Victor stood and addressed the troops. "Time to saddle up, boys! We've got supplies for a few more camps like this until we reach the Undying Fortress." He spread his arms wide as a hint of worry flashed across his face.

The platoon cheered and whistled for their mounts to heel.

Boris's kytling nipped his hand as he tried to mount; he lost balance and fell into the long grass.

The king chortled. "Be gentle, Boris! They're smart and require a lot of patience."

"I try, Sire, but she's a stubborn gal—more than the rest, methinks." He rubbed his backside, then reached over to pat the neck of his mount. He mumbled a few soothing words, then managed to climb into the saddle, and together they fell into formation.

In a low voice, Sir Victor expressed some concerns. "Sire, I've heard many things about the Forsaken and I've fought a few in battle. It wouldn't be beneath them to simply kill us on sight."

"I know, my friend. I too, am afraid. Tomorrow we face a potentially perilous ride close to Wolven territory. Let's just pray it isn't the last morrow we see… "

Chapter 3

The Forsaken

King Areth and his company made camp on the border of the Darklands. The grass thinned out and grew patchy, fading into ash, dust and rocks. Rough winds stirred up perilous dust clouds, restricted vision to just a few feet, and created a perfect shroud for the Fortress.

The old texts say the Darklands used to be a prosperous and fertile place, home to many cities and farming colonies. That was, until the Wyrms cremated every slither of life in the entire region. After the Great Wyrm came and laid waste to what was left, nothing was able to grow or thrive here and the land was evacuated and forgotten. Of course, most citizens believe that to be fictional; it was widely believed the true cause of the wasteland was the foul immorality of the undead residing within.

Somewhere in the middle of this dire expanse of land, stood the Undying Fortress, home of the Forsaken. The Fortress lay deep enough into the Darklands to be a safe and secretive place for this race of outcasts to reside.

Sir Victor stood and faced the other men as they sat around several campfires, flickering away among a handful of tents. The soldiers gobbled their rations of bread and water, storing energy for a potential clash with the Forsaken. The kytlings lay on small islands of grass, chewing on hunks of meat, cooing and purring with blind satisfaction.

"Men!" he bellowed as he pointed to the creeping nothing behind him. "Soon, we shall be riding into the harshest land we will ever see. We ride to meet Queen Lucia of the Forsaken and to request her alliance at a great cost. It is possible we won't return. It is also possible we will return stronger than ever.

"Each of you has been selected for your strength and vigour in battle. Our good Sire, King Areth III, has tasked us this mission in the hope of a more peaceful world..." Here the huge knight punched the air as a flourish. "... so let's give it our all!"

Soldiers, including the king, climbed to their feet and cheered at his speech.

Sir Victor added, "Oh and Boris, try to not stab yourself this time." Laughter erupted, and Boris went rather red-faced, only managing to cover half with his scraggly hair.

King Areth lifted one hand, settling the crowd. "Remember, the Forsaken have a ruthless reputation. They may try to anger you, but I urge you all to keep a level head and absolutely do *not* strike first. That is a direct order."

The smiles and laughter dropped from the faces of the soldiers as the reality of their mission set in, accompanied by fear. A few moments of deafening silence passed.

"You heard the Captain. Let's saddle up and head out." The king stepped over to Violetwing, and began adjusting her saddle.

The camp was quickly packed away, and the men mounted up, ready to make the final stretch of the journey. Boris caught his foot on the stirrup of his saddle and slipped over, pulling his kytling with him; she snapped at his arm and hissed as she scrambled to her feet. Laughter rang out once more at the clumsy soldier, as he succeeded in his second attempt to mount.

"Hey Boris, you have a great bird there, she puts up with a lot, having you as a rider," jeered a soldier from across the V-shaped formation.

Boris flushed red as he strove to ignore the crowd.

A white flag was raised high above the party, flapping in the breeze, as a signal for peace when they approached the Fortress. A cacophony of sharp whistles ripped through the air and the kytlings strode off, carrying their riders into the blackened land sprawled out before them, their talons leaving deep impressions in the dust.

* * *

As they advanced deeper into the Darklands, their sense of fear and foreboding grew. The landscape grew dark, as thick dust and sand choked out the blazing sunshine, threatening to suffocate the men and their kytlings. One by one, the soldiers lowered their protective visors, in an attempt to prevent the soiled air from getting into their eyes and throats; although, it didn't do much to stifle the hideous, stale smell of the charred land.

The sounds of flowing rivers, rustling trees, and singing birds behind them faded into a disturbing silence, the stillness broken only by the muffled clomping of kytling feet on scorched ground and the rattling of steel armour.

What seemed like an eternity, of riding through the rubble of razed towns, passed. The dark, thick air made it difficult to tell which direction the group was headed, yet they pressed on, following their king and his enormous mount. The kytlings grew tired and slowed as they struggled for breath, coughing and spluttering.

Suddenly, they all came to an abrupt halt, let out ear-splitting screeches, and refused to take another step. The majestic birds struggled and pulled at their reins with closed eyes, irritated and distressed by more than just the air. The soldiers tilted their heads up, mouths agape, and saw it. Before them in the murk, stood a colossal shadow.

"There! The Undying Fortress," yelled King Areth behind his beak-like visor, the sound muffled by the dust storm.

"Look at the size of that thing! Where does it end?" Sir Victor pointed. "Where's the top?"

Standing proud and strong, no more than a short run ahead of them, loomed the outer wall of the Undying Fortress; a tower lurked behind it, disappearing high into the storm and dwarfing the walls.

"Careful men. It's likely we've already been spotted. Forsaken eyesight is many times sharper than our own. The watches atop the walls likely saw us the same time as our kytlings saw them." The king waved his arms to order a dismount, and pointed to the outline of a recess in the wall.

Boris plucked the pouch of fireballs from Violetwing's saddle. "I'll keep them safe, Your Highness," he said as he secured it to his own belt. The company began to march forward, but stopped at the sound of a gate cracking open. The drumming noise of hooves grew louder until the silhouettes of six horses galloped out from the recess in the wall each carrying a fearsome rider.

Sir Victor glanced at the now grey flag and gritted his teeth. "Steady your weapons and hold your ground! We are here for peace, do not forget that!"

The riders approached and circled the group, grunting and grimacing. The soldiers huddled together; their weapons remained sheathed, but they gripped the hilts of their swords in preparation. Fear swept the small group as the armoured black steeds kicked up more dust, further shrouding the faces of their riders. The piercing red eyes of the soldiers cut through the dust like sunbeams through water.

The mark of the Forsaken.

The men in the outer ring shielded their faces from the dust and sand until the sound of the hooves stopped. When the king lowered his arm, he was met by the sight of one of the Forsaken riders, spurring her steed steadily forward and raising her arm. The other black riders glared with malice, awaiting the order to dispatch these living visitors.

Sitting tall and darkly beautiful atop her steed, the rider with the raised arm addressed them. "When my arm drops, you will all die. That, gentlemen, is a fact. To stop that from happening, you will answer my questions quickly and clearly. Do you understand, King Areth?" A subtle smirk appeared to creep across her smooth, pale face as she spoke.

"You know me?" His brow furrowed.

"I am Captain Levana of the Forsaken, sent to deal with you by Queen Lucia herself. Yes, I know you. It is the only reason we haven't killed you already. State your business, outsiders."

The king lifted his visor, revealing his strong face in full detail. "As King of the race of Man, and by the flag raised above me, I come to Queen Lucia in peace, bearing an offering in return for her allegiance. Will you take us to her?"

Levana's smirk broke into a full smile, revealing a perfect set of pearl-white teeth. Her smile grew wider and wider, until she erupted into laughter. The horses still surrounding them shuffled their hooves and whinnied.

"You have the same determined look in your eyes that he had. The first King, that is . . . so handsome, so tragic . . ." Captain Levana's attention seemed to drift away for a second, then she snapped back. "What makes you think the Queen will accept an alliance with Man? Tell me why my arm should remain in the air any longer!"

"Captain Levana, please. I do not wish to see my people suffer. Likewise, I do not wish to see any of your people suffer. We will relinquish our weapons if we have to, but you must bring me to the Queen at once."

Their gazes locked and both remained silent. The fire in King Areth's eyes shone through, and eventually Levana sighed. "Very well, but on our terms. You and your men will be unarmed and you alone will see the Queen escorted by four of us. Your men must wait outside under guard."

He faced his men, studying each of their hopeful faces in turn.

I risk their lives, their families... but it is my duty as King to ensure their safety. The risk is worth it.

He stepped towards the Forsaken Captain. "I trust our weapons will be returned afterwards?"

"That depends on what the Queen wants, *Sire*. Oh, and I'm going to need your helmet. The Queen will want to see that handsome face of yours."

The king removed his kytling helmet, stared at it, then handed it over. "Very well. Men, hand over your weapons."

Sir Victor objected to this. "Sire, I have to come with you!"

With a warm smile, King Areth gave his breastplate a subtle tap. "Do not fear, my good Sir. I trust that I will be unharmed."

At an order from Captain Levana, the Forsaken riders gathered the entire company's weapons—including the pouch of Fireballs hanging on Boris's belt. The Forsaken rider who grabbed the pouch took a rather keen interest in what they were, opening the bag and examining them with a curious eye.

Boris stretched his arm toward the warrior. "Careful with those! They are—"

A menacing red-eyed glare and a disgusted grunt cut him off.

* * *

After traversing what seemed to be thousands of uneven stone steps, they faced a set of thick double doors. With a flick of her hand, the Captain dismissed the other three escorts and grinned. She pushed open the doors and shoved King Areth inside. He stumbled into the pinnacle chamber—Queen Lucia's throne room.

"Look what I found, Lucie! Says he wants to..."

"King Areth..." interrupted the Queen, gazing out of one of the three windows overlooking the whole Fortress. The onyx hair that flowed down her back like a midnight waterfall stopped just above her waist.

Her rich, purple dress followed her swing as she turned to face them. An unassuming size, coupled with a sweet, innocent smile, made it difficult to believe this woman was the ruthless ruler of the Forsaken. "Levana dear, you can go now. It seems the good King and I have important matters to discuss."

With a respectful bow, Captain Levana backed out of the room, shutting the doors behind her.

"How did you know it was me, Your Highness?"

"Oh please," scoffed the Queen. "I'm in this tower and you think I can't see who approaches my gates?"

"But the dust storm. You can barely see the ground."

"Yes... the storm has been nasty the past few days hasn't it, dear?"

Something about the way Queen Lucia spoke unnerved the king. She seemed too calm, too delicate to be dangerous, yet her reputation as a merciless ruler preceded her. She drifted across to the great Triash throne and placed herself upon it, adjusting her tight dress for comfort. With an elbow on one of the carved skulls on the arm of the throne, she rested her soft chin in the palm of her hand and, with her free hand, gestured for him to speak.

Lost for words and stuttering, he began to speak of his plan. "Y-Your Highness, I umm..." His head bowed for a second, then he cleared his throat, took a deep breath, and looked up again, stronger than before. "I come to you personally, as we are equals; not a single one of my men could relay the message and offer of peace I bring today."

Queen Lucia let out a mocking laugh. "Oh, you're serious, aren't you?" She collected herself a bit. "You have the same eyes as him and the same steely stare. It's cute, almost like an old love rekindled." Her free hand twiddled the black lace on her dress as she seemed a bit lost, or maybe enthralled.

"I assume you are referring to my ancestor, King Areth I?"

"You even sound like him! It's uncanny! It's as if I didn't bring him his true death."

Her sly smile fuelled a brewing irritation within, yet he remained calm, mindful of the mission at hand. "With respect, Your Highness, his son, King Areth II, banished your people and created this rift between our races. I am here to reverse that decision and heal that rift. I'd like to form a mutually beneficial alliance between our people." He stepped forward, adding weight to his words.

Queen Lucia rose from her throne to pour herself a goblet of wine from an iron jug. "Wine, Sire? Alcohol no longer has an effect on me, but I like the taste," she remarked, as if he hadn't said anything at all.

The king paused, then accepted a silver goblet and sipped it. The queen's crimson eyes pierced his soul, making him squirm and shuffle in his armour. "Well, Highness? What are your thoughts?"

She took another sip and placed her goblet on the table. She smiled and glanced around the hexagonal chamber, her eyes shifting from the throne, to the windows, to the weapon stands dotted around. Finally, her eyes came to rest on him once more. "My thoughts? I'm wondering what would happen if I were to kill you and your men now."

Is this a dark joke? Is she really threatening me?

"But your offer has piqued my interest, my dear. Let's not dress this up; you tell me what you want and then tell me what I will receive in return. I have little time to waste." She folded her arms and leaned against a nearby wall, watching his lips.

"Okay then. Simply put, I ultimately want peace. I want our people to unite as a demonstration to the rest of Naeisus that peace is possible. I want our combined forces to bring order to the rest of the world. If we combine our efforts and find the shards together, we can all benefit from the reward."

Queen Lucia's face failed to give away her thoughts. She simply gestured for him to continue.

"As for your benefit... I will freely offer you the Mys shard, as well as my forces in combat."

"Adding your forces to mine would be as helpful as adding a bucket of water to a lake, dear. As for offering us the shard? Well, it seems your reputation as an intelligent ruler is false."

Through a clenched jaw, he responded, "That is my offer, Your Highness. Take it or leave it."

* * *

Sir Victor and his men stood agitated outside the closed gate, their weapons just beyond and within their sight, almost mocking them from the wrong side of the portcullis. Their kytlings screeched out, just beyond the edge of visibility in the dust, still refusing to draw closer to the Fortress.

Captain Levana arrived at the portcullis to stand watch, atop her grand obsidian steed. The mare's elegant black armour and embroidered saddle furthered an already intimidating appearance. Sir Victor walked over to her, clutching his ram's-head helmet, his fingers twitching along the intricately forged horns, which coiled up like snakes on either side of it.

"Where is King Areth? He's been gone a while," boomed the knight, trying to conceal his inner anxiety.

Captain Levana dismounted and stood opposite Sir Victor, the portcullis between them. She looked up at the bearded face of the massive man, smiled, and then bowed her head. "I'm sorry… " she started.

"Sorry?" shouted Sir Victor as he stamped a foot forward.

Captain Levana put her hand to her face, trapping some of her long black hair between her hand and face, then threw her head back in amusement.

"Oh Sir Victor, you are most loyal. What would you do if I told you he was dead? Would you kill me?"

Sir Victor dropped his helmet, slammed his heavy hands against the iron, and growled at a hysterical Levana. "Tell me! If my good King has been slain, the wrath of Mankind will fall upon you, here and now!" The knight's hands coiled around the thick iron grating and his knuckles turned white as he gripped it.

"You have foolishly walked into our territory, relinquished your weapons, and allowed your leader to speak with ours alone. What did you think would happen?!" The Captain's arms flew out as she laughed harder and harder.

The other men gathered around Sir Victor, some clutching their helmets like makeshift weapons. The guards inside the fortress readied their swords and bows as tensions climbed, and Captain Levana continued to giggle away at the trouble she stirred. She signaled to her troops to lower their weapons, and they obeyed. Boris stepped forward and placed a gentle, reassuring hand on the broad shoulder of his superior.

"Sir, the king is okay; she is just trying to anger you. Remember, we are here for peace, not war. I have faith in King Areth; he will come out soon." The shaggy haired soldier glanced away from the knight, and his eyes shot daggers at Captain Levana, who returned nothing but an amused grin.

"Hey, this's a smart one!" The Forsaken Captain lowered her tone a bit. "Relax, if we were going to kill you, you'd already be dead. We still might, actually, I just need the word from the queen. Although . . . " she paused for a long moment for effect, ". . . if my Queen is unable to give the order, then I may just act on my own volition."

Grunting at the her, Sir Victor walked away and began to pace the ground, biting his grubby fingernails.

Captain Levana swept her hair back from her smooth pale face and mounted her horse. As she rode away, she glanced over her shoulder with a smug look, taunting the knight beyond the gate with menacing eyes.

* * *

"So then... you chose to approach us. The Forsaken. Let's say I agree, take your shard, and then kill you. Or better yet, I kill you now and attack your weakened cities for the shard. What then?" Queen Lucia made the proposal, assuming that the king hadn't thought his plan through at all.

Smirking and gaining confidence, King Areth took a few steps forward, paused, and seated himself on the throne, stroking the solid Triash skull-carved arms.

"Why is that notion so amusing to you? You think I won't kill you?" The Queen folded her arms and huffed.

The king leaned forward on the throne, with a smug smile. "Because, *my dear*, I am not stupid. I know that you stand to gain much more with my help than by inciting another war with my people. You know me, and you are fully aware of my reputation. What do you think will happen if I die here? Can you really withstand my armies, on top of the Wolven onslaughts you so frequently encounter?" He sat back, and watched as the queen stepped towards him.

Her arms dropped, and a subtle smile returned to her face. She enjoyed intelligence and knew the words to be true. Her hips swayed as she walked closer to the confident king. Upon reaching the throne, she placed herself on one of the arms and slung an arm around Areth's neck. She ran her ice-cold fingers across his face and stared longingly at his stern lips.

His breath grew a little sharper as her finger ran across his lip, and his eyes closed as a freezing sensation trailed behind it.

"He and I were lovers, you know. Your words, your looks, even the way you conduct yourself... you bring such positive memories to me, dear Areth." The queen's voice softened, and her sharp fingernails continued to trace his cheek.

"If you were lovers, why did you so carelessly end him?" demanded the king as he pulled away from her.

"You think I killed him for fun? For power? Areth, I'm shocked and upset that your opinion of me is so low!"

Her face turned to sadness at the accusations as she averted her gaze. Taking a deep breath, she continued. "My dear, your ancestor was the first. He became so corrupted, so twisted with revenge and malice that he became a threat to us all. Every shred of humanity had left him; what remained was nothing more than an evil shell, consumed by hatred. He was no longer capable of leading, so for our own safety, I did what needed to be done. It broke my heart, and it breaks again with your accusations."

King Areth's gaze dropped. "I . . . I'm sorry. I do not intend to walk that same path. As I've said, it's only peace I want."

Queen Lucia focused her attention out of the window as she stared into the empty distance.

"Your Highness, please. I have to know if you will accept my offer of allegiance."

Queen Lucia's fingers returned to caressing his stubbled face, and she remained silent. Suddenly, she swiped a sharp fingernail down his cheek, creating a small gash that began seeping blood. A gentle, white glow emanated from the cut. The delicate glow swirled around and quickly sealed the wound, leaving only a trace of blood.

He clapped a hand to his cheek and glared at her, furious.

She buried her face in her hands and burst into laughter. When she settled, she lifted her head again and smirked. "You actually brought it with you! I could smell the desperation on you when you walked in the room, but never did I believe you were actually foolish enough to bring the Mys shard into my city!"

"What of it?" he snapped. "It's my only form of protection around you."

"Oh please," she jeered, "as if that thing would help if I really wanted to kill you—you are unarmed and I have thousands of Forsaken surrounding us."

"Regardless, I'm done with your games!"The King thumped the throne with his fist. "I demand to know your answer."

"Relax, Areth. My answer was always going to be yes." She flashed her uncomfortably sweet smile as she spoke. "Is it a crime to want to enjoy your company for a little longer though?"

Reeling himself in, he stood and paced the room. "We must discuss the terms of our alliance, before I can hand the shard over, you understand."

Queen Lucia walked to the window, once more gazing across the Fortress as the storm outside began to subside. She shrugged and waved. "I'm listening . . ."

* * *

The monarchs emerged from the throne room hand-in-hand, both smiling. Queen Lucia held the Mys shard loosely between her fingers. The gentle footsteps and light clinking of Captain Levana's armour echoed from the spiral stairwell, and she emerged still smiling to herself. She abruptly stopped, startled to see the pair of rulers just pulling the Triash doors shut behind them.

"Ah, Captain Levana. Just in time! Be a dear and bring the good King's men, inside will you? We have an announcement to make," ordered Queen Lucia.

Captain Levana stood still, perplexed for a moment, and then glanced at the shard in the Queen's hand. She grinned and bowed her head, before turning on her heels and walking back down the stairs a little more heavily footed than when she came up. The monarchs followed her down the cold, winding stone staircase through the swirling dust for a long while. Upon reaching the bottom, the Captain mounted her steed and headed toward the entrance of the Fortress.

"This looks different from when I was here last." The king took the time to scan the environment.

"That's because last time, my dear Areth, our men were red with the blood of yours in the heat of battle," responded the Queen begrudgingly.

"I apologise; I hope our newly formed alliance can dispel any hard feelings."

"I can't say my people won't be displeased, they do hate the living after all. However, they will follow my rule or be killed."

King Areth nodded at this, unsure of how to react to such brutality.

Queen Lucia glanced at him and scoffed. "When you've been ruling for hundreds of solar cycles, it becomes apparent what works best." With that sentiment, the queen smiled almost psychotically through strands of jet-black hair before brushing it all back.

Captain Levana returned with the king's men striding behind her, still without their kytlings. As they walked towards the two leaders, a nearby Forsaken Wolven growled and snapped at the living.

Queen Lucia glowered, curling her fists before whistling sharply and pointing at him. As soon as the whistle left her lips, an arrow shot through the air and pierced the skull of the disobedient undead Wolven. His body slumped to the floor as his soul seeped out through the arrow wound, finally claimed by Knas.

King Areth's jaw dropped at the display, only able look to his new ally for an explanation.

"My people will learn to accept you as allies, as per our agreement," stated the serious-looking queen. "There will be no objections."

Captain Levana beamed at the death and let out a hearty laugh as she drew near to the monarchs. She dismounted and introduced the living men to the queen. They all sighed with relief to see their king alive and well. Sir Victor stepped forward to hug his leader and friend.

"My friends, my good people," began Queen Lucia. Her stern voice carried out over the group. "The good King Areth III, ruler of the race of Man, and I have had a lengthy discussion about the state of all of our people and about Naeisus as a whole." Dust swirled around them and receding winds tousled their hair and loose clothing as the storm weakened.

The queen held up the shard for all to see, its beauty captivating everyone nearby as they stared in awe. "The good King and I have discussed many things, including the transfer of the powerful Mys shard to our nation. We have decided it beneficial to end the conflict between our two races, so may I be the first to announce the alliance between Man and Forsaken."

Captain Levana's face dropped.

The ears of nearby onlookers pricked up, but they made no noise out of fear of the queen's ruthlessness, despite their displeasure with this news. Some low mumbling rumbled around the group, but dissipated as King Areth III stepped forward to speak.

His heroic voice rang out more powerfully than the queen's. "I know many of you will not take this news well, but I assure you that our interests lie only in the preservation of peace in the land we all inhabit. From this point forth, all Forsaken will be permitted to come and go in peace to any of our cities. Likewise, the Queen has assured me that we are welcome here." He looked to the Queen for reassurance and she nodded in agreement.

"Some of my men will head back to Straeta to inform my people. I hope that we can finally put our differences aside and work together. It will take some time, I know, but I sincerely hope we can all honour this alliance from the goodness of our hearts."

The king bowed and stepped backwards, allowing Queen Lucia to finish the announcement. "Any betrayal of this alliance will be viewed as a betrayal of me personally, so think before you act. Our first mission as allies is to seek out Ulv Nikos and request he joins the alliance. This will stop the Wolven attacks on our cities and further our ultimate goal of completing the Yultah Crystal."

The queen smiled her familiar, sweet smile and dismissed the onlookers with a dangerous crimson glare. "My dear Levana, accompany one of King Areth's men to calm the kytlings outside the Fortress and lead them to the front gate. Then gather up a handful of your best riders and meet us outside the main gates." The queen retained a piercing look that terrified even the bravest.

"My Queen—" objected Levana.

"Now, Captain."

Infuriated, Captain Levana stormed off to follow her orders.

"Areth dear, it is approaching sundown. You and your men may rest here overnight; if you trust us that is." She smiled from the side of her mouth, a smile that the king found alluring.

Reluctantly, he nodded, accepting her curiously generous hospitality.

"Great." With a darkening glare, she added, "Then tomorrow, we begin the journey to pay the Ulv a visit."

"Certainly my Queen," he said in an attempt to hide his nervousness.

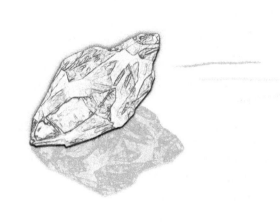

Chapter 4

The Wolven

The titanic plaited trees of the Triash Forest towered far above the band of Man and Forsaken. King Areth's army gazed around in wonder, their mouths agape at the magical sight of the forest.

"You've clearly never been here before." Levana raised her palms and shook them. "Oh, wow—awe and fascination. Let's just get on with it shall we?" she said, rolling her eyes and stomping her way through the brush.

Everything about this place seemed almost hand-crafted, from the Triash trees, each of which was woven from three separate trunks, to the glowing mushrooms which carpeted the ground. Thorny vines hung from every branch and dangled from the canopy. Fireflies buzzed around in their thousands, glowing bright within the darkened forest. As the trees grew denser, so did their thick, sweeping leaves, blotting out more and more sunshine. The king absorbed his surroundings in astonishment, basking in the gentle cyan glow of the detritus beneath his feet.

This is wonderful! Such a feeling of security and privacy under this magical canopy... this forest is utterly enthralling!

Despite the beauty, the party moved with great caution, listening out for any suspicious sounds.

The queen whispered, "This is Wolven territory. If we drop our guard at any point, we're likely to be ambushed. Stay alert." She tugged at a strap on her snug-fitting leather battle armour, pulling it tighter.

Captain Levana smirked. "Comfortable? The jerkin allows for more freedom around the joints and the tight fit ensures no snagging in thick brush or undergrowth. I told you, Lucia, I know my combat gear."

The queen remained silent, focused on pushing forward.

"The forest is too dense ahead," whispered King Areth. "We can't all push through together, especially with our mounts."

Queen Lucia nodded, and addressed the group. "You will all have to wait here and keep guard. Areth, Levana, and I will go ahead on foot, to meet the Ulv."

"Sire, three of you won't be enough." Sir Victor thumped his chest. "Allow me to accompany you. If you get ambushed, I can provide a vital means of support."

Captain Levana rolled her eyes and folded her arms; turning her back to the group, she kicked the bright ground.

"Of course, Sir Victor." Agreeing to bring his best knight along helped the king conceal his worry about a Wolven onslaught. "Boris, I need you to lead everyone back to the rim of the forest and wait there for us. If we do not return by sundown, ride home and notify the council of our fate."

Boris bowed. "Understood, Your Majesty."

Some of the Forsaken grunted, so the queen spoke up. "Robert, do the same will you, dear?"

A gruff, gravelly voice came from one of the larger Forsaken warriors. "My Queen."

Captain Levana scoffed in disbelief at this display of alliance and shoved her way deeper into the forest. "Are you coming or what? Let's get this over with."

* * *

Violetwing cawed after her master as Boris led her and the others away. He looked over his shoulder as the silhouettes of the four nobles disappeared into the murky blue haze beyond the trees, then returned his gaze to the rather large Forsaken man riding alongside him.

The Forsaken man met Boris' stare and growled. "What is it?!"

Boris jumped at the rough, yet almost ghostly voice of the undead warrior. "Oh, um... you... you're Robert Drake, aren't you?" he quivered.

"Yes, what of it?"

Boris' eyes glinted, almost star-struck. Strands of scraggly, muddy hair partially covered his gawp.

"Well? Speak, man!"

Boris jumped. "I... I've read a lot about your conquests with King Iain IX. You were a great warrior—"

"Were? I still am," snapped the legendary knight.

"Of course, I'm sorry."

Robert grunted and pulled ahead while Boris failed to avert his gaze. Without thinking and desperate to satisfy his curiosity, Boris called out, "What's it like being dead?"

He immediately regretted asking as the darkest crimson stare and a hefty growl met his question. He jumped again and stared straight ahead of him in complete silence.

Robert pulled on his steed's reigns and fell back level with Boris, his eyes softening. "It hurts." As he spoke, he put one armoured hand to his face, stroked his cut and scarred cheek, and sighed, turning his gaze to the floor.

"Oh . . . then why do you choose it?"

"Stupid man! I didn't choose this."

"I mean no offence! I'm just trying to understand." Boris raised a palm as a display of non-aggression, which Robert seemed to acknowledge.

"The living run when they see us. We are unnatural. You are different. Why do you show such interest?"

Boris looked to his saddle, believing he'd never hear the answers he longed for. "I'm just curious, Sir. I've read much about you, you're a famous warrior. We are allies now and I'm curious as to what changes when you die. "

Robert sighed and stared into the distance away from Boris, concealing a small smile that turned his lips at the corners. "You care, don't you lad?"

"I guess I do, yes. Sir Victor teaches us to look out for our brothers and sisters over ourselves. You are our brother now."

Robert smiled at Boris, and cleared his throat. "When a living creature dies, the Yultah Knas pulls its soul away from the body. If another Forsaken wishes it, they can pull the soul back into the body of the fallen, providing they are powerful enough. Once reattached, the soul will expend most of its power to repair any fatal damage—like the Mys shard does—only with us, it works just once. We still feel Knas constantly pulling our souls; we have defied her, and she wants what she is owed.

The smile faded from the undead man's face. "We no longer need to sleep or eat, we do not fatigue, and our bodies no longer repair damage, as you can see from my cuts—while they look fresh, some are decades old." He stared into the distance, seemingly troubled by the reality of his existence. "On top of all of this, Knas is waiting. If we fall again, there is no going back. She will not be beaten twice—one fatal blow and our souls will pour from these vessels we call bodies."

"Knas is real? You've seen her?! What is she like?" Boris' eyes widened, like a child witnessing heavy snowfall for the first time.

"Mhm. We all have, yet I cannot possibly describe her. Our memories of her are tied to the fragment of soul she still holds, like leashed hounds."

"If it's such a curse, can't you just . . . y'know . . . end it?"

"Then who would fight for us? We Forsaken need that crystal as much as you. You would not understand the reasons."

"But we're allies now; surely you can—"

"Enough! I've spoken to you long enough for one day, you insufferable man," Robert turned his face and put his hand to his mouth to cough, concealing the smile that lit up his undead face as they led the rest of the troops from the looming reach of the forest canopy back into the sunshine.

* * *

The dwindled group of four pushed their way deeper into the brush and thickened trees, often having to slice a path through the dense thicket.

"How do they live in such a place?" Levana hacked away at some vines with her quickblades.

The king glanced over his shoulder at a low grumble— one he presumed came from Sir Victor in reaction to the brash Forsaken Captain.

With a few more quick chops, Levana opened the way to a small clearing and beckoned the others to follow her. The clearing itself only served as a short respite from the tireless cutting. The group began arguing about how to find the Wolven den in this vast, sprawling forest.

At a loud grumble, Sir Victor interrupted. "What was that?!" The huge knight scrutinised the treetops.

All four readied their weapons, scanning every direction in an attempt to discern where the grumble had come from. Back-to-back in the centre of the clearing the small group huddled, gripping their weapons tightly.

"Show yourself!" roared Sir Victor.

A hulking Wolven dropped out of the trees and landed with poise, claws ready.

"Keep your guard, they travel in packs," ordered King Areth.

Another dropped from the trees behind them, then two more.

The threatening beasts surrounded them, standing on their hind legs with menacing claws raised, ready to pounce. The thick, smoky fur coating their bodies stood on end and gave the illusion of even greater size and threat.

Two of the Wolven barked to one another, while the other two listened. After some more growling and barking, the creature facing the queen grunted at her and bared its teeth.

"Lay down your weapons," instructed Queen Lucia. She dropped her rapier on the ground and it disappeared underneath the blanket of fungus and ferns.

"Are you serious?!" The king's brow dripped with sweat. "They look ready to rip our throats out."

"They know who we are and said they'll take us to the Ulv if we relinquish our weapons."

"How do you know that?" Sir Victor gripped his sword tighter.

"Did you not notice the Forsaken Wolven at the Fortress? We have learned to understand their language. You must watch their bodies as well as listen for the signal sounds. Now trust me, and drop your weapons."

With quivering hands, the other three softened their grips on their weapons and, finger by finger, let them drop to the ground.

The Wolven, with immense agility and synchronicity, hurled themselves at the group. The beasts grabbed them, hauled them over broad shoulders, and concealed the direction in which they ran.

* * *

The Wolven scouts threw the four nobles to the floor with a crash. They were in an underground room, dug out of the earth and tree roots. One large tunnel trailed off behind them, winding around several corners and disappearing down multiple offshoots, presumably the way they came in.

A series of tangled tree roots formed themselves into a thick throne-like structure. A large Wolven, very different from the rest, sat atop the throne. His thicker, jet-black fur differed from the multitude of greys and browns of the other Wolven. Guards stood either side of him, one almost matched the gigantic size of the Ulv—both were hunched in an aggressive attack pose.

King Areth noticed their confiscated weapons heaped in a pile beside the throne. He reached for his sword at his hip as an automatic response, but his hand passed over empty space. The four of them helped themselves off the ground and faced the great black Wolven.

Queen Lucia spoke first. "Ulv Nikos, I was hoping we'd see you…"

"Silence, Forsaken!" barked the Ulv in a frightening tone.

"My, my, someone's in a bad mood today," scoffed Levana.

Ulv Nikos growled and snarled a series of hostile noises. His tail whipped back and forth, thumping against the Triash roots.

The queen raised her palms. "No, please, Great Ulv; hear what we have to say, and then make your decision."

Ulv Nikos raised a claw and directed it at King Areth. "You. Speak."

The king stepped forward, somewhat impressed at the Ulv's command of their language. He spoke with the same passion and enthusiasm he'd poured into his entire mission. "Your Majesty, I am Areth III, King of Man, and I come to you today seeking an alliance. As you can see before you, we have already made peace with the Forsaken. We urge you to join us for the benefit of our people, and for Naeisus."

"Alliance?" roared the Ulv. His claws dug into the roots that formed the arms of his throne.

"Yes. We presented the Forsaken with the Mys shard as a symbol of our dedication to this alliance. Unfortunately we cannot offer you the same gift, as we only have one shard between us, but I'm sure—"

"Man King. Me have angry. You tell me. What me get?"

"Ulv Nikos, with the greatest respect, do you still want to fight? I want to make peace with all races; to find the shards together and live in a world that suits all of us. Surely that should be the ultimate goal?" The king stepped forward and the two guards tensed, teeth bared and claws at the ready.

"Peace," barked the Ulv.

"Tell me, Ulv, why have you been scouting our outposts?"

"Me want shard! Me want Man gone. Me want Forsaken gone. Me want Marusi gone!"

Sir Victor pulled King Areth back a little, growing more terrified for his safety.

Captain Levana smiled. "Look, *dog*. Either you join with us and we find these things together, or you stand against us and we crush you."

The larger of the two guards raised a lethal claw, snarling and barking.

The Ulv grew angrier, and his claws dug deeper still into the roots that formed the throne's arms. He snarled and salivated as his black eyes threatened the throats of the disarmed group. Ulv Nikos lashed out and grabbed the wrist of the larger guard, before he could take a swipe at the Captain. He pulled the guard close, grasped his throat, and stood on his hind legs, lifting the struggling Wolven closer to his face, and in the Wolven tongue he said, *"They are MY prey."* He squeezed his giant hand tighter.

The Wolven guard thrashed and flailed, gasping for air, scratching at the Ulv's arm.

The group took a few steps back; sweat beading on Sir Victor's forehead.

The Ulv tightened his grip further and his razor-like claws pierced the neck of the yelping Wolven. Blood flowed down his arm, soaking his fur, and dripping off his elbow. Life slipped away, and the Wolven guard went limp before the Ulv dropped him and faced the group once again.

The other guard whimpered, and scampered from the room.

Ulv Nikos fixated on King Areth, oblivious to his surroundings as he lurched forwards, towering over all but Sir Victor. "You come to *my* den. You have friend to *my* enemy. You ask peace to *me*?! You insult. You mock. You think to me have weak. Me Ulv! Me decide to you have death!"

With Ulv Nikos distracted, Captain Levana edged her way along the wall to the Wolven corpse. She crouched and whispered an ancient language in his lifeless ear. A white glow surrounded the corpse and lifted it a few inches from the ground. Light entered its skin from every direction, coursed through the body, and reanimated him, different parts at a time. As he settled to the floor, this glow shot out through his eyes and faded into the air, leaving behind the infamous red glare of a Forsaken.

"Welcome back," whispered Levana. It will take time to adjust; I'll explain later. Right now we have a bigger problem."

Healed, the seething Wolven clambered to his hind legs. He snarled, teeth dripping with revenge, and he leapt upon Ulv Nikos. Aggressive grunts and snarls bounced off the earthen walls as the two Wolven clawed and ripped at one another, locked in animalistic combat.

Captain Levana picked up the group's weapons and tossed them to her colleagues. She led the escape down the only tunnel from the chamber. As they ran, echoes of yelps and howls chased them.

Sir Victor halted and rested his hands on his knees, panting. "We should help him!"

"No, Sir Victor, we have to get out of here." The king continued to run, beckoning the others to follow suit.

They reached an intersection, where tunnels branched off in different directions. "Which way now?" asked Queen Lucia. "There are dozens of tunnels leading to a dozen more."

"I can feel wind on my face coming from this way, hurry, and quietly! We can't be caught." The king made a sharp turn, and the others followed him down one of the winding tunnels. After a few more moments of running, the tunnel began to open up.

Captain Levana stepped in front of the king and came to an abrupt halt. She and the others skidded to a stop and looked ahead in horror.

They stood in one of hundreds of entrances to a superbly vast chamber. The two Forsaken squinted, barely able to make out the opposite wall. They looked down and recoiled; gigantic winding tree roots—many of which appeared to serve as dwelling spaces—intertwined and entangled the empty space. The party gaped in fantastic shock as hundreds of Wolven pounced and leapt across the roots, with an unparalleled agility.

"Quick, against the wall." Queen Lucia pressed against the soft earth.

A slow patter of feet echoed through the corridor and approached from behind. Their hearts sank like stones in a lake.

Captain Levana drew her quick-blades. "Looks like we're fighting our way out of here."

"Be cautious, Captain. On my signal..." Queen Lucia drew her slender rapier.

King Areth and Sir Victor followed suit, drawing their glimmering Eveston steel broadswords in preparation for an ambush. They waited, ready to attack as the footsteps grew closer and heavier.

The queen took a few steps forward and lowered her blade, peering around the corner into the darkness. She raised her palm behind her as a signal for the others to lower their weapons, then turned and smiled.

The source of the footsteps—a limping, blood-soaked Wolven—hobbled around the bend, bringing relief to the party. He clutched his stomach, trying desperately to stop the bleeding.

"Well, well; it's the rogue dog." The Captain paid no mind to the blood flowing out of the creature. "What happened to the Ulv?"

Gasping for air, the damaged Wolven replied in whimpers and low growls.

The queen's smile vanished as she relayed the message to the two men. "The fight was fierce, but the Ulv is coming for us. He has already alerted others and word spreads quickly." She gestured to the red-eyed Wolven. "He is going to show us the way out."

Sir Victor was skeptical. "Why would he help us?"

"For giving him a second chance. But now's not the time to quibble. We have to go. Now." The queen gestured for the Wolven to lead the way.

Using his keen sense of smell, the newest Forsaken directed the group through what felt like miles of tunnels, excavated by the Wolven several hundred solars ago.

Captain Levana attempted to spark a conversation with their new ally. "You. You make a pretty good fighter. What's your name?"

The Wolven shook his head, as he led them through yet more winding tunnels and steep inclines.

"No name, huh? How about we call you Wrath? The spirit of vengeance!"

The Wolven didn't react. He pointed ahead to a sliver of light squeezing its way between some roots and leaves.

The party increased speed as they dashed towards the promise of an exit. They burst through the brush and back into the murky glow of the Triash Forest; while the men stood by a nearby tree to catch their breath, the Forsaken surveyed their surroundings.

Wrath grunted at Captain Levana with a nod.

"Good, then Wrath it is!" she replied. "Don't get soft on me though, dog,"

Amazed, King Areth stepped closer and scanned the Forsaken. "Your communication skill with these creatures has proven invaluable, My Queen."

The queen flashed her perfect teeth and winked. "There's more to me than just looks, my dear." She flicked a strand of silky hair from her face.

"But there is one question... how is the Ulv able to speak our tongue?"

"All Wolven are capable of learning our tongue, but only the Ulv has a need to use it. Traditionally, the Ulv is the only one who uses it often enough to not forget."

Snout to the sky, Wrath sniffed the air and growled.

"He's right," said Queen Lucia. "We need to move."

Wrath turned to retreat back inside the den, but stopped short at Captain Levana's bellow.

"Wrath! Where do you think you're going?"

He responded in grunts and growls, gesturing to the den.

"Yes, and then you'll get ripped apart. You're a Forsaken now, dog. You're with us."

Wrath barked and bared his teeth at her insulting tone.

She laughed and walked closer, unintimidated by his threat. "You saw her, right? I brought you back from Knas and you helped us. Why would you want to go back now?"

A series of vicious barks and snarls followed, terrifying to all who couldn't understand the Wolven language.

"Ha! Of course he'd kill you. He's already done it once! Come with us, I'll teach you our tongue. There are many Wolven Forsaken at the Fortress already."

Wrath paused then grunted at the Captain.

"Well, you'll be the biggest one by a long way. Aside from the Ulv, I've never seen a Wolven as big as you are. You'll be an asset to my army."

Wrath nodded and barked once more, to which Captain Levana laughed.

"Don't push your luck. I'm not about to go soft on you, *dog*."

"Captain, please; there is no need to insult him," interrupted the queen. "We need to get out of this place and regroup with the others."

"Agreed. Let's go," added the king.

Captain Levana glared at Wrath and beckoned him to come along. It took a moment, but he followed along, keeping his snout to the sky.

Wrath's pointed ears flicked up and he sniffed the air behind him. Sensing danger, he growled and gestured for the others to stay back.

"What is it?" asked Captain Levana, readying her blades.

As she spoke, two Wolven emerged from the bushes behind them and another two dropped from the trees at either side. Without hesitation, they attacked.

With amazing speed, Wrath clamped his powerful jaw around the throat of the closest Wolven. His teeth soaked with blood, he dropped the lifeless corpse and pounced on another—a little too hastily. This Wolven swiped and caught Wrath's face, leaving a deep gash down his eye. Wrath caught the creature's other arm as it came in for another swipe, and pulled the Wolven towards him. He raised his hind legs, using them as a lever against the body of the beast, and wrenched the arm from its socket. An ear-splitting yelp carried out through the forest, silenced with an accurate claw to the throat.

King Areth and Sir Victor watched in bemusement and shock at the sheer speed and strength of their newest ally.

Captain Levana wore a manic grin as she looked on. The scene rang out with a multitude of barks, growls, and yelps as the two remaining Wolven fought against their much larger undead counterpart.

Queen Lucia stepped forward to help, but a third Wolven's life-blood poured out onto the forest floor in a horrific display of combat. The fourth beast scampered off.

Wrath pounded into the dense thicket, hunting the escaping survivor.

"Wrath! Let him go. We have to get back to the Fortress," called Levana.

He stopped in his tracks. Reluctantly he barked at the Captain and bared his teeth.

"No. You will follow my orders like a good dog."

Queen Lucia glared at her Captain's continued use of insults.

Unamused, the Captain grunted."Just follow my orders. We go. Now!"

With her final word and no objections, the party pushed on towards the exit with Wrath begrudgingly leading the way.

* * *

The party emerged from the forest and met the rest of their troops. The majority of King Areth's men paced on the backs of their kytling. The Forsaken troops sat calm and collected on horseback.

Queen Lucia gestured for Wrath to follow her toward the Forsaken knight, Sir Robert Drake. The king's men gaped at the size of this beast, following the Forsaken ruler like a pet. "Forsaken, we have a new member. His name is Wrath. Sir Robert, the shard, if you would be so kind." The queen held her hand out.

"My Queen." Sir Robert bowed.

Sir Robert pulled the shard out from a small pocket in his jerkin and handed it to his queen.

"Thank you, dearest." She put the shard into the pocket of her leather breeches.

"How did it go, Sire?" Boris asked King Areth.

"Not well, my friend. We need to go, and fast."

The king turned to face the Forsaken and cleared his throat, a steely look of determination on his face. "Queen Lucia, you and your troops head back to the Fortress; we will head back to Straeta to plan our next steps. Everyone shall be informed of the day's events."

The queen folded her arms and a smug smile crossed her lips as her gaze traced him from head to toe. "Of course, Areth dear. But what now? The plan to ally the Wolven has failed. Your master plan to unite every race has come to naught. As it stands, you have lost your only shard to me, with only my word of allegiance."

"I saw you back there, Lucia *dear*."

The queen unfolded her arms and scoffed.

"We work well together, and you know it. Neither of us would have come out alive on our own. We've proven what we can do, so let's build on that. It failed with the Wolven, but we go on to the Marusi; they will be far more willing to talk. We know they possess a shard, which means we still have options. Do not be so quick to abandon hope, My Queen."

Queen Lucia huffed in disbelief and mounted her horse. "Then for now, *My King*, we part ways. I hope to see you soon dear, we have some unfinished business." She winked at him and took the lead back towards the Fortress.

Her Captain and the rest of the troops followed with an unmatched discipline.

"Sire," interrupted Sir Victor.

"Yes?" King Areth broke his gaze away from the queen. "Yes! Sorry, my good man. Is Violetwing ready?"

Sir Victor presented the king's beautiful kytling, who shuffled to her Master and cawed with affection.

"She's missed you, Your Majesty." Boris handed Violetwing's harness over.

The large mount ruffled her almost luminous purple feathers and bowed her head, rubbing her neck against his head as he stroked her.

"Hey, girl! Let's go home." He checked the harness and bellowed. "Men! We ride straight for outpost Markuss! I need to discuss some important matters with the Captain there. I fear some trying times are ahead of us all.

"Boris," he pointed to a large black bird happily cawing away overhead. "Send your raven off to Straeta with a message informing them of our success. Also send an order that my children are to be escorted to the outpost. I fear I'll not get much time with them.

"At once, Sire." The soldier grabbed a message scroll from his bag and whistled sharply. The raven responded with a piercing caw before swooping down to land on his shoulder.

The king donned his helmet, hooked onto his saddle, and mounted the kytling. He pulled down his visor to cover his troubled face, as his mind drifted to unfavourable potential futures.

Chapter 5

Attack

Queen Lucia sat, legs folded, atop her great Triash throne and studied the most recent reports from Rogue.

REPORT 11,347 — TRIASH FOREST, WEST DIONUS REGION

RUMBLINGS NOT AS PROMINENT HERE. WOLVEN ARE SPREADING THROUGHOUT THE TRIASH FOREST. SUSPICIOUS ACTIVITY FROM WOLVEN IN RECENT DAYS, DISAPPEARANCES OF WOLVEN FORCES, FEWER SCOUTS, ULV NOT SIGHTED. WILL MONITOR AND CONTINUE DAILY REPORTS. CURRENTLY MOVING TOWARDS TRIASH MOUNTAIN.

REPORT 11,289 - TAKTUUN, SOUTH EAST BUI'INAR

ODDLY ENOUGH, RUMBLINGS ARE JUST AS PROMINENT HERE AS THEY ARE AROUND THE GOLZHAD VOLCANO. HERE, HOWEVER, THEY ARE MORE CONTINUOUS. LITTLE EVIDENCE OF TAKTUUN RUINS REMAINS. NO SIGN OF KORKRENUS - LIKELY EXTINCT. WILL SEARCH FOR THE SOURCE OF RUMBLINGS AND CONTINUE DAILY REPORTS. CURRENTLY MOVING TOWARDS JOKTUUN.

Her chin rested in the palm of her hand.

Over four-hundred solars and still no Korkrenus sightings. They can't have disappeared into thin air.

Distant memories played out in a haze of horror, at the demonic destruction these ancient Naeisen titans had wreaked.

The heavy throne room doors burst open with a crash and Captain Levana stormed in. She handed the queen a scroll tied with a sturdy length of grass, bearing the signature of Rogue.

"Lucia, I think you'll want to read this report immediately. The warrior who presented it felt it was of such importance that he told me its contents."

Queen Lucia unfurled the report. Her smile vanished and her eyes filled with fear, yet she remained collected and cleared her throat. "Captain, when is this due to hit?"

"If they've already mobilised, no more than three days."

"Send a message to King Areth calling for his aid. We will suffer great casualties alone against such a large force of Wolven, especially if they are led by the Ulv."

"It'll take a messenger three days to get to Man's outposts! We don't need their help! I can—"

"Now, Levana." The queen's face darkened.

Without so much as a retort, the Captain bowed and turned to follow her orders.

The queen called, "Levana, my dear, when you're done arranging the message, take this to Rogue." She strolled forward and placed the brilliant white Mys shard into the Captain's palm. "I don't trust anybody else with it."

Levana closed her fingers. "But if I'm gone, who will lead the troops against the incoming attack?"

"Wrath will know more than the other Wolven Forsaken, let him take this one."

"But he's a recruit, he doesn't know—"

"I have faith in him," interrupted the queen yet again. "You will give him this chance."

"Lucia, please, I—" replied the Captain, raising her voice in increasing frustration.

"Are you disobeying my orders, Captain?"

"Perhaps. Are you trying to replace me?"

Queen Lucia approached the Captain and stood mere inches from her face. The two locked eyes. "Need I remind you that I am the queen? There is a reason I chose you to be my Captain. Don't make me regret it. Now, follow your orders and return to me when they're done."

Captain Levana growled and stomped out of the room with the shard clutched in her hand.

* * *

Late summer sunlight glared on outpost Markuss and bathed an array of emerald leaves in a warm, settling glow. King Areth brought his children to the meadows surrounding the outpost as he checked the status of the previously sighted Wolven scouts.

Sir Markuss and his men guarded the Northernmost of the four outposts, strategically built many solars ago on hills several miles out from Timbrol East. They spanned the narrower part of the land where the Kingdom of Man kept a watchful eye, and acted as an impressive early warning system. During these ages of war, this system proved vital in giving the leaders time to organise proper defences and repel incoming attacks. The outposts sat in a direct line of sight of at least one other outpost, each with a beacon poised atop a central tower which was lit when necessary. Since their construction, these beacons had only been lit once, when a grand and fierce Wolven force attacked.

The beacons proved effective; the system had been used to prepare traps, diversions and to coordinate enough opposing force to drive back the attacking army, and ultimately win the fight.

The king stood with his son near the beacon at the top of the outpost, still wearing his signature armour, now sporting the addition of his royal purple cloak.

Prince Areth rested his hands on the low wall overlooking the breathtaking sea of hills, covered in different coloured flowers.

The king's three daughters made daisy chains in the field below, blissfully unaware of the nearby soldiers.

Areth looked to his father. "Father, I've never been out beyond the towers. What's it like?"

The king placed a reassuring hand on his son's shoulder. "My boy, I'll take you out beyond the towers someday soon. Perhaps you can accompany me to the Undying Fortress one day, to meet Queen Lucia of the Forsaken!"

"A real Forsaken?! I've only heard stories! You must take me, Father!" The boy's grin widened.

"You have grown fearless in your pursuit of knowledge, my son. Consider it a promise; you will need to meet our new allies, if you are to become the future King." He returned the smile and held an arm open for his son.

"I promise to be as brave and courageous as you, Father."

Areth hugged his father and a full blown smile jumped onto his face at the prospect of adventure. The king always tried to encourage his son's inquisitive nature, although it seemed he feared more for Areth's safety than the boy himself did.

Sir Markuss stooped as he came out of the doorway from the central stairwell.

The king looked up and greeted him with a warming smile, reaching for a handshake. "Sir Markuss! It's great to see you. How goes it here?"

The knight grasped the offered hand with a firm grip and bowed. "Sire, since your visit to the Triash Forest there have been no Wolven sightings. This worries me, considering your negotiations were unsuccessful. It all seems too calm."

King Areth's smile faded and his brow crinkled. He stroked his rough beard, his mind already racing through defence strategies. "It unnerves me as well. What precautions have been set in place?"

Sir Markuss pointed to a plume of smoke on a hill in the distance. "We have a small encampment there looking out for any incoming troops or messengers, and they will alert us with a smoke signal. It is the quickest possible way of preparing, in case of an attack."

"Genius idea, my friend!"

As if in response to this news, the smoke from the encampment began to change. Small, quick plumes rose from the flames and puffed out into the sky. The king looked to his knight, ready to receive dire news.

Sir Markuss eyed the smoke for a moment and then breathed a sigh of relief. "No need to panic, Sire. There is a lone horse rider approaching; most likely a messenger. It will take some time to arrive at current speed."

"A messenger? One of ours?"

"Impossible to tell at this distance, Your Majesty."

King Areth gazed towards the smoke.

"What of the other outposts? Have they had any news?" The younger Areth glanced at his father for confirmation, and received a gentle smile and nod in return.

The king looked to a surprised Sir Markuss to answer his son's question.

"An excellent question, young Prince. You'll be a fine leader one day, much like your father." Sir Markuss bowed his head. "We have stationed additional troops at each of the other outposts, as immediate back-up. Outpost Johan has nothing to report; beyond them to the south, outposts Baer and Sasha report tremors in the ground, different from the ones coming from the southwest. They are not sure of the source, but they seem to be more frequent—at least three reports have come in during the past lunar cycle, compared to at most one in previous cycles. I have no further information, but Sir Baer and Lady Sasha, will no doubt be able to provide more detailed accounts."

"Thank you for your continued work, Sir Markuss. We shall go to speak with the other outposts to find out more." The prince beamed at this successful interjection, and he looked to his father once more to await instruction.

"No need to travel, Sire," a strong female voice answered from behind them.

The king grinned with delight, and they all turned to see Lady Sasha Swiftblade bowing before them.

"Apologies for dropping in unannounced, but I heard His Majesty and young Prince Areth had come to visit," she announced with the utmost seriousness. "I felt I should report my findings in person."

Lady Sasha took her role as commander of Outpost Sasha with all the gravity she felt it deserved. Her reputation, as a valiant and fair commander, preceded her. She often used her wealth of experience and expertise to help younger recruits grow into fine soldiers. She had earned the name 'Swiftblade' by demonstrating exceptional skill with a sword. She'd refined her style and focused predominantly on speed and quick, fatal strikes.

"Wonderful, Lady Sasha! What do you have to report?" asked the king.

"Sire, the rumblings do not correlate to that of an approaching army. To our knowledge, there doesn't exist one large enough to generate such force. Even if one did exist, it would have been sighted by now. The fact that Outpost Baer are feeling tremors too, and more powerfully than we are, suggests that they are not coming solely from the Golzhad volcano like we first suspected. Observations of the volcano conclude that it does seem to be active again, but unless there were an eruption, Sir Baer should not be able to feel it at his southern outpost. As of now, there are no theories on why this is happening, and I would suggest sending a long-range scouting party to try and locate the source of the rumblings."

"Could it be Wolven tunnelling underneath us?" asked the king, concern on his face.

"Wolven could not generate a force big enough to shake the ground simply by digging. We have men patrolling the area, but they have seen nothing."

"Thank you for your report, Lady Sasha. Keep up the good work."

"Sire." Lady Sasha bowed, turned on her heels and walked back down the stone steps to the base of the tower.

King Areth walked to the inner side of the tower and peered over the edge to check on his daughters. They waved, showing off the various lengths of daisy chains.

Evelyn yelled, "We made this one for you, Father!" She sported a daisy-crown.

Warmness filled his heart, and a loving smile crept across his face. "It's beautiful, I'll collect it later."

The shadow of the tower protected the girls as they frolicked amidst the flowers in the long grass. The delightful sound of their giggles drifted on the air.

"Your Majesty!" shouted Sir Markuss from across the top of the outpost. "A Forsaken rider approaches."

"Remember, Sir Markuss, they are allies; show the rider no hostility."

"Of course, Your Majesty."

The knight bowed once more and rushed off to prepare his men for the arrival of the messenger, ensuring they would heed the king's words, despite his discomfort with the situation.

Prince Areth tapped his father's shoulder. "Father, can I meet the Forsaken with you?"

The king pondered for a moment before nodding and grabbing his son's shoulder with a firm hand. "Very well my boy, but stick close to me. They may be our allies now, but we still must be cautious and mindful at all times. Remember…"

"Rule with my head, not with my heart," concluded the boy.

King Areth chuckled and beamed with pride. "You're a good lad. Come on, let's go."

"Yes!" The prince gave the straps on his breastplate, a smaller version of the one his father wore, a quick tug and offered his father a confirmative nod.

The king led his son to the bottom of the outpost, where they regrouped with Sir Markuss, who waited for the rider, now visible in the distance and approaching with great haste.

King Areth walked to his daughters and crouched. Evelyn presented him with the daisy-crown, but her gift was met with a solemn look. "Not now, my sweet. A messenger from the Forsaken is on his way to bring me some news. I want you all to wait inside with Lady Sasha."

"Why Daddy," questioned Eleanor, "is he a bad man?"

"No, he's not a bad man darling, but he may be bringing bad news. Please wait inside, I'll be back soon to claim that wonderful crown you all made for me!"

Evelyn and Eleanor clambered to their feet, and the king picked up Anya, who threw her arms around his neck. He followed the two older girls to the outpost entrance and handed a reluctant Anya to Lady Sasha.

"I won't be long; I love you all very much. Lady Sasha, thank you. Keep them safe."

"With my life, Sire." Lady Sasha comforted Anya and started to lead the girls inside.

"Father why does Areth get to go?" yelled Evelyn as she spotted her brother.

"Evelyn, your brother is older than you, and one day he will have to conduct these talks himself."

"But why can't I?"

"You are too young, my Princess. Now please, go inside and argue no further!"

"I want to come too!"

"Evelyn..." started the king, his temper rising.

"Sire, if I may be so bold," said Lady Sasha. "Evelyn is nearly eleven solars now; if we are to be allied with the Forsaken, don't you think it would be wise to negate any fear she may have developed for them, before mistakes of the past are made again?"

"I do not wish to put them in any danger, my Lady."

"But you would put your son in danger? If we are truly allied with them, what real danger is there? Look around you. There are many troops surrounding us and but one Forsaken rider."

"No, but... I..." He met Lady Sasha's intense stare, then dropped his gaze to Evelyn's eager face. Knowing he was out-maneuvered, he sighed heavily and motioned for the girl to come along.

Unlike her brother, Evelyn was not dressed for combat; She wore a flowing white dress made for playing in the warm summer sun.

"Stay close to me, okay?" He turned and addressed her younger sister. "Eleanor, I need you to look after your little sister, can you do this for me?"

Eleanor saluted her father, then took the daisy-crown from Evelyn. "I'll keep this safe for you too."

"Good girl, thank you. Now we must go and see what news approaches."

Anya's gaze was strongly fixed on Lady Sasha's shaven head as the knight led them inside. She smiled and winked at the littlest princess. "It makes sword practice easier; hair gets in the way."

King Areth and Evelyn joined the prince as Sir Markuss strode towards them, with Sir Robert Drake in tow.

"Sire, may I present—"

"Sir Robert! My friend how are things?" The king reached for a handshake as Sir Markuss bowed away from the pair and stood to witness the exchange.

Sir Robert towered high above the king's two eldest children and glared at them with piercing crimson eyes; he shifted his weight, uneased by the presence of children.

Evelyn cowered behind her father's leg, but Prince Areth stood strong and hid his fear in the presence of the undead soldier.

The Forsaken knight shook the king's hand with a puzzled look.

"Sir Robert, may I introduce my son, Areth, and my eldest daughter, Evelyn. I apologise for the way they look upon you; they've never met any of the Forsaken before."

Sir Robert nodded, then spoke with a sense of urgency. "Your Majesty, the Undying Fortress is soon to be attacked by a large Wolven force. We estimate one-thousand are amassing, and are being led by Ulv Nikos himself. There is no way we can fight them alone—we require your assistance."

The king's face dropped, and he pondered the situation. "How long do we have?"

"Unfortunately we do not know when the Ulv started moving, or exactly what route he's taken. It's likely we are already under attack. "

"How many warriors do you have?"

"Just under two-thousand, but this won't be enough against the ferocity of the Wolven, especially in such a large pack. I need to deliver your response to the queen at once, Sire."

"Sir Robert, ride back and inform Queen Lucia that a further one-thousand able fighters are on their way. Unfortunately, that is all I can spare at this time."

"The queen sends her thanks, I'm sure."

Sir Robert bowed, hurried to his horse, and heaved his huge frame onto its back. "It was nice to meet your children, and indeed the future of Man." He rode off at great speed.

King Areth stood in silence, still stroking his beard. His children and Sir Markuss all looked to him for guidance, but he had already fallen deep into his thoughts.

Prince Areth tapped his arm several times to get his attention. "Father... Father! What happens now?"

The king jolted from his trance and placed both hands on the young boy's shoulders. "Areth, are you able to take your sisters back home to Straeta? I can get an escort to meet you at the port in Timbrol West."

"Yes, Father. Will you go to fight the Wolven?"

"I'm not sure; either I go myself, or I send Sir Victor in my stead."

Evelyn clutched her father's waist. "Please come back safe, Father."

"If I go in person, I will remain cautious, my sweet." He gave the girl a quick hug. "Now please go with your brother and help him care for your sisters."

Without question, Evelyn and Areth ran off hand-in-hand to collect their siblings and make the journey to Straeta Keep.

"Sir Markuss, send a raven to Lissy. Have her meet the children at Timbrol West and arrange an escort to ensure they all arrive home safely. Also, I need you to send word to Sir Victor to assemble his army—we must leave as soon as possible. It's at least two days to the Fortress; I pray to Mys we can make it."

"So, you are going?"

"I fear I must. It is necessary to prove I am taking this alliance seriously."

"Well, if you can make the Fortress in two days, I'll be impressed, especially since it will take Sir Victor at least until dusk to assemble his men and lead them here."

"That's what I'm worried about. The Fortress is designed to keep attackers out so I hope it will stall the Wolven long enough for us to arrive."

"I hope you're right about this, you're a much respected leader and . . . well, just come back safe, Sire."

"Thank you, my good man. Please, join me inside. I must draw up a plan of attack and would value your input; Wolven are not exactly easy foes to fell."

Sir Markuss nodded and gestured toward the doorway, allowing the king to enter before him.

* * *

King Areth sat with Sir Markuss on cold stone stools, a large map unfurled on the floor between them. Torches on the walls flickered, bathing the room in a dim, orange glow. Sunlight leaked in through the open door and illuminated the map.

The hand-drawn map pinpointed the exact locations of every known landmark. A stone replica for each outpost sat in their rightful positions for easy and efficient military strategy. The men studied the map using coloured pebbles to represent armies and their locations. With no more information to go by other than the Wolven's imminent attack, they applied their best guesses.

King Areth was a genius and tactically brilliant when it came to battle, but he could not accurately predict how an individual conflict between Wolven and Forsaken armies would pan out.

"The Wolven will most definitely be attacking from the Triash Forest to the west; it makes sense for the Forsaken to defend the western wall more heavily than the other fronts. To arrive quickly, we have to come from the south. Coming from the east or west would add too much time to the journey, so the Wolven will be attacked from the east, and the south." The king drew his fingers across the map and moved stone markers into position.

"But what if the Wolven surround the Fortress? We know their pack mentality when it comes to fighting . . ." Sir Markuss shuffled the pebbles around surrounding the castle-shaped marker representing the Undying Fortress with enemy troops. ". . . they surround the enemy."

"Hmm, good point. Well, if they are in one large group on the west wall, we must come from the south and envelope them; this will force them against the walls and allow the Forsaken to dispatch many of them them from above. If they surround the Fortress, we can't surround them; our men would be spread too thinly." Again, the king moved pebbles around to prove his point. "But then, the only gate is on the southern wall. Surely the Wolven will want entrance to the Fortress, which means they will have to attack from the south. We would arrive after them and could flank them—that would be a sure victory."

"What if they have already gained access to the Fortress? Would we admit defeat? I say our main target is the Ulv, so we should focus the whole fight on him." Sir Markuss picked up a dark pebble and moved it aside.

"No... if he goes down, another Wolven will just take his place." The king placed another large stone in the same spot. "They are not lost without a leader; they work by strength only."

The knight stood and groaned as he stretched his legs. "I shall check on the preparations."

* * *

Sir Markus returned to the king's side. His brow furrowed as he studied the map and coloured stones, resting his hands on his waist. "Dusk is closing in, Sire. What have we decided?"

"We are fighting this battle blind. We cannot know the situation until we arrive, and when we do, we will need to adapt quickly." King Areth sighed and brushed his hair from his face, his eyes still locked on the map.

Sir Markuss knelt and scratched his bald head, going over all the information previously discussed. "Ah! Sire, there is an avenue that could win us this fight. I mentioned their pack mentality—"

"Yes, it makes them all the deadlier."

Sir Markuss began to move the rocks around again. "I've fought the Wolven a few times, but never more than a small pack—fifteen or twenty. I've never known them to split up voluntarily. They communicate incredibly effectively using short grunts and body language, meaning their synchronicity in battle is unparalleled. The most effective method I've used is to force them to separate into smaller groups."

He separated the group of rocks into two. "They panic, get aggressive, lose control and make a lot more mistakes. It's not easy to do, but I suggest using a spear-head formation, and driving right through the centre. Although with such a large army you may just end up with two packs."

"Hmm. What if we were to use several spearheads and split them further?"

"By doing so, you risk spreading your men too thinly, Sire."

"Of course, I see. So, we split into two groups, flank them, and spearhead from opposite sides. This will cut off half of their force from the attack on the Forsaken, and give us both a more even footing."

"I can see it working, but you'll need another force to prevent your troops from being flanked. If the Wolven's attention focuses on your army and not the Forsaken, you will easily be surrounded."

"This is too difficult to plan blind, for all we know we're wandering right into a Forsaken trap."

"You don't trust our new allies, Your Grace?"

"No, no, it's not that I don't trust them; let's just say I like to think of every scenario. It is a possibility."

"Of course, Your Majesty. I think it best to witness the situation and then act accordingly. It's risky, but it seems to be your only option."

With this, Sir Markuss stood and checked outside. "The sun will be setting soon, Sir Victor assured us the men would be ready by sundown."

"Very good. Is Violetwing ready?"

"Almost, except she won't let us saddle her up tonight."

"I'll see to her, thank you, Sir Markuss."

King Areth rose from his stool and strode outside to watch the sunset. He paced the grounds waiting for Sir Victor. His hand cupped the rugged beard on his crumpled face once again retreating into his thoughts. The ground began to vibrate, and a low rumble rolled in. The king stopped and whistled for Violetwing, who came bounding at his call. He adjusted her saddle, and scanned the horizon in a wash of panic then sighed.

Sir Victor thundered towards him, leading a mighty force of capable men and women riding an array of kytlings and horses with supply caravans in tow, all prepared to lay down their lives for their King.

The king climbed aboard his large affectionate kytling and waited for the advance of his army. When they reached earshot, he unsheathed his sword and raised it to the sky. "We do not stop! We fight for our alliance—for peace!"

"Fighting for peace? Ha! Whatever it is, we're with you," hollered Sir Victor.

Almost in unison, the army lowered the visors on their helmets and began their ride to the Undying Fortress.

* * *

As they rode through the Darklands, the sun crept over the horizon. Hefty plumes of smoke originated from the Fortress. The troops and their steeds felt the strain of the impending battle already.

The smoke in the distance made the king's heart heavy and he spurred Violetwing to ride faster. He pulled ahead of his army with panic squeezing his chest.

As the monstrous Fortress came into view, there seemed to be no sign of a Wolven army. Instead, hundreds of Wolven and Forsaken corpses littered the ground surrounding the walls. The great portcullis stood intact, a detail which gave King Areth a spark of hope swimming in the sea of anxiety within him. As

Man's army rode within a stone's throw of the walls, the portcullis raised to let the king and his knights through without question. Sir Robert Drake, looking pained and battle-torn, met them just inside. Fresh gouges in his armour told the king all he needed to know.

"King Areth, you are too late. The queen wishes to speak with you at once."

"We came as fast as we could; the queen is unharmed?"

"Luckily, yes. Please, this way. Your troops will be provided for shortly."

The Sire looked back at his army, now all stationed just outside the walls, and gave them a solemn nod before following Sir Robert to the top of the central spire.

In the main throne room, Queen Lucia sat in her usual place looking as elegant and resplendent as ever— only this time, she appeared incredibly unsettled.

She looked up and dismissed Sir Robert with a wave of her hand. As soon as the door closed, she sighed and shot King Areth a malicious glare. "Here at last, my dear." Her eyes dropped to her hand, picking at the wood on the arm of the throne.

"I'm sorry, My Queen. I have been informed we are too late. We rode as fast as—"

"Thanks to you and your *plans*, the Ulv came for more than revenge. He came for the shard and when he discovered it wasn't here, he destroyed some of our buildings and left." Her voice grew dark and unnerving.

Unperturbed, the king took a stride forward and raised his voice. "You agreed to this when you agreed to an alliance. Did the Wolven acquire the shard?"

"And *you* agreed to protect us when we needed it. Of course they didn't, do you think me a fool?"

He averted his gaze. "I understand your—"

"You understand nothing!" Queen Lucia stood and stomped to the window to gaze over the destruction.

He clenched his fists and ground his teeth. "How did they get in? The gate is intact."

"Over the walls," replied the queen curtly. "The agility of these beasts while they're alive is incredible. They helped each other climb and jump their way over our walls, into the Fortress."

"How many did you lose?"

"Enough... but it's not all bad I suppose. There is a handsome new battalion of Forsaken Wolven lying around outside."

"Is there anything my people and I can do?"

The queen turned, still scowling, and approached him, standing mere inches away. "We need to show the Wolven this won't stand. We need to tear. Them. Down."

His Majesty refused to break eye contact. "Okay."

"What did you say?" Queen Lucia's jaw dropped, and she stepped back.

"I said okay. We'll do it."

A grin broke out across her face, shattering the tension in the air. "The King of Peace . . . will exact revenge?"

"If it cements our alliance, yes. The Wolven bow to power only, so it's time we show them what real power is."

A manic laugh erupted out of the queen. "So then, what do you suggest, my dear?"

"Leave that to me. Focus on rebuilding here. I will leave some of my troops to assist you, providing you can keep them well, and I will send a messenger when the time is ripe."

The queen circled, dragging her finger across his chest and shoulders as she went. "Don't leave me waiting, dear Areth..." True death smiled through her eyes.

A chill washed down his spine as he took a deep breath and headed to the base of the spire.

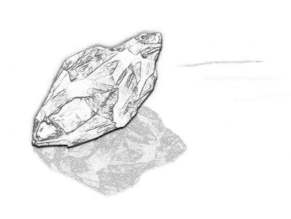

Chapter 6

The Island

The transport ship docked at Timbrol West's magnificent dockyard after an exhausting journey and the gangway lowered onto the wooden boards with a thump. King Areth led Violetwing out with sadness in his eyes.

Sir Jacob galloped to meet the disheartened king, carrying important news. "Your Majesty! I am delighted to find you are safe and well."

The king brushed some of his golden hair from his face. Fewer than half of the soldiers departed the ship with him. His chest was puffed, but despite this air of confidence, his gaze seemed to pass through Sir Jacob, settling far into the distance.

"Sire, where are the rest of the men?"

"We were too late. The Wolven had won, but they didn't get the shard. I've left half of our men behind as a precaution and the outposts are all on high alert." The king glanced behind him and signalled for his remaining troops to be dismissed.

"Has this affected our diplomacy?"

"I am unsure, my good man. I spoke with Queen Lucia personally." He stroked an ever-growing beard.

"She was reasonably angry at first, but I think I calmed her—although we will have to change strategy. She is unstable and I'm not entirely sure I trust any of the Forsaken."

Sir Jacob interrupted. "What's the new strategy? If you don't trust the Forsaken and the Wolven aren't willing to ally, it seems we are at a loss."

"The Wolven would not listen to reason, but perhaps the Marusi will."

"With respect Your Grace, the Forsaken and Marusi are hardly the best of friends; they—"

"Neither were we if you recall correctly. Still, I have hope they will uphold this alliance. They seem to be sticking to the agreement currently."

"Understood, Sire." The knight sensed his angst and did not want to exacerbate it. Sir Jacob disagreed, but he trusted the king's judgement, as did everyone in the kingdom.

King Areth massaged his eyes with his thumb and forefinger as a gentle sigh left his lips. "I apologise for my frustration. It's been a long and stressful ride back, and the fate of Naeisus is still far from positive."

"Of course, Sire. I understand. I do not wish to add to your burden, but I have information to report about a recent discovery."

"Before I hear the report, please, tell me how my children are."

"Lady Lector has been very kind to them, as usual. They are looking forward to your return." He chuckled, glancing towards Straeta before adding, "She is a fine woman; she cares for them as if they were all her own."

The king looked at his feet and grinned. "Indeed, she does."

"Sire, one of our fishing vessels has discovered a new island to the far north, about half a day's sail." He pointed to the horizon, his gaze following his finger to where the setting sun dyed the clouds a brilliant array of orange and rose.

The king repeated with piqued interest, "A new island?"

"Yes, Your Majesty. You see, the usual fishing shoals have been migrating further north recently, which may be related to the rumblings being reported by the outposts. Our ships have had to sail much further to catch a good haul."

"Has anyone set foot there yet?"

"It appears not, but from a distance it seems it may be a good source of ore. It's not a very large island, perhaps smaller even than Straeta, but if there is a rich ore deposit beneath it, it could be of great value to us."

King Areth's hand found his chin, massaging the thickening beard. Crinkles appeared on his brow. "Interesting; Sir Jacob, I must go home to see my children. His fingers fiddled with the straps on Violetwing's saddle. I can't help but wonder how long they will be safe from the Wolven."

"But Sire, Mannis is a difficult island to get to without ships; I do not feel the Wolven will be a threat here."

"Seeing their resourcefulness has sewn seeds of doubt in my mind. It will put my mind at great ease to make further preparations. Ready my ship for tomorrow morning. We will bring my son, and William Stone, to this new island and scout. We will soon see if there is anything of value there."

"Very well, Your Grace." Sir Jacob bowed with respect.

With that, King Areth hauled himself onto Violetwing's back, and tapped her neck.

* * *

The rising sun crested over the Straeten Keep, flooding in through Lissy's spare room window and bathing the king's face in warmth. It was his decision to not go home the previous night, but instead stay here with Lady Lector and his children; he would be leaving the girls with Lissy again today while he and the prince explored the mysterious new island.

He dressed in light leather armour, suitable for exploring, before helping Areth don similar gear. Together, they walked downstairs to meet the girls for breakfast.

Chatter exploded around the table as everyone spoke of what exciting possibilities awaited them on the island.

"Maybe there is a big castle there," exclaimed Evelyn with a mouthful of egg.

"And a big field with lots of daisies." Eleanor waved some bread around.

Anya giggled along with her sisters. "And shiny trees."

"Shiny trees? My, my, I'd love to find one of those, my little one." Lissy placed another piece of bread in her own mouth.

As the laughter settled, Areth took a solemn look at his father. "Father, will it be dangerous?"

The king placed a hand on the young prince's shoulder and smiled. "Perhaps, my boy. That is why your sisters cannot join us until we know it's safe. Now grab your sword, we must meet William and Sir Jacob in Timbrol West before the sun has fully risen."

"Father, do you have to leave already?" groaned Eleanor, sadness etched on her adorable face.

"It's okay, Eleanor," chirped a beaming Evelyn. "It's his duty as King, but he always comes back for us! Right, Father?"

"Yes, you know I will always be back, for all of you." Eleanor's face lit up as her father's rugged hand brushed her cheek.

Lissy ambled to the door, checking over her shoulder at the king and his son following behind. Her golden hair came to rest down the front of her silk nightclothes.

She looked Prince Areth in the eye and rested a hand on his shoulder. "Look after your father, okay?"

"Yes, My Lady." The prince returned her sweet smile.

She turned to the king and stroked his cheek, before pinching it to amuse herself. "And you look after him! Don't worry about the girls, I'll take care of them as well as I always do."

Lissy glanced at the princesses. Their giggles and idle chatter about the mysterious island filled the room with a pleasant aura. Lissy caught Anya glancing up and beaming. Her heart flooded with warmth and her eyes softened.

"Areth, go and see to our kytlings, I'll be there shortly," King Areth ordered.

Without question, the young man disappeared around the side of the house to prepare their birds for the ride to Timbrol West.

Lissy waited until she was sure Areth was out of earshot, then with an affirmative nod, she folded her arms and leaned toward the king, against the doorframe.

"It means the world to me that you let me spend so much time with my daughter, Areth," she said, in a loud whisper. The three girls inside the house played and joked, too caught up in their fantasies to pay any attention to the quiet conversation at the door.

"I would hate to part from my children, so I would not keep your child from you." His Majesty glanced at his daughters. "I'm happy that you treat them all equally.

The other three don't have their mothers any longer, but they still need a mother figure in their lives. I'm confident they all see you as that."

"You never speak of what happened to their mothers. Why?" asked Lissy with a sympathetic expression.

King Areth inhaled deeply and held his breath. He exhaled with an uneven breath and responded with the aptitude one expected from a king. "Areth's mother died from disease, when he was very small, and Evelyn and Eleanor's mother . . . she . . ." He took another deep breath and held back a surge of emotion, collecting himself before continuing. "She was a fierce warrior, but was bested by Wolven shortly after Eleanor's birth."

"You truly loved her." Lissy placed a reassuring hand on his arm.

He shook it off and straightened. "I do not wish to speak of her further, please."

"Do you not think they deserve to know?"

"Areth knows of his mother. I will tell the girls about theirs when the time is right. Please, Lissy, you cannot breathe a word of this to them." He flung his hand out and gripped her shoulder.

"You can trust me, but they must know soon, Areth."

"Of course. They will—but they also cannot know that you are Anya's real mother right now. It would break them apart, to know that only one of them still has their mother around."

"I know. I am aware, and I will always see them all as my own."

His grip loosened and he softly stroked Lissy's arm. She bid him farewell with a hug and headed inside to attend to the girls. Muffled laughter spilled from the door as King Areth sighed.

From around the corner, the footsteps of his son and the kytlings grew louder, before all three stopped beside the king.

"Father, we are ready."

"Good work, my boy. Come on, let's go."

The kytlings rustled their wings and squawked with excitement as the men climbed on their backs and rode off towards the main gate of Straeta.

* * *

Shuffling hooves on cobblestone echoed around the empty streets of Timbrol West as the sky began to lighten.

"What do you really think is on this island, William?" Sir Jacob steadied his restless steed.

"I dunno, but I'm 'oping it's a ton o' ore!" A wide, toothy grin swept William's face. "We can use it to forge grea'er weapons an' armour fer the troops, fortify the walls, even better shoes fer the 'orses!"

Sir Jacob's mouth opened, but no words fell out. Instead, he diverted his attention to the unmistakable patter of Violetwing's talons.

As they arrived at the ship, William Stone flung his arms wide open and a deep chortle escaped him. "I was jus' tellin' Sir Jacob 'ere that with the resources we find we could reinforce the walls, build more outposts beyond the four we 'ave, and give some ore to Philos in Eveston fer more weapons an' armour." William ran a hand over his beard, his full cheeks flushed red with excitement.

King Areth chuckled at the enthusiasm of his trusted friend. "We don't know what's there yet, good Sir! Still, the day is bright and warm, and it will be a fine sail, even if we return empty handed."

"Aye." William punched the air.

"Huzzah!" Sir Jacob beamed with delight.

"Sire, we must depart at once." William's voice rang out across the quiet, early morning cobbled streets of the city. "I'm enthused to see what this island holds fer us."

The king looked to Sir Jacob with a grin, awaiting confirmation.

"The ship's ready. On your command, Sire."

"Then, my friends, my son—" He looked at each in turn. "We depart!" He finished with a subtle bow, sweeping his arm toward the gangway. The men boarded the royal ship and set sail for the mysterious island to the north of Mannis, dreaming of the wonder that lay ahead.

The king had an unsettled look plastered on his face, as potential dangers of the unknown swarmed his over-worked mind.

As the ship sailed onwards, waves began pounding the hull. Gently at first, but beating harder and harder the closer they got to the island. Storm clouds drew in like a curtain, almost completely obscuring the midday sun. Rumbles of thunder growled in the distance.

Sir Jacob scrutinised the rain-soaked island ahead. "This is most odd."

"What is, my good man?" asked the king. "The storm?"

"When my men first reported this island, they were forced to turn back due to a storm despite it being clear and calm all day. I simply assumed it was bad weather." Sir Jacob furrowed his brow and rested his chin in his hand. "I find it strange that there is still a storm."

"It's just an unlikely coincidence. The storm doesn't seem all that bad. We are almost there, let's push on."

The ship sailed on until it lurched forward, its keel scraping the sand. William strained and groaned as he hauled the anchor overboard. The ship came to a dead stop a little way out from the rain-soaked beach and aggressive waves lashed at the oak hull, thudding and thumping against the wood. The ramp released into the water and the small group of explorers stepped out, leaving their horses and kytlings aboard the ship, sheltered from the awful weather.

They squinted through the pounding rain at what appeared to be a silhouette of a ruined structure in the distance. A handful of oak trees dotted the island, and various sized rocks made up the rest of the landscape. The men used their arms to shield their faces from the spray of the sea washing over them.

King Areth scanned the area then raised a hand. "Look, to the east, and then to the west," he shouted through the howling wind.

"I see nothin'," yelled William.

"Exactly, now look south, behind the ship!"

"Still nothin', Sire!"

"It's not raining in those directions, Father. Just here." said Prince Areth.

"Exactly, my boy! I think there's more to this island than it first appears."

The other two men scratched their heads as they surveyed the scene.

"I think we should find some shelter and assess that structure up close." Sir Jacob pointed toward the ruin. As they stepped foot on land and headed towards the strange building, the rain intensified. Thunder rolled out across the sky as the strong wind turned into a gale and became difficult to walk against. Pushing forward became more of a task with every step, until it became too much for the young prince.

"Areth, turn back! The storm is getting too dangerous." The king pressed his hands against his son's back, supporting him through the aggressive winds.

Areth wiped away the water streaming into eyes and nodded.

On his return, his steps became easier; the wind eased more and more until he arrived at the ship with just the heavy rain.

"Father!"

No reaction.

"Father!"

Still nothing.

Prince Areth could do nothing but watch as the three men forced their way forward, arms crooked around their faces and toes digging hard into the ground. The king, Sir Jacob and William Stone continued to fight hard against the increasing storm until they reached the edge of the structure. They found a small, broken wall and stood behind it, recovering their energy from the trek to this point. Pieces of rock crumbled and broke away from the unrecognisable cobbled stone structure.

Again, thunder rolled throughout the sky, and this time lightning thrashed the ground with violent force as the rain pelted down upon them with unmatched intensity. The three men all pressed their backs to the ruined wall as they scanned the drenched environment for whatever clues might help determine the past life of the ruins.

"Look." Sir Jacob pointed to a scorched spot in the centre of the structure. "The lightning is only striking in that one spot." He spat water as he spoke.

"The man's right! That's mighty strange. I reckon this 'eld some impor'ance one time or another," roared William.

"Something underground is drawing the lightning to that spot. Perhaps a chest or some other treasure?"

"I reckon there's some kind o' hidden trap door that leads underneath, there's gotta be! Ain't nuffin else 'ere!" William's voice cut through the gale, but fell on deaf ears.

King Areth's face unscrewed and he clapped with excitement. "Men, stand back!" He unsheathed Ichtheon, a glorious short sword, from its leather scabbard. He stood close to where the lightning struck and watched. After every crash, he mouthed, "One, two, three—" CRASH! "One, two—" CRASH! "One, two, three—" CRASH! A smirk formed on his lips. Timing it right, he leapt and jammed the sword into the ground.

CRASH!

A bolt of lightning lashed the pommel of Ichtheon, narrowly avoiding the king as he pounced away.

William and Sir Jacob looked on, their hearts in their mouths. Fear soon turned to amazement as the lightning struck the blade, no longer blackening the ground it previously battered.

King Areth turned to his men and wiped away some of the water streaming down his face before pointing to the sword. "We must move quickly, whatever is attracting that lightning is buried there! Take caution, the lightning is still close and immensely unpredictable."

"Man's a genius," responded William. He bolted for the stricken patch, dropped to his knees and used his huge, calloused hands to grab at the scorched sand. A lifetime of manual work had made his hands so tough the heat didn't bother him enough to make the dig a challenge, especially after the rain cooled it a little. His fingers scraped something hard and he dug faster, revealing a glass sculpture, which emanated a red glow.

William's eyes widened as he battled against the rain water trying to fill the hole back in. He dug harder and faster until he could grab the strange object and give it an almighty heave. As it loosened from the ground and broke away, William fell flat on his back clutching the object to his chest. It rested on his leather jerkin radiating an impressive crimson light that stunned the men. He began to sit up, still gripping the jagged edges of the glass object.

William yelped and tossed it high in the air, shaking his hands and blowing on them. "Blasted thing!"

It came crashing down to the ground, landed on a stray rock and shattered into thousands of glistening pieces which reflected the pouring rain. The king shielded his eyes from the exploding glass. As he dropped his arm, he saw it; amidst the pieces of broken glass, it shone brilliantly.

The men gawped in sheer awe at its strangely familiar beauty, drawn to the power.

"Bloody Knas! It's one o' them shards from the Yultah Crystal," exclaimed William.

"It seems so, my good man." The mystified king reached out with caution to pick it up. The shard was almost identical in size to the Mys shard and glowed deeper than the deepest ruby-red as he lifted it.

The lightning stopped at once and the rain reduced to nothing more than a drizzle. The sturdy oak trees nearby, close to snapping in the gale, seemed to sigh as a cool breeze drifted across their leaves. The men all looked to the sky in wonder, rainwater still running down their faces. They returned their gazes to the shard still resting in the king's grip.

"Which one do you suppose it is?" asked Sir Jacob.

"I'm not sure, we only know of three. The white Mys shard that can heal wounds; the Marusi's blue Bui shard, which is said to be able to control water; and the green Tur shard, lost in the Korkrenus city of Joktuun. The other three are still missing; well, two now."

"I wonder what power this one possesses." Sir Jacob was lost in the infinite wisdom swirling around within the gem.

"Something to do with storms, I would guess. We must get it to Philos in Eveston. He can analyse it and tell us exactly which shard it is and what it can do. We must also send an envoy to Queen Lucia and inform the Forsaken of this incredible discovery. Perhaps this at last will convince the Wolven to join us."

With that, King Areth stuffed the shard into his trouser pocket and reached for his sword.

William screamed. "Careful, Yer Majesty!" William flung an arm out to stop him. "That'll burn to touch. Allow me." He pulled a dirty cloth rag from his belt and used it to hoist the sword from the ground before tossing it into a nearby puddle where the blade hissed and sizzled as it cooled.

The king thanked the Master of Resources as he picked his sword up and examined the freshly melted pommel with dismay. "This is going to have to be reforged." He sheathed the weapon.

As they made their way back to the ship, the clouds began to clear. Rays of sunshine pushed their way through, drying the sodden ground.

Sir Jacob looked at the ruins they left behind. "With your permission, Sire, may I return and study this place further?"

"Permission granted, Sir Jacob. Although I suspect there is nothing more here now."

"If there's ore," interjected William, "I'd like permission to mine it an' use it."

"Of course, my good man. You may do what you will with this island." The king looked over the land, then stopped the others, a seriousness in his eyes.

"There is still a gravely serious matter we must discuss, men." King Areth placed a hand of each of their shoulders.

Worry filled their eyes.

With a grin, he asked, "What are we going to name this little land?" He slapped their backs and laughed at the slight panic he'd caused.

William and Sir Jacob joined the laughter, and began suggesting names—some silly, some serious.

"Sir Jacob's island," started Sir Jacob. His suggestion was refused by the other two.

"Little Mannis," suggested William with a hearty chortle.

"Traegor," shouted Sir Jacob.

"Traegor... " said the king. "I like that. Did you make it up?"

"As far as I'm aware, it's ancient Maurish for storm."

"I didn't know you knew ancient Maurish," responded the king in astonishment.

"I don't, really. I've picked up a few words while studying the Marusi. When I was overseeing Timbrol and the crossing, I thought it best to be prepared for anything that might surprise us. It made sense to learn what I could about the amphibious Marusi, in case they surfaced from the water."

"Sir Jacob, you have just demonstrated perfectly the reason I appointed you as overseer of Timbrol. Traegor. I really do like that. Henceforth, this island shall be known as Traegor. Perhaps an ancient Maurish name will help us establish peace talks with the Marusi."

The three men began to chuckle at their incredible luck as they made their way aboard the ship ready for the journey back to Timbrol West.

* * *

The king and prince lay on the ship, listening to the gentle hiss of the ocean waves soften in the distance.

"Father, what will you do with the shard?"

"I will go to Eveston." He faced the prince. "Philos has a vast wealth of knowledge on these matters, and surely he will be able to unlock its power."

"Shall I tell Lissy and my sisters?"

"You're coming with me, my boy! We'll inform them when we return from Philos. How's that?"

The prince gave a subtle nod, before a yawn forced its way out.

"Get some sleep, my boy. We have a long day's ride tomorrow."

The gentle ringing of the harbour bell alerted them both that they had reached Timbrol West. The king and his son gathered their things as the sun began to set.

Sir Jacob shuffled below deck. "Forgive me, Sire. I must retire home for the night."

"Of course, good Sir. After spending the day sailing us back, I think a rest is much needed!"

Sir Jacob bowed and took his leave, dragging himself to his steed.

Mounted upon their kytlings, King Areth and the prince saluted William Stone and began their ride to the industrial city of Eveston.

Mannis' luscious green meadows and rolling fields seemed to glow at night. The moonlight from both Bo and Dalon glinted off dew droplets in the thick grasses, twinkling like a sea of scattered diamonds.

* * *

The sun crested over Eveston's city walls, and the silhouettes of tall, winding buildings cast shadows for miles across the plains, as if stretching out to reach them.

The guards spotted the pair heading for the elaborate gates. The iron portcullis was raised, but revealed no greeting party.

Prince Areth scanned the impressive city. "Wow, Father! Eveston is beautiful! How come the architecture is so different from Straeta? The buildings here seem taller."

"Eveston is much younger than Straeta, my son; we've learned much about construction since then.

We've also poured more iron and steel, hence why we can add aesthetics such as those twisting spires and bulbous watch towers."

"The colours are brighter here, look at all these purples and blues! Even the roads are level and smooth!"

"Philos discovered the secret to making metal shine with a specific hue. The man really is a genius."

Areth's mouth fell open as they rode past interesting statues of kytlings and horses. He pointed at a large circle on the ground with a locked trapdoor. "What's that?"

"Ah, that is the well, which leads down to the mines. It's where Philos finds all the resources he needs to make Eveston steel and continue his technical research. Only people authorised by me or him are allowed entrance. This entire city was built around that well. Without it, or Philos, we'd not be half as prosperous as we are today."

As they rode towards Philos' laboratory on the far hill, Prince Areth continued to marvel at the intricate patterns detailed into every building and structure. A few guards patrolled the streets, all recognisable by their silver-trimmed Eveston armour. The king and his son dismounted their kytlings and let them run free around the surrounding grassy hill.

His Majesty knocked at the door.

It creaked open to a hunched over, bony old man. He looked up through bushy white eyebrows leaning on his staff for support. He broke into an airy, crackly laugh. "Your Grace. I saw you coming through the gate."

"It's good to see you, Philos! You remember my son?"

Philos squinted then broke into a toothy smile. "How could I forget the young Prince! You've grown since I last saw you, my boy." He patted Areth on the arm.

The prince bowed. "Thank you, Sir. You're looking well."

"Please come inside. We have things to discuss." Philos led them to some finely constructed Triash chairs, positioned beside a roaring fire in a stone fireplace.

The old man sat, leaned forward, and watched King Areth reach into his pocket to pull out the brilliant gem. Philos' eyes widened, and his bony hand slithered towards it, enthralled by its power.

"Philos!" The king snapped him out of the trance. "We found this on an island to the north of Mannis. We know it's a shard, but we don't know any more than that. Can you tell us more?"

"Yes... yes... this is unmistakable. May I?" Philos snatched the shard from the king's hand and examined it from every angle. He stroked every facet, obsessed with the power radiating from within the crimson exterior. With eyes squinted, he fondled it, even sniffed it at times, then yelped in excitement.

On the edge of his seat, King Areth asked, "What is it?"

"Did you notice anything strange around the shard when you discovered it?"

"Yes, the whole island was engulfed in a storm, yet the skies were clear around the island. The moment we excavated the shard, the storm cleared. Lightning had struck the sand so many times, glass encased the shard."

"If I recall correctly, the Dion shard possesses the power to manipulate the clouds and the wind." Philos was unable to avert his gaze from the gem. "The holder of this gem may decide when and where it rains, the wind direction and speed, even where lightning strikes. If my texts are correct, of course."

"Fascinating," added Areth.

The king held a hand out, but Philos cradled the shard and wrapped his fingers around it, eyes closed. He focused then glanced at the window. A faint tapping came from the window. Rain began to fall around the laboratory. Philos grinned and then attempted to place the shard in his pocket.

"Excuse me, my good man." The king thrust his palm forward, narrowing his eyes.

"Apologies, Your Majesty. Please forgive a senile old man, heh. A simple mistake." Philos removed the shard from his pocket and reluctantly handed it to his leader.

"Of course," the king replied with a warm smile.

Prince Areth eyed the old man and glanced over at his father, who put the shard in his own pocket. He noticed Philos's face turn sour but chose to keep quiet for now.

"So, tell me, have you any further technologies for the kingdom?"

"Ah yes, Sire! Do you remember those Fireballs I gave you at the council meeting a while back?" Philos appeared to forget about the shard.

"Yes, we've not used any yet, but I still have them." King Areth's tone was somewhat apologetic.

"Never mind that; I've decreased the size of the orbs and increased the potency. I'm working on crafting a device to project the orbs over a distance so that one may target an enemy from afar." His fingers came together and tapped against one another as he explained.

"That sounds incredible! Please keep me updated with any progress you make. I'd like to see a prototype when it's ready."

"Of course, you will be the first, Your Majesty." His eyes sunk deep below huge eyebrows giving his face a sinister turn. He coughed and sputtered a little before continuing. "I've also managed to extract some more purified coal from beneath the well, so we can increase our production of Eveston steel. I've taught many of the blacksmiths here how to use it to increase the temperature of their furnaces and imbue more into their crafts. Our weapons and armour will be strengthened upon your command, Sire."

"Excellent!" The king drew his damaged blade. "As you can see, my sword has suffered and will need reforging, if you would be so kind."

"I'll deal with that for you. Return in two days and it will be done." Philos shuffled in his seat, shifting his weight. "Eh, if I could be so . . . bold, Your Majesty, I'd like . . . I-I'd like to use the shard to experiment with for a few days, if you'll allow it?" He rubbed his hands together, like he was expecting a hearty meal.

"Unfortunately not, my good man. I need to inform the Forsaken of this find and together we will decide where it should go. Perhaps we shall keep it here, or perhaps offer it to another nation for their allegiance."

"As you wish." Philos's voice was sharp and he spoke through a clenched jaw as he ground his teeth.

"We must ride back to Straeta, my friend. I apologise that the visit was so short." The king stood and made for the door.

"No apology necessary. Thank you for dropping by."

King Areth and the prince left the laboratory, and the door slammed shut. They whistled for their kytlings who came sprinting up the hill to greet them.

"Father, I don't trust Philos."

"Philos is a good man—just old and weathered. His temper gets the better of him, but he will do us no harm."

"Remember what you taught me, Father. Don't be blinded by friendships, always remain aware."

"You're a smart boy, but you must also trust my judgement. I have known Philos since I was a boy, and he has always offered a helping hand."

The prince simply nodded, unwilling to argue with his father, and mounted his kytling. "What now, Father?"

"I need to speak with Queen Lucia once more. I only pray that she has looked after our troops and still honours the alliance." King Areth furrowed his brow.

Our goal of peace is getting closer, I can feel it. I just need to convince the Wolven to join us without causing damage. That will surely cement a unified future. After that, the Marusi . . .

Chapter 7

Counter Attack

King Areth stood with Queen Lucia at the throne room window in the Undying Fortress and admired the grand army assembled on the esplanade.

Queen Lucia smirked. "I'm glad you came so quickly, my dear."

"Well, now we have the Dion shard and this magnificent force, we're sure to beat the Ulv into submission." Areth grabbed her hand, almost recoiling at her inhumanly cold skin. "I hope this proves my resolve to the alliance, Your Grace."

Lucia smiled that infamous bitter-sweet smile and nodded. "With our combined forces there are nearly six-thousand warriors. A force this large hasn't been witnessed for centuries, at least not all in one place."

These former enemies now stood shoulder-to-shoulder against a threat that obstructed the path to true peace. The king and Sir Victor's cohorts consisted largely of cavalry armed with spears, and kytling riders behind them wielding swords. Two huge groups of archers, led by Queen Lucia and Captain Levana, flanked them. Forsaken Wolven backed them all as foot soldiers, armed with nothing but their own teeth and claws, and hungry for living flesh. Sir Robert Drake and Wrath fronted these groups with a fierce leadership that none dared contest.

The army stood poised and ready. Captain Levana and Sir Victor Blackrock rode side-by-side, screaming words of encouragement and raising morale. Their troops returned a ruckus of thunderous cheers and battle cries. The force looked frightening.

King Areth's troops bore Man's sigil on their shimmering armour. The near-white colour of Eveston steel radiated and brought a proud sense of grandeur, which contrasted sharply with the Forsaken troops, wearing whatever armour they salvaged from the land around them and previous battles. One-hundred of the best fighters wore custom steel armour, gifted to them by King Areth and his blacksmiths.

Queen Lucia grinned as she fondled the ends of her hair. She rested her dainty, pale hand on King Areth's thick pauldron, then leaned in and kissed him on the cheek.

Resolute, he continued to scan the troops, watching as the four commanders rallied their battalions into fighting frenzies.

The Queen chortled to herself and spoke softly. "You're a man of your word, aren't you, my dear?" The tone sent chills down his spine.

"How many Wolven did you say attacked the Fortress?"

She tapped her sharp fingernail against her chin. "It was hard to tell. I'd estimate it to be around one-thousand."

"Before your eyes are nearly five-thousand warriors, many of which used to be Wolven." King Areth averted his gaze from the window and focused on his ally.

"Don't forget, we are fighting on their grounds. The Triash Forest is thick. We couldn't get five-thousand warriors in there at once. All they have to do is separate us off and take us out groups at a time." The Queen moved her finger to his chin and dragged it down his throat. "If that happens . . . if your plan fails—"

The King grabbed her wrist and pulled his face uncomfortably close to hers, glaring into her eyes.

She pulled her arm free and laughed in his face.

He raised his voice, refusing to back away. "The Ulv's rage and arrogance will betray him. He will be easily lured out of the forest once he sees our small scout group approaching over the ridge."

Queen Lucia scoffed and turned to the window once more, resting her hands on the ledge.

"By sundown today," the king said from behind her. "We will either have a new ally, or the Wolven will not be a threat for some time."

"Or your dream comes to an end, my dear. We shall soon see."

* * *

Queen Lucia made the final adjustments to her new battle armour. The king stepped in and pulled the leather straps tight, jerking her tiny frame.

"Watch yourself, Areth," she grunted.

Pulling harder, he secured the straps in place. "I know how this armour is fitted, I had it made for you, just like mine."

Queen Lucia huffed as the breastplate squeezed her chest. "Yes, and I do adore it. This floral design that runs down the arms looks just divine; I especially love how the stems morph into blood and thorns. I hope you're not trying to hint at something."

"You're the Queen of the Undead, what was I supposed to have the smiths etch? Bunny rabbits and rainbows?" He placed the similarly designed rounded pauldrons on her shoulders and passed the straps around her arms. "Look, the blood-drop crest on your breastplate has the same hidden shard compartment as mine. You can hide the Mys shard there—it will still be close enough to your body to work."

The queen ran her fingers over the cold metal and a smile crept across her face. "Thank you, my dear, it's perfect."

As the two monarchs exchanged gazes, a cloud of silence lingered in the air. He basked in the moment, entranced by the depth of her crimson eyes. A freezing sensation engulfed his cheek and he brought his hand up to meet hers.

As the two drew closer, the mighty roar of Sir Victor's rallying cry broke the spell.

The king cleared his throat. "We should go. Our armies await us."

* * *

King Areth and Sir Victor nodded at one another in confirmation of their departure. The large knight slid on his angry-looking ram helmet, the tightly coiled horns completing the intimidating look.

In turn, Queen Lucia nodded at Captain Levana. The captain's favourite quick-blades rested in their sheathes, strapped to her back. Two short, curved daggers with a grip near the centre. She had designed these blades herself to allow freedom of movement and speed while battling, and there was no finer user of the twin blades.

Raising his renewed Eveston steel blade high above his head, the king reared Violetwing around to face the masses of troops. "Look at what we have achieved! Two races, once enemies for no better reason than the difference in our mortality, now fighting side-by-side. Look to the brothers and sisters on either side of you, look to them and protect them. We win by fighting together, united. The Wolven are not to be underestimated! Their coordination and strength are unparalleled, but the might of our alliance will break them. Our aim is to capture the Ulv, not kill him, but you may do what you wish with the others."

He paused to take in the flood of support from this rallying speech. He looked to Queen Lucia and Captain Levana, both unable to hide a hint of worry about the King's immense leadership skills. He pointed his sword at each of the battalion commanders in turn, then raised it to the sky once more. "Men! Women! Forsaken! To battle!"

A cacophony of battle cries dominated the land and echoed out for miles. Six mighty leaders mounted on kytlings and horses led an unstoppable force westward through the Darklands. The army thundered towards the Triash Forest with such force the ground shook with tremendous power.

* * *

Ulv Nikos bolted upright on his makeshift wooden throne.

New guards on either side of him bared their claws, preparing for something big. The thick black fur on the Ulv's back stood on end making him appear even larger. His eyes tightened, his tail flattened, and he snarled orders. He spat, voice low and gravelly, almost demonic as he aimed a claw at one of the guards.

The guard scampered from the room, hoping to get some information from the scouts who were due back any moment.

Ulv Nikos lifted his wrinkled and scarred snout to the ceiling, sniffing the air. He paced out of the room, beckoning the other guard to follow as he made his way toward the giant central chamber. The Ulv dropped his front claws to the ground and broke into a sprint. His attuned sense warned him that the rumbling he'd detected meant something large, and possibly dangerous, was headed in their direction. He reached the central chamber and loosed an almighty howl, which echoed throughout the entire Wolven complex.

From the many tunnels leading to this chamber, Wolven poured in, all answering the call of their strongest and scrambling to find places to perch where they could both see and hear their leader. The first guard rushed in followed by three scouts.

They panted and barked the news. *"An army of no more than five hundred Man and Forsaken rides towards our forest. King Areth and Queen Lucia ride at the helm, your Strongest."*

Ulv Nikos scoffed and spat his orders. *"Every Wolven capable of fighting meet me on the surface immediately. We charge to dispatch of this pathetic threat once and for all. Any not willing to fight, speak now, so I can end your worthless existence."*

The Wolven obeyed and hurtled towards their nearest exits. On the surface, the Triash Forest's trees jostled and rustled, as two-thousand Wolven gouged through tree bark and uprooted shrubs.

Ulv Nikos hunched over and panting, led with sheer rage. He let out a mighty howl and bared his teeth, salivating, grinding, snarling and spitting. A cacophony of deafening shrieks, cries, grunts, and growls responded, as the Wolven began to work themselves into a blind frenzy. It sharpened their senses, honed their reflexes, and pumped them full of adrenaline, turning them into merciless killing machines.

Ulv Nikos put one of his clawed hind paws in front of the other, each step quicker than the last until he picked up speed. He dropped his arms to the ground and darted along on all fours at an incredible pace, backed by his army of wild beasts.

* * *

Smirks formed on the faces of Queen Lucia and Captain Levana as the distant howling of the Wolven army drifted through the air. The Queen maintained her elegant poise, raised a dainty hand and pointed.

The Wolven cry shook many of the warriors—their palms began to sweat as they gripped their reigns tighter. Nevertheless, they pushed on, determined to finish what they started.

As they approached a ridge, a halt order was called. From here, they could make out the tops of the trees in the Triash Forest and miles of flat battleground ahead. The ridge itself concealed the true size of their army from the fast approaching Wolven. The king forced his arms in opposite directions and the small advance group spread.

The queen watched with a hint of jealousy in her eyes at the respect commanded by this magnificent man. Even her own troops followed his orders without question.

The opposing armies came into view where the sand and rocks from the Darklands began to show signs of green grass and life from the edge of the Triash Forest.

King Areth signalled his troops to stay in formation, expecting the Ulv and his Wolven army to mirror them, but they pounded on, relentless in their charge. A full-scale charge of hulking, salivating creatures, ready to shred apart anything in their path.

"Hold your positions! Cavalry! Spears!"

The army obeyed without hesitation. Hundreds of spearmen followed him to the base of ridge and lowered their weapons. They stood ready to catch the heads of any Wolven foolish enough to charge them.

"Archers! Take aim," followed the queen. Hundreds of archers drew their first arrows and aimed for the sky. Captain Levana and the rest of the army waited for the signal before they charged forward.

As the Wolven drew nearer, Queen Lucia let her arm fall from the air and screamed, "Loose!" Thousands of arrows whistled through the air, arcing over and hailing down on the Wolven army. A handful of Wolven dropped. Dozens more continued their assault, completely unaffected by the arrows sticking out of their limbs.

"Charge!" The rest of the army pulled into view, swarming the brow of the ridge. The Wolven didn't appear to notice as their pace only increased, continuing their charge with even more ferocity than before.

The king glared at Queen Lucia. "What are you doing?! Send another volley. Now!"

Queen Lucia's jaw dropped and a nasty glare shot from her crimson eyes, but she nodded and ordered another volley of arrows. A group of Wolven took arrows to the face, killing them instantly. She issued a third order to fire; arrows soared through the air and rained down on their targets. A final handful of Wolven dropped to the ground, but the rest drew too close for another ranged barrage.

The front line troops braced themselves for impact, digging their toes into the ground. The Wolven leapt over their spears; landing in the middle of the army. They slashed wildly, ripping at shields and armour, and cutting through steel and flesh alike. Some were impaled when they fell short and landed on the spears, but this only served to anger the other Wolven troops.

The two armies crashed together with a thunderous roar. Blood spewed in every direction as the massacre raged on like wildfire through a dry forest.

* * *

Ulv Nikos made a dive for King Areth and missed as Violetwing threw her master off. Instead, the Wolven leader landed on the brave kytling, knocking her to the ground. Anger coursed through his veins and the screeches of the kytling enraged him further. Narrowing his eyes, the Ulv lurched towards the unguarded king with a vicious growl in his throat.

"Give me shard!" demanded Ulv Nikos with his claws bared.

"Join us! It doesn't have to be like this." His Majesty readied Lycanire and his round shield.

Ulv Nikos dug his clawed foot deep into the dirt and churned up the soil as he stomped closer. "Give me or die!"

Violetwing reared up and snapped a chunk from his ear. She flapped her wings, and using her wickedly sharp talons, gouged his face.

The Ulv yelped in pain and swiped at the kytling.

"Violetwing, get back! You foolish bird!" screamed King Areth.

The giant bird turned to run, but before she could escape, the Wolven leader sank his claws into her ribcage and tore through a lung. She screeched in agony and collapsed.

The king looked on in horror. "You bastard! I just want peace!" He charged at the Ulv.

Queen Lucia, in an uncharacteristic act, fought her way to the injured kytling and knelt. She placed her hands on the grievous wound now gushing with blood and used her mind to activate the Mys shard in her breast plate. A swirl of light worked its way around Violetwing's body, shining with brilliance.

The Ulv turned to witness the healing light, leaving himself wide open to a mighty pommel strike to the back of his head. He collapsed face-first to the hard ground.

King Areth panted above him, sword raised.

"Areth, no!" screamed the queen.

Ulv Nikos lashed out, kicking his leg out and leaping to his feet. Several of the king's men rushed to his aid, but the Wolven leader effortlessly tore them down with a few skilful strikes. He leered at the Queen. "You! Give me now!" His rage seethed so absolutely, he disregarded the rest of the battle and stomped with blind ferocity towards the tiny queen.

Unperturbed by his intimidating demeanour, she laughed. "You'll have to pry it from my cold, dead hands you animal!"

Captain Levana and Sir Victor stood on either side of the queen and shielded a quivering Violetwing.

"Deal," growled the Ulv. His rear claws tore up the ground as he approached her relentlessly.

* * *

Sir Robert Drake directed his steed to a hilltop for a better view of the battle. He ordered his battalion to keep pushing forward through the ranks of Wolven. From the hilltop, he watched the Ulv advance towards Queen Lucia. He scanned the environment. His troops were segregated from the rest of the army, putting them at a great disadvantage.

A smaller group of Wolven broke from the pack and focused on devouring Sir Robert's battalion.

With eyes narrowed, the Forsaken commander reared his steed around. "Unit one, West. Unit two, East!" His face wore an expression of satisfaction as his plan unfolded, exactly to his design. With the Wolven pulled in two directions, their advance on the front of his battalion halted, and disarray began to set in.

Sir Robert's army circled back and formed a threatening perimeter. With an intimidating grunt, the army stamped forward, and forced the Wolven tighter together. Another grunt and another stomp, the circle closed in. With shields raised and spears pointing forwards, the Forsaken troops advanced another step. Ear-splitting howls pierced the air, but once again the army stepped forwards. Growling, snarling, and spitting the Wolven retaliated. Spears pierced the throats of many Wolven, but their claws slashed through helms, collapsing some Forsaken troops.

The battle erupted into a brawl, yet the perimeter held. For every Forsaken troop that fell, so did three Wolven. One by one the enemy yelped in agony and collapsed to the sodden ground. With a loud whistle from their commander, Sir Robert's troops stopped the attack and held a perimeter around the frightened beasts, who were now lashing out in undirected terror.

Sir Robert's horse leapt into the circle, its rider soaring through the air as he leapt off its back. The legendary warrior swung a gigantic steel hammer above his head, as if he were Knas's chosen warrior. He fearlessly brought his weapon down with such force that he crushed an unfortunate Wolven's head. He bellowed a blood-curdling battle cry and hauled the hammer high once again. Decorated with bone and fur, his weapon dripped blood as he charged.

The remaining Wolven fought back with all they could muster, but shock inhibited their communication, snuffing out their pack-fighting skills and making it easier for the Forsaken knight to dispatch them. A heart shattering yelp pierced the sky as the final Wolven's soul was torn from its body by Sir Robert's hammer.

Victorious, his troops cheered, but he silenced them and barked orders. "Go and assist the queen at once!"

Without question, the warriors turned and reinforced their monarch's position while Sir Robert scanned the battlefield once more.

* * *

Wrath had learned much of the Forsaken language, despite his reluctance to obey orders. He proved himself a mighty warrior and valuable leader, hence his position here on the battlefield. Sir Robert's battalion was clear of threat and charging the bulk of the Wolven forces, but Queen Lucia was in imminent danger—although it wasn't this fact that drove him to fight against his own on this day.

The bulky frame of the Ulv lurch towards the queen and scowled, baring his teeth. Wrath's lust for revenge fuelled him, but he wasn't getting anywhere near the Wolven leader until he cleared the pack of Wolven who were dominating his regiment. He howled and growled at his troops, before barking direct orders in their own tongue, "Push forward!"

The Forsaken unit dug deep, advanced, and dispatched the Wolven troops in their path. The enemy pack pushed back harder and skilfully dispatched another row of Forsaken warriors.

Wrath seethed with Wolven frenzy and slashed at the enemy. He closed his crimson eyes and relied on his other finely tuned senses. He merged with the Wolven fighters. Pretending to fight, he slipped to the back of the pack, leaving his regiment alone. With his snout raised to the sky, he let out a mighty howl, drawing the enemy's attention. His troops cut down a large chunk of Wolven foes before the confusion dissipated and their focus returned to fighting.

Fuelled with an insatiable sense of revenge, Wrath turned his back on the fighting and bolted in the direction of the Ulv, his visage nothing more than a blur as he hurtled with tremendous speed. His heightened reflexes caught any warrior that stood in his way, Wolven and Forsaken alike. With rapid slashes of his claws, troops fell—dismembered and writhing in agony as punishment for standing in his way. His troops fell into disarray, making themselves easy pickings for the tremendous power of the Wolven pack.

Wolven tore the limbs off those who let their guard down. Man and Forsaken thrust blades and points into the flesh of any Wolven foolish enough to turn their backs. Arrows flew through crowds, often hitting the wrong targets; horses and kytlings alike fell alongside Man, Forsaken, and Wolven fighters.

A few Forsaken warriors crouched near freshly slain corpses and attempted to bring them back—some successfully, others not. Warriors leapt from the lifeless bodies of their counterparts to gain a height advantage over the towering beasts, but were often caught mid-air and slammed to the ground with a fatal thrash. A handful of the larger Forsaken fighters could stare the Wolven in the eye. These troops wielded two-handed broadswords and some found the strength to thrust one, hilt-deep, down the throats of their enemies.

The dismembered bodies and limbs of fallen warriors littered the battlefield—trampled on, used as shields, and even used as weapons. The fight lost all honour and descended into a bloody brawl between man and beast, between the living and the dead.

* * *

Queen Lucia pointed her slender rapier at Ulv Nikos and flashed a threatening smile.

Captain Levana slashed the throat of a nearby Wolven and jumped to her queen's side, brandishing her lethal curved twin blades.

Sir Victor glanced at the assembling defence. He kicked a Wolven corpse from the end of his mighty claymore and joined the women as they faced the advancing Ulv. Three Wolven began to sprint to their Ulv's position.

King Areth dipped his hand into a hard leather pouch at his side and pulled out one of the two Fireballs he had brought. With careful aim, he hurled the metal sphere at the Wolven, scoring a direct hit on the snout of one of them. The sphere erupted with such force that it blew the teeth of the unsuspecting target through its skull.

The Wolven soldier dropped to the floor as his comrades looked on in horror. The king reached for another Fireball and with careful aim he slung it in the direction of his enemy. This time he missed, but the impact of the ball on the ground triggered the explosion, sending both Wolven hurtling backwards. Their bodies lay motionless on the floor.

King Areth drew his focus inwards. Without warning, it began to rain; lightly at first, but within seconds it escalated to a drenching barrage of pouring water, hammering the battlefield.

The king's hands reached to the sky, still gripping the sword. He smiled into the downpour. "It's working." His unarmed hand reached out. "Lucia, the Mys shard."

The queen slid her blood-drop crest to one side, revealing the shard.

The Ulv's eyes narrowed as he barked and threw himself forward. Captain Levana and Sir Victor jumped in his way and fought together, fending off his desperate attacks. No matter how hard he tried, he couldn't get past the pair's defenses.

Queen Lucia pulled the Mys shard from its cradle and aimed for King Areth. With a deceptively strong arm, she hurled it over the Ulv's head.

The huge Wolven leader reached out a clawed hand and, ignoring the blades of his adversaries, he pushed off the ground. He stretched, and as he was about to scrape the shard with a claw, a hand snatched it from his reach. Infuriated, he looked backward at Sir Robert Drake, who landed on the ground and made a dash for King Areth.

Fuelled with frustration, the Ulv landed a kick, knocking over the giant Sir Victor. He slipped the Captain's attack, and screaming in anger, made a charge for Sir Robert. He made ground fast and quickly caught up to the Forsaken knight. He dived and grabbed Sir Robert's leg, his claws piercing the armour like butter.

Ulv Nikos started to drag the knight backwards, but released his grip and yelped in agony as several sharp points pierced his back. He turned and used his powerful hind legs to launch Wrath through the air.

Sir Robert handed King Areth the Mys shard, much to the queen's relief.

Rumbles of thunder and flashes of lightning now filled the dark sky, as a brewing storm grew stronger and louder. With Ulv Nikos distracted, the king broke into a sprint, fury dripping from his eyes like sap from a tree. A gut-wrenching battle cry emanated from his lungs and reverberated as he sailed high into the air, leaving small craters in the soft mud.. He landed on the shoulders of his adversary and wrapped his legs around the Ulv's neck. The stench of wet fur and blood filled his nostrils.

With the Mys shard in one hand, King Areth aimed his sword to the heavens with the other.

An almighty crack drowned out the deafening ruckus of battle as the king called forth a wicked bolt of lightning. The fierce surge of electricity pounded through the sword and into the Ulv beneath him, yet any damage sustained was instantly healed by the power of the Mys shard. The Wolven leader's entire body radiated a brilliant white, as he screamed in agony.

The lightning seared and tore through flesh repeatedly, only to be rebuilt each time by the shard. Lightning consumed Ulv Nikos, paralysing him.

As suddenly as the lightning strikes started, they stopped, and the pair collapsed on the muddy ground. Smoke from singed fur rose through the rain. The king fell hard and motionless, and the Mys shard rolled from his limp hand.

The battlefield fell silent.

Every clash halted. All screaming stopped, and the ringing of steel on claws transformed to nothing more than a whisper on the wind.

Queen Lucia snatched the shard from the ground, dropped to her knees, and removed the king's helmet. The rain dissipated and the black storm clouds rapidly cleared, making way for sunshine once again.

Upon witnessing the collapse of their Ulv, the Wolven howled and retreated toward their home in the Triash Forest, abandoning the battle and their fallen leader.

King Areth's eyes heaved open, and he was greeted with a wide grin from Queen Lucia. Her drenched charcoal hair dripped water onto his face.

The queen stood and helped him to his feet, smiling sweetly. "That was quite a display, Areth." She eyed him up and down. "Okay, I believe you. You are indeed a man of your word."

Bodies of the slain littered the once untouched landscape. a few Forsaken analysed the corpses, resurrecting a handful of the deceased to recoup numbers lost in the blood-bath. The men roamed the fields looking for any signs of life and dispatching those Wolven who hadn't yet died from their wounds.

Queen Lucia held her palm to the King's cheek. "Areth, I'm relieved you're well and impressed you pulled that off."

Captain Levana scoffed.

"Do you have a problem, Captain?"

"No, My Queen. No problem at all." Levana paced away, avoiding the confrontation.

At King Areth's feet lay the motionless, hulking body of Ulv Nikos.

Sir Victor stood beside his king, with his sword still drawn as a precaution. "He's still alive, Your Majesty."

"Good, Sir Victor... Good." The King crouched beside the Ulv's gigantic head and grabbed his snout. "Ulv Nikos, wake up."

The great Wolven stirred with a grunt and flitted his eyelids open revealing his deep amber eyes. The king released his snout and stood, offering a helping hand.

The Ulv sat upright, swatted away the hand, and growled. "Why you no kill me?"

"I told you last time, Ulv Nikos, I want an alliance between us all." He glared into the face of the Wolven leader.

The Ulv traced his eyes across the surrounding landscape only to find his subjects gone. Ulv Nikos growled under his breath. "Me strong, no stupid."

He steadily helped himself to his feet, rising far above the people surrounding him. Wrath barked and bared his claws, looking ready to strike.

Captain Levana pointed a dagger at him. "Pipe down, dog!"

Wrath spat back at her. "Try it! I will show you true death."

She thrust the blade at the unstable commander, and he backed down, curling his claws into fists.

Ulv Nikos looked to each of the commanders in turn, then to Queen Lucia, and finally down to King Areth who refused to avert his gaze.

"What you give me?"

"Our loyalty, our men, our aid, peace." He sheathed his sword.

"Me want shards. Me want power," hissed the Wolven.

"Between us, we will get the shards. If we utilised the power of the completed crystal as allies, do you not think we could shape the world to a state that suits us all?"

"Me no have trust to you. You use us. You save crystal." The Ulv glanced to Captain Levana with this response. She grinned from ear to ear, Wolven blood splattered heavily across her face.

The king's voice raised, and he stomped a foot. "How do we know you won't do the same? You answer to strength, and I have defeated you. If you cannot answer me now, I will be forced to defeat you again, but this time it *will* be permanent."

Ulv Nikos responded with a snarl and shifted his focus between the faces of the commanders. All stared back at him, expectant of an answer.

Ulv Nikos sighed and bowed his head as a mark of surrender. "You have strong. You defeat me. If return, pack see me weak." Worry coated his gravelly voice.

"You are still the strongest Wolven. Prove to your people you are still capable of leading."

The Wolven King narrowed his eyes and glared. Finally, he huffed, "You win, Man King. Me yet have no trust you, or Forsaken. If you betray, me have promise. Me destroy all you."

King Areth broke into a relieved smile and held his arm out, offering the Ulv a handshake. "Good! Well, it seems that's the best agreement we're going to get."

With a grunt, Ulv Nikos engulfed the king's hand in his own mighty clawed one and shook it firmly, cementing the agreement and establishing an alliance. The Wolven leader looked to the Triash Forest and raised his snout to the sky. He sniffed, then crouched and without another sound, sprinted after the fleeing pack with immense speed.

Queen Lucia applauded and grinned at this. She strolled over to King Areth and looked at his rugged face, almost longingly.

"Well played, my dear. It seems your plan is back on track and the Wolven's allegiance is no longer an issue. That is, if that beast can convince his *people* to still follow him." She raised an eyebrow, expecting some sort of witty retort.

Instead, he glossed over her words and continued with the plan. "We've secured a Wolven alliance for now; that is all that matters. Now only the Marusi remain."

Sir Victor raised an arm and asked a question that lurked in the back of everyone's mind. "What about the Korkrenus? They haven't been reliably sighted since the shattering and reports are that their two cities are empty. Nobody is even sure if they still exist, but I think they are merely hiding."

"Sure, but if they don't exist, that's one less alliance to worry about." Captain Levana interrupted rather brashly, still wearing a manic grin. "I'll bet they were burned to charcoal during the Age of Fire."

"With respect, Captain, a race of sixty-foot tall earth demons doesn't just vanish overnight."

"With respect, *Sir*," sneered the captain, "why has nobody sighted one, despite expeditions to both Joktuun and Taktuun?"

"I don't know," said Sir Victor curtly. "All I'm saying is to not be so hasty as to assume they are extinct."

"The evidence is in front of you, Victor." She became angered. "Every race has many scouts. Every corner of Naeisus has surely been scouted in the last three hundred solar cycles."

"What evidence? If anything, there is a lack of—"

"Our priority," interrupted King Areth, "is the Marusi. We will worry about the Korkrenus if and when we find them. My Queen, what are your thoughts? You've been quiet." He turned to the Forsaken monarch waiting for an answer but shifted his weight uneasily at her gaze.

Queen Lucia stroked the King's jaw before mumbling to herself. "So much like him..."

A disgusted look passed between Levana and Sir Victor.

The queen snapped out of her trance. "You've done all the work thus far, my dear. Please, allow me to speak with the He'en of the Marusi. We Forsaken still know a little of their tongue, albeit an older dialect." She smiled.

"Are you sure? It's imperative we get them on our side."

"Yes. I'm sure. You go home and spend time with those darling little children of yours. Allow me to prove the value of the Forsaken on this mission."

Something about the tone of the queen's voice put him on edge, but this often seemed the case whenever the two conversed. The king brought his hand to his face and pondered the potential of this plan for some time. He spoke through his palm, offering a handful of his thoughts aloud. "So, you go and speak to the He'en of the Marusi. We know they possess the Bui shard and now between us we have the Dion and Mys shards. Perhaps we can use them as a bartering tool for their allegiance; maybe we should go together."

Captain Levana lurched forward. "No!" She quickly took a step back.

Confusion plastered the faces of the onlookers.

"No, you can't. Alkra is mostly underwater, right?" A devious flash crossed Levana's crimson eyes. "Forsaken don't need air anymore, therefore we can speak to the He'en in his or her own environment."

Sir Victor scratched his head. "You Forsaken are such unnatural beings. How can you not need air?"

His thoughtless question provoked the volatile captain, who stepped forward to offer her response. "I'll make it simple for you. You're alive, Knas is happy. I died, she is owed my soul. My soul was snatched away from her, and Knas grew mad. Following so far?"

"Yes,"replied a mildly vexed Sir Victor. "Continue."

"She now has a grip on my soul and is pulling it back, and let me tell you, that bit hurts. The only thing keeping my soul here is this body. It's become a kind of . . . jar for my soul. It no longer needs to support life—it simply needs to hold my soul. Break the jar, the soul is released. Get it?"

Sir Victor put a hand on the hilt of his sheathed sword. "A jar? So, if I cut you now, you'll collapse for good?" he jested.

"It takes more than a cut... and you can try, old man." She readied her own blades and narrowed her eyes.

"That's enough!" King Areth bellowed. "Queen Lucia, would you and Captain Levana be able to navigate Alkra successfully enough to speak with the He'en?"

The queen nodded.

Captain Levana raised a hand. "There is one more thing. Can we swap shards?" Her maniacal grin softened to a sweet smile.

The king eyeballed her. "Why would you want to swap shards?"

"Don't you trust us?" She looked to the queen for support.

"I do but—"

"Great! So, we'll need the Dion shard to help us ally with the Marusi, and you can take the Mys shard back as a guarantee we won't run away." She lurched toward the king with her hand outstretched.

"First tell me why you need this shard instead of the Mys shard. Your motives are unclear and make me uneasy, Captain."

"I feel it would benefit the alliance talks more. It would carry more weight with the Marusi than would the Mys shard; it would also serve to assist our journey to Alkra. The road is treacherous and wild beasts roam the land. A clear sky would serve to make this whole thing happen more quickly."

Again, the captain looked to her queen for back-up. This time, Queen Lucia noticed and stepped forward, holding out the Mys shard for the king to take.

"She's not wrong, my dear. The road is not safe and the Mys shard would do little to help us Forsaken."

Reluctantly, King Areth sighed and pulled the Dion shard from behind the crest on his armour, dropping it into Captain Levana's already outstretched hand. She grabbed the shard and held it to the sky, eyeing its beauty in the sunlight.

"Only because I trust you as allies. Do not fail, I urge you."

"We will not fail," reiterated the queen as she handed him the Mys shard. She looked at her captain with narrowed eyes.

Why would she make that pointless trade so suddenly and without discussion?

"Come, Sir Victor," said King Areth, holding the Mys shard up. "We should assist with the injured." He bowed to the Forsaken. "I bid you both good luck, and look forward to promising news soon." A nervous smile painted his face, as he led his head knight away, stepping around the litter of bodies to offer aid to the injured.

* * *

Queen Lucia watched them walk away. Her eyes narrowed as they moved out of earshot, then she grabbed Captain Levana's arm and looked her in the eye.

"Are you trying to make me look a fool? Why did we need to make that trade?"

"My Queen, I apologise. As I told His Majesty, the road to Alkra is dangerous and I hear the Marusi are even more dangerous. I only seek to bring it for protection."

"You are the most skilled fighter I know, why would that be an issue now?"

"I didn't want to have King Areth doubt we can pull this off. The more help we can get, the more chance we have of success, right?"

The queen let go of the captain's arm and stared her in the eye for a little longer.

"Do you trust me, Lucia?" The captain furrowed her brow.

"If I didn't trust you, my dear Levana, you would not be my Captain. I listen to your council, I consider your suggestions, I even go ahead with your ideas much of the time."

"Then allow me go see the He'en alone." Her eyes brightened, seeming to hold a grave secret behind them.

"What? A leader must see a leader!" replied the queen through gritted teeth. "The He'en will not consider an alliance if it appears I cannot be bothered to show."

"If you come and they decide to execute you, what then? The alliances fall apart. All your dear king's work for nothing. However, if I go alone and they decide to kill me, you and Areth can still consider other options."

A great deal of logic surrounded Captain Levana's words.

"No... I can't..." said Queen Lucia hesitantly, considering the outcome of her true death at the hands of the Marusi.

Captain Levana grew more intense as she spoke. "You can't let the king down, right?" Greed and fire filled her eyes and certain darkness seemed to cloud her person. "Your true death would break him. It would break everything he has worked for."

She tilted the Queen's chin up a little to look her in the eye. "Let me go. I will tell the He'en that if he wants to meet you personally you shall come, but only on the word of his allegiance."

"I'm still unsure. Allow me time to think about it. We'll discuss it further on the way back to the Fortress."

"Please consider it deeply, My Queen." The captain bowed with respect.

"Of course, my dear. Gather whatever Forsaken we have left. We'll resurrect any we can and head back."

Queen Lucia and Captain Levana began resurrecting a select few bodies.

Wrath watched in awe as the Forsaken selected a body, knelt beside it and whispered some words. Beams of light emanated from the body and then collapsed back into themselves. Moments later the body stood with red eyes aglow; the birth of a Forsaken. He strode over to the Queen. "How does this work? How did you bring me back?"

The queen picked another body and knelt. "What do you remember about death, Wrath?"

Wrath clutched his head as if the thought pained him. "A voice. A void and a voice. A shadow."

"That was Knas. Nobody can remember what she looks like, but we've met her." She cradled the head of the slain warrior beside her. "This woman is still warm. She is meeting with Knas right now; all I have to do is give her the strength to fight, to return to her body."

"Can I help?"

"It's unlikely. Not many of us can do this—it's complex." Queen Lucia leaned in and whispered into the fallen warrior's ear. "Now we wait. Sometimes the soul is happy and chooses to stay with Knas, sometimes it returns."

Right on cue, the body shuddered as the mystical light surrounded it and sucked back inside it like a vacuum. The fiery-haired woman groaned and sat upright. "What happened?"

"You need to recuperate, my dear. Head over there for treatment." The Queen pointed.

Wrath looked to the floor and furrowed his brow. "How did the first Forsaken come back?"

Queen Lucia's gaze drifted off. "That was my darling, King Areth I. Never has there been one like him. He fought against Knas alone and brought many of us back himself. He was already Forsaken before even my great, great grandparents were born. He saved me from disease and we ruled together for hundreds of solars."

She bowed her head, cleared her throat, then darted her gaze to Wrath's eyes. "Then I killed him. He became so corrupt with the pain of death that he posed a threat to us all. I brought him his true death."

Wrath swallowed hard as the Queen's gaze burned into his mind, like she threatened him.

Her gaze broke. "All I want is to be alive again. I want that crystal so I can oppose Knas and claim my life back. Besides, Naeisus needs us..." She stood and strode off in search of Captain Levana, leaving Wrath to ponder alone.

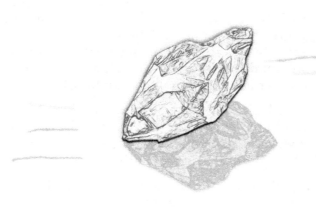

Chapter 8

The Marusi

In the dizzying heights of the central spire, deep within the Undying Fortress, Queen Lucia sipped scarlet wine from her goblet.

Captain Levana sat opposite and glared at the queen's throat as she swallowed. The Dion shard shone like a star in the centre of the table, illuminating the captain's fingers.

"Levana, my dear." Queen Lucia sipped. "I'm trusting you with this, so go through the plan one more time. It needs to be perfect."

"Of course, My Queen. I will ride to the Shu'ung lake where Alkra lies, along with ten of King Areth's men and ten of our own."

"One of whom will be Robert Drake." The queen rolled her eyes.

"Yes, Robert too," replied Levana through gritted teeth, while she fixated on the gem. "Once there, we request entrance to Alkra to speak with the He'en and offer to lay down our weapons."

"Good." The queen gestured with a delicate wave of her hand. "Continue... and remember, the entire Bui'inar region is under Marusi control; it's not our territory."

"Yes, but the Marusi are not a particularly aggressive race. They've always preferred to live in seclusion, so we're unlikely to suffer an attack. Creating an alliance with them will be a breeze." Levana waved her fingertips, mimicking the wind, and smiled.

The queen huffed. "Don't underestimate them, Levana. You're fully aware of what this mission means."

Captain Levana let her hand flop to the table with a thud. She pulled in closer and eyeballed her superior. "If all goes well, we are taken to the He'en's chambers where I confirm the alliance with ourselves, Man, and Wolven. I display the shard, inform him of the other one we share, and then I tell him how this allegiance will be beneficial to us all." Levana adjusted her seating position confidently and let slip a subtle grin as she glanced at the shard.

"Good. Very good. If he rejects the alliance, what do you do?"

"Keep calm, and arrange a council with the leaders to convince him otherwise."

"And if he gets violent?"

"Do what I can to protect myself and my men, and get back here to you. We send word to the other leaders, and await further instructions."

Queen Lucia leaned back again and twiddled her fingers. "Excellent, my dear. Stick with that plan and don't let me down, I don't take kindly to failure. Once the great alliance is complete, we can make our move."

The Forsaken commanders shared a light chortle before the impatient Queen interrupted. "How long will it take you to get there, Captain?"

"Two days, maybe more. I have not ridden across the Bui'inar region for quite some time, but Shu'ung lake is large enough to find from a distance."

Queen Lucia smiled once more and slowly slid the Dion shard across the table toward her Captain. She hesitated, then removed her fingers. "Take it and leave when you are ready." She rose from her seat.

Without a moment's pause, Levana snapped up the shard, flicked it high into the air, and caught it with the same hand. She tucked it behind the black leather bracer on her other arm.

"I won't let you down, My Queen." Levana bowed and headed out to prepare her troops for the long ride to Alkra.

Sir Robert Drake hailed the captain as she walked out onto the Fortress streets and then marched alongside her. "Captain Levana, the troops are ready for departure. It's a long way to Alkra, we should bring extra supplies."

"I'll tell you whether we need extra supplies or not, Drake. We'll be there in two days, maximum. It's not like we need to eat—only the living Man soldiers need food, and if we keep sleep to a minimum, there will be no problems."

"Two days? To make it in that time, we'd need to find a way to cross the Shu'ung strait. You are aware we have to ride South, following the river Inar, until we reach Serpent mountain?"

Captain Levana glared at the unperturbed knight. "Yes, then we climb the mountain, follow the ridge around Shu'ung lake, descend into the valley and follow it to Alkra. I'm not stupid. We can do it in two days."

"But, Captain—"

"Two. Days. Assemble the party at the front gates; we leave now." She stormed off, distracted by her thoughts as she headed for the stables.

* * *

The party stood atop Serpent mountain, staring at the Shu'ung lake nestled in the centre of this mountain range. The magnificent domes of Alkra's land-dwelling portion obscured a large piece of this sprawling body of water. The rest of the city dove into the depths of the lake, like shining grapes hanging from a vine—an amphibious city, for an amphibious race.

One of the king's men gawped at the silvery, pearlescent sheen of the spheres, clinging to land like frogspawn. "By the hand of Bui, look at that city! Is it made entirely from steel?"

A Forsaken soldier pulled level with the man. "No. It's called Deepset Coral. It grows at the bottom of deep lakes and the sea, set into the rocks. The Marusi extract it, dry it and heat it. It's incredibly versatile when heated and strong enough for them to make weapons, armour, and the plates to create these domes. Once they temper it, it becomes one of the strongest materials known to Naeisus."

"Seriously? Why aren't the rest of us using this stuff?"

"Only the Marusi know where it is and how to extract it, and they're not willing to share the information."

Captain Levana turned her steed to face her troops. "Time to descend the mountainside. Once we're there, leave the diplomacy to me. With any luck, the He'en will invite me into his chamber at the bottom of the city." She mumbled, "I bet that's where the Bui shard is."

As they guided their horses cautiously down the treacherous valley, rocks and pebbles tumbled around them. Boots and hooves slipped on the steep decline as every Man, Forsaken, and horse attempted to keep their balance, until at last they reached the bottom.

Captain Levana faced the small band following her, with darkness in her glistening crimson eyes. "Sir Robert, step forward."

Sir Robert Drake stepped forward to meet his Captain, as she slid her hand down her own leg. Covertly she pulled a small dagger from a holster strapped to her thigh. She reached up and ran her fingers down Sir Robert's cheek, smiling sweetly.

A hint of evil flashed across her eyes as her face twisted into anger. She swiftly brought the dagger up, jammed it through the eye socket of her best soldier, and ripped it across his face.

With a lifeless thud, Sir Robert's body collapsed to the floor, his soul now released to Knas. The other soldiers flinched.

King Areth's men drew their swords and readied their stances.

Levana kicked the body at her feet and flipped her dagger in the air catching it by the handle again. "Oh please, I have a shard. Are you really going to take me on? Do what I say or you all die. Do we have any objections?" A grin swept her psychotically gleeful face.

Nobody stirred. The men still gripped their swords but stayed silent. The Forsaken soldiers maintained a forward stare, unable to make eye contact with their commander.

"Good." Captain Levana gestured at the shining collection of bubbles behind her with her dagger. "New plan. In that city there is a shard. We need the shards. We *don't* need more pathetic allies. Using our shard, we will take theirs by force and you will all help me. Got it?" She squinted and dragged her leer across the terrified faces of the troops in tow.

"You're a monster," yelled a woman's voice from the back rank. "I'm informing the king!" One of the horses pulled away and galloped towards the mountain path.

Captain Levana put her hand to her head and brushed away some of her shimmering black hair. "I warned you..." She took aim. With a mighty hurl, her dagger flew at incredible speed and embedded itself into the neck of the fleeing soldier. She fell from her horse and it stopped galloping.

"Anyone else?" Levana flung her arms wide and scowled at the warriors.

The soldiers sheathed their swords and trembled at her insanity.

"Good." She glanced at Sir Robert's lifeless corpse. "Ugh. Please get rid of this lump of flesh; it doesn't send the best impression."

Captain Levana spotted two Marusi guards emerging from the closest bubble, utterly dwarfed by the structure. As they marched nearer, the tips of their Deepset Coral spears reflected into her eyes. The captain held her ground and greeted the Marusi with a glistening smile as they halted.

They stood as tall as Wolven, with droplets of water glimmering on their blue skin. Their clawed, webbed hands gripped the elegant harpoon-type spears they carried, and their feet splayed out on the ground. Swishing their long, slender tails behind them they stared and spoke in a dialect only the captain understood. "Hva eresk suktil Alkra?" The male guard's voice was rough and grating.

Levana admired the long, sky-blue fur shrouding their shoulders. She stepped closer and stared at the closed gills on their slender necks.

The guards readied their spears, preventing her from advancing further.

"Relax, we are messengers of..." She hesitated, glancing at the troops. "We're messengers of King Areth III. He seeks your He'en's allegiance."

The guards stood at ease then looked at each other through their large black eyes. The two slits on their faces flared open and closed as they breathed the salty air.

Captain Levana stepped forward again, more cautiously than before, and examined the strange creatures more closely. "It's been an exceptionally long time since I last saw a Marusi. Your armour looks magnificent; it glimmers with the same sheen as the city itself!"

She lightly poked the fishlike scales that hugged their muscular bodies, held up by two crossed leather straps passing over their furry shoulders.

They each blinked two sets of eyelids. "Stol ce'ease," growled the taller Marusi. Their elegant language was complex and had many words impossible to pronounce without gills.

This time, the female spoke in Captain Levana's own language. "Why would King Areth send a Forsaken messenger?"

Levana scoffed. "You are aware that Man and Forsaken are allies now? He trusts me. We wish to speak with the He'en. We have an offer—"

Another voice came from one of the King's soldiers, "You liar!"

The captain bowed her head and rubbed her eyes with thumb and forefinger. She sighed and turned her back on the Marusi guards.

"Why? Why was there any need for that—you dumb bastard? Men, kill these Marusi." She stormed towards the soldier with a face of thunder. "I'm dealing with *you* myself."

The Marusi reacted instantly, twirling their spears with immense skill and precision, as they fended attacks from the charging Forsaken soldiers. King Areth's men banded together and charged Levana as she unhooked her quick-blades.

The captain ran toward the advancing horses, blades ready to strike, and leapt into the middle of the warriors. She dragged her blades across two throats before they had time to think. Blood gushed from the gashes and their bodies fell from their steeds with a thud. She spun, twisted, and jumped with perfect precision. Hundreds of solar cycles of training brought expertise, as she parried and countered. Soon, eight of the men who charged her lay on the ground, dead. The ninth crawled away from her, blood gushing from a snapped elbow.

Captain Levana stooped over his quaking body, as he pathetically slid on the hard ground. "How dare you attempt to ruin my plan?"

She slowly pierced his stomach with one of her blades. Steadily, she drew the blade towards his neck. "Now look at you, bleeding out, flesh torn..." Her eyes traced the path of the blade and glimmered as his blood spilled out.

The man's screams intensified as his ribs cracked under the pressure of the sharp blade working its way up his body. His blood drained fast and his skin washed out.

The snapping of his bones caused a manic grin to appear on the Forsaken captain's face. "Will you stop screaming over me?" She applied more force to the agonising blade.

The man mustered all the strength he had left and spat blood into Captain Levana's intimidating face. Her smile disappeared and her eyes narrowed. "I'm done with you." She removed her blade and walked away from the soldier, leaving him alive but slipping out of consciousness.

Her anger intensified as she saw only one blue corpse lying among a few of her own. She stamped her foot before inhaling deeply and exhaling, calming herself. "No matter, the real plan can still begin."

The Forsaken Captain rubbed her hands together with delight. As her face contorted from psychotic glee to terrifying rage, she raised her arms to the sky. Her bracer seeped brilliant red light from the shard as storm clouds converged into an angry, dark swirl.

The winds gusted. Clouds twisted, merged, and violently funnelled to the ground. Rain poured, and thunder rolled out across the sky. A cyclone formed in the lake near the city stirring up a lethal maelstrom, which was fed by the growing storm, as waves crashed and tore into the bubbles of the city. Lightning smashed the glistening domes with such force that chunks were sucked into the vicious tornado, whipped around, and hurtled back, smashing into the city.

Captain Levana manipulated the wind, focusing the current to Alkra's land section. Bolts of lightning crashed into the connection between it and the water section, severing the two. Hundreds of Marusi emerged from the city—most were pulled into the surrounding maelstrom, while others swam or scrambled away.

A Marusi with a spectacular coral headdress clawed his way onto land, with a small object clasped in his hand.

He faced the lake and revealed a perfect blue gemstone within his fingers. Concentrating hard, he aimed this shard at the heaving and writhing body of water tearing the city apart. Streams of sapphire shot from the gem, diving deep into the lake, and settling the waters instantly, despite the raging storm. The waters stayed calm long enough for thousands of Marusi to evacuate the lake via the Shu'ung strait.

The power of the two gems clashed violently.

Captain Levana focused harder and the wind screamed, thumping into the lake and dragging waves around with it.

The Marusi struggled to keep his focus on the waters which stirred again. He poured all his energy into the powerful shard, yet the light from the shard flickered and faded. The maelstrom reappeared with a vengeance, only matched by the power-hungry Captain of the Forsaken.

Levana marched to where the weakened He'en lay and stamped on his wrist. The blue Bui shard fell from his grip and she snapped it up. Greed emanated from her eyes as her hunger for power grew with the addition of another shard.

The Marusi hauled himself to his feet and lunged for her, only to lose his footing and fall again.

"Ha! Pitiful fool. Who are you to try to attack me?" She circled him and planted one of her heavy boots into his ribs and kicked him towards the lake.

He coughed and spluttered, his upper body supported by his slender arms. "I am Sha'koth, He'en of the Marusi, and you will pay for this."

"Well, Sha'koth, I am the one with two shards in my hand right now, so go ahead." Captain Levana stomped her feet and taunted the Marusi leader. "Make me pay."

Panting and clutching his ribs, Sha'koth hissed and sank his claws into the earth. He squinted at her with the fury of the Yultah inside him before noticing one small detail.

"Your eyes…" The He'en backed away from the looming terror. "Prepare your Fortress, Forsaken. You and the Man King have picked the wrong fight." He frantically scanned his surroundings and spotted some of the king's men dead on the ground near his own guard. The searing pain in his side coupled with the sheer exhaustion in his muscles made his vision less than reliable, but he recognised the armour.

The captain marvelled at the desecration around them, then clapped with a laugh. "Fortress? Oh no, no. I come by royal appointment from King Areth III himself! He just doesn't like you! You know we are allies now, right?"

"I don't believe you. He is a hon—" started the He'en.

"The king. Sent. Me. And now I grow tired of this chatter." Captain Levana pulled one of the blades from her back. Slowly she stepped toward him, grinning and taunting Sha'koth with every foot of ground gained.

His large, shadowy eyes widened further, and he bared his pointed teeth, hissing and growling. He dragged himself backwards toward the lake, slithered over the edge into the water and with a splash, disappeared into the depths.

Captain Levana stopped and scoffed at the cowardice of her opponent. She tucked the two shards into her bracers and turned on the four remaining Forsaken soldiers. Hurling herself in their direction with blades drawn, she cut them all down in an instant. They fell from their horses, collapsing in motionless heaps on the ground.

"It's a shame the Marusi got to you." With an evil grin, she mounted her steed. She basked in the storm and the chaos it left behind, puffing out her chest.

The lower half of Alkra now sank helplessly to the bottom of the lake, while the broken husk of the top half lay in tatters on land. Bellows of smoke rose from the ruins of a formerly proud city. The gigantic domes that stretched far across the land reduced to nothing more than a collection of shattered eggshells on the shoreline.

The captain galloped toward the mountain path, congratulating herself as she went. She skirted around the mountains to the river Inar, following it north until it disappeared, then riding further northwards into the desolate wastelands she called home.

* * *

The exhausted steed trotted through blowing sand and dust, to the gates of the Undying Fortress, Captain Levana swaying upon its back. A few yards from the portcullis, she dropped the reigns and her arms fell to her sides. The horse stepped forward and the captain's body slumped and crashed to the hard ground. A dust plume launched into the air and dissipated on the breeze.

Queen Lucia rushed out, accompanied by two Forsaken soldiers. They scooped up the captain and brought her inside to the nearest tavern, Death's Arms. A crest hung from a round wooden plaque outside the door, depicting two outstretched skeletal arms gripping tankards of ale and clinking them together. A checker-board pattern served as the backdrop for the crest as it swung, creaking in the breeze.

Inside, Forsaken of various backgrounds sat and chatted while drinking a wide selection of ale. The ale no longer made them drunk, but they continued to drink out of habit and enjoyed reminiscing their living days—the days where it didn't hurt to exist. Heavy cloth obscured most of the light from the filthy windows, giving the place a dank demeanour and a musty smell. The mismatched furniture was carved in an assortment of shapes from a variety of woods and served no aesthetic purpose. Still, it was a popular place. The queen pulled out a rickety chair for Captain Levana, the wooden legs clunking against the uneven floorboards.

"A drink for the captain," she ordered the barman.

With a nod, the large, heavily scarred Forsaken stopped polishing a metal tankard and poured a brown, frothy liquid from one of many tapped barrels. He brought it over and dropped it on the table with a grunt.

"For the captain, it's on the house." He shuffled away as Levana untied her bracers and allowed the two shards to drop onto the table.

The queen dismissed the Forsaken guards and pulled up another chair, awed by the shards. The captain grabbed her tankard, poured half of the contents down her throat, slammed it onto the table, then dragged the back of her wrist across her mouth.

Queen Lucia gawped at the fascinating gems and their awesome power. "How did you . . . my dear, tell me the news. Where are the others?"

"We got there, they attacked us. Sha'koth, the newest He'en, didn't want to listen. I tried to talk to him, but they overpowered us." The breathless captain snatched her tankard.

"I don't understand. Take me through it. Did you tell him that I sent you on a peace mission? How did you get their shard?" The queen looked up at Levana.

Taking a deep breath, the captain leaned forward and detailed her version of events. "When we arrived at Alkra, two Marusi guards met us. I told them we wanted to speak with the He'en about an alliance, but they didn't believe us and turned aggressive. King Areth's men rushed in to attack; I tried to stop them, but they wouldn't listen. Then the Marusi threatened our men, so I was forced to use the shard. Sha'koth emerged with his shard and used it to kill Sir Robert and the others." The captain paused and held a fist to her mouth, pretending to choke on her own words while concealing an emerging smile.

The queen reached out and placed a reassuring hand on the captain's, using her eyes to urge Levana to continue.

"I only escaped because of the Dion shard I brought with me, but not without damage. As for their shard,

Sha'koth was a poor fighter. I couldn't help myself—I wasn't going to leave without some kind of result. I apologise if this was a poor decision, My Queen." The captain slammed her fist on the table and looked down. Her hair fell into a curtain around her face and concealed her delightful grin.

"Oh, my dear." consoled Queen Lucia. "If you are sure they didn't want to talk, then I guess taking their shard brings us one step closer to our goal. That's two for us to the king's one. Unfortunately, we have no idea where the final three are."

A few moments of silence passed and the queen let go, picking up the two crystal shards, still fascinated by their power. The Bui shard glowed deep sapphire, perfectly contrasting the Dion's ruby-red aura.

Captain Levana took another hefty swig and waited for direction.

"We must inform Areth right away. Captain, can you send messengers to him as soon as possible?"

The captain flashed her sickening smile. "Leave it to me, My Queen."

The queen pulled herself to her feet, the chair screeching against the floorboards as it slid. "Are you not joining me?"

"I'm just going to finish my drink. You go."

"Very well."

Queen Lucia scooped up the two shards and placed them in a small pocket in her elegant dress. She bowed to her Captain and drifted out of Death's Arms. The door fell shut with a bang.

Levana remained for a long while, sipping at the remainder of her ale, mulling over the message she would be sending to the 'good' King Areth.

* * *

Captain Levana sat at a sturdy writing desk in her quarters, penning a letter to King Areth. She glanced around her at the unusual tidiness of the room, as if searching for inspiration.

Pairs of quick-blades adorned the walls, one set for every circumstance she may encounter. All pristine, polished and sharpened, ready for action at a moment's notice. Mannequins stood at precise points around the edges of the hexagonal room, each displaying a different set of armour. Some were thicker and solid for heavy combat, others were more basic leather protection— but all were engineered for her speed and agility by the best Forsaken armour smiths in the Fortress.

A chest sat proudly against one wall containing her favourite spoils of war. Among these were old Wolven claws, decayed Marusi tails, and strange webbing rumoured to be from the wings of the mythical Wyrms that once dominated Naeisus. She tapped her feather quill against her delicate chin repeatedly, before staring blankly at the parchment sprawled out on the writing desk. Dipping the quill into the ink and tapping off the excess, she wrote.

King Areth,

Forgive us. Our mission to seek an alliance with the Marusi was only a partial success. Your men, intimidated by the Marusi, blindly attacked them. We tried to subdue the situation. However, the Marusi would not listen. A small battle ensued, and we secured the Bui shard from the He'en, but destroyed their city in the process.

The He'en got away but assured me he would come back for you and then for us. Please prepare your men.

Unfortunately, we cannot spare any troops. The queen regrets that she cannot deliver this message personally but tells me she needs some time away from you and yours. She feels that this latest development with the Marusi may spell bad news for our alliance, especially now. We have two shards and are not prepared to give one to the Wolven as you would want.

For now, the alliance remains, but the Marusi's next move will prove critical in deciding our fate. Queen Lucia does not wish to anger you, but she hopes you understand her situation. We have not yet informed the Wolven of this, we will await your response first and foremost.

Regards,

Captain Levana.

She leaned back in her chair with the letter in one hand and the quill resting against her chin. The captain read what she had written with great distaste. Sighing with disgust, she held the corner of the parchment to a freely burning candle and watched the flames engulf it, burning their way to her fingers. She let the last corner float to the floor and smoulder, before grabbing another sheet.

This time, she smiled as she wrote—that same, manic, corrupted smile that made even the hardiest of creatures uneasy. Her writing speed increased until it seemed she was scrawling on the page. She studied the revised letter with menace, rolled it up and tied it off with a hair from a horse's mane.

The captain left her pristine room and headed out towards the scouts to give them the letter for delivery. She smiled, sure that this letter would result in some form of thrilling chaos. More fighting, more warfare, but most enjoyably—more killing.

Chapter 9

Discord

The laughter of children filled the Straetan Keep gardens, as King Areth and his young ones frolicked on the freshly trimmed grass. It wasn't often he spent time with his beloved children, so when he did, he treasured every moment. Thick stone walls shaded them from the unusual autumn heat. The sun shone brightly onto the array of flowers in the flowerbeds surrounding the grass and bathed them in nourishing light.

A royal gardener wiped the sweat from her crinkled brow as she tended to myriad flowers on proud display at the borders. She smiled at the sound of the children as they played and danced.

Little Anya's ginger ringlets bounced as she ran, her hair closely resembling the same style and fiery auburn shade as her siblings, and indeed, her father. A gentle breeze rustled nearby trees and the chirps of flying birds faded into the distance. These more immediate noises blended with the ambient plethora of critters creating the most wonderful melody.

The rest of Straeta bustled with markets.

Traders from all over the land littered the long promenade leading to the Keep. Fishmongers from Timbrol, weapon and armour smiths from Eveston—all competing to sell their wares to any passer-by catching their eye. Even a Forsaken merchant had set up a stand selling popular wares from the Darklands. People haggled and bartered, and argued and fought over the prices of everything from salt to steel.

The Straeten inns and taverns heaved with merry folk. They drank their body weight in ales and wines from all over Mannis, as song and dance burst from their inebriated bodies.

On cold, shadowy street corners, beggars knelt on tattered blankets and scrounged for a loose coin to pay for their next meal. A host of different street entertainers hoped to earn their own coin. Storytellers and bards acted out wondrous tales of past glories, exciting the imaginations of the children. Stories about the mythical Wyrms from the Age of Fire, the towering Korkrenus, and Man's most fabled warriors proved popular. Citizens marvelled at dancers, jumping and twirling to the music played by bards in an impressive range of routines. Poets spilled satirical and light-hearted verses about any person who stopped to listen to their work. Painters and tricksters alike were eager to show off their talent.

This whole community of vibrancy and colour earned Straeta its wonderful reputation. All of them dependent on this one man, sitting on the grass in the Keep gardens, playing with his four beloved children. This was one reason King Areth was so popular and much beloved. To him, royal boundaries were blurred, nothing was too much trouble, and when it came to tough times, he had the heart to make the necessary decisions to ensure the safety of his subjects.

Deafening, battle horns roared throughout the city.

Citizens stopped dead and panic washed over their faces. Repeated drawn-out calls from the horns signalled the populace to head inside and the army to assemble. Market sellers cobbled together all the wares they could carry, beggars and entertainers hurried to find shelter, and armed soldiers trickled onto the streets heading for the eastern gate.

The king bolted upright and shushed his children. "Quick children, inside the Keep, there is danger approaching." He hurriedly bundled them inside, carrying Anya.

"What is it, Daddy?" she asked, almost on the verge of tears at her father's expression.

"I don't know, my sweet, but I need to find out." He smiled, soothing her at once. "Stay in Areth's room, look after each other, and don't come out until I come and get you okay? I'm sure it's nothing serious. Areth my boy, you're responsible for everyone's safety here."

Young Areth took control of the situation and led his younger sisters to the security of the bedroom.

King Areth hurtled down the hallway to his own bedroom and threw on his armour. He grabbed

Ichtheon, newly re-forged, before rushing outside and meeting his army at the gate.

A large force had already assembled and more were seeping in by the second. Sir Victor stood tall, already prepared and waiting with his signature ram helmet gripped in his hand.

"What's going on?" shouted the king over the horns.

Sir Victor waved at the horns. "I don't know, but something's coming, Sire!"

"Who in Naeisus could..." King Areth stopped, as realisation flashed across his face.

"What is it, Sire?"

"Marusi. It has to be! Wolven and Forsaken would have needed to pass the outposts and use the Timbrol crossing to get to us. Sir Jacob would have warned us long before they could reach us. The Marusi would not need a crossing. I'm assuming the queen's negotiations failed, but if that was the case then why would the Marusi be coming for us? Unless . . . No! She can't have!"

Anger swept him and he bellowed into the wind. "What in the name of Knas has she done?" He gripped the pommel of his sword so tightly his knuckles flushed white.

"Your Majesty, with respect, you're not making any sense," yelled Sir Victor.

The king shouted to one of the horn-blowers on the wall. "You there! What is it? What do you see?"

"Marusi, Sire. Coming from the shoreline, thousands of them. Armed." He resumed the warning calls.

"Damn those Forsaken!" Blind rage filled him. "I should never have trusted them... but why are the Marusi coming for us?"

Sir Victor gripped the hilt of his broadsword. "Sire, surely you don't think the queen betrayed us?"

"I don't know, Sir Victor." He took a few deep breaths and looked his friend in the eye. "I apologise. This is not your fault. We need to go and speak with the He'en before this gets worse. I need you by my side. Order your men to stay here but stay alert—this might turn nasty."

Sir Victor roared, "You heard His Highness, men! Stay vigilant, but stay put!"

King Areth pointed to the gatekeeper atop the wall and whistled for his attention. "Gatekeeper! Open the gate but leave the portcullis down!"

"Yes, Sire!" He turned one of the two heavy locks which slowly pulled the inner wooden gate upwards.

Pebbles jostled and buildings quaked, as the thunderous footsteps of the Marusi drew nearer to Straeta. Their clawed, webbed feet churned up the soil. Sunlight glistened off droplets of water in their fur, like shawls of diamonds.

As they closed in on the city, the leader of the large army thrust his spear sideways, and then in the opposite direction. The Marusi fanned out, spreading their force. With organised precision, they surrounded Straeta and began tapping their Deepset Coral spears against the wall. A sinister click-clack of thousands of spears flooded the city, growing faster and faster.

King Areth strode to the portcullis with aggressive confidence and confronted Sha'koth, who paced the ground on the other side.

The He'en approached the portcullis, towering above the king. He pulled back his thin lips, baring his sharp, pointed teeth. His tail whipped the air behind him and he dragged the solid coral tip of his spear along the metal, with an ear-splitting screech.

His Majesty looked up at the He'en's pointed coral crown and lay his sword on the ground. "You must be the He'en. Why do you bring your army here? We have no quarrel with you."

Sha'koth spat ancient Maurish words before translating to the common tongue. "I am Sha'koth, and you ask stupid questions, King Areth!" He snarled; his nose slits vibrated and the long fur on his shoulders stood on end making him look more intimidating.

"Please, my friend, whatever the problem, I'm sure we can work through it."

"My quarrel? You destroyed my city, now I shall destroy yours."

Sha'koth's tail raised and the furry tip swished around sending subtle messages to the army behind him. They readied their spears.

Panic settled into the king's heart. Desperate to cut the rising tension he raised his palms. "Wait! Me? My understanding was that Queen Lucia came to see you about an alliance!"

"No Queen came to visit. Instead, a Forsaken warrior—claiming to be sent by you—came with a great power. She destroyed my city, killed my people, and stole my shard!"

Sha'koth faced his army and yelled orders in ancient Maurish.

King Areth's eyes narrowed as he judged that the order wasn't a peaceful one. The grand Marusi army fell into several block formations and advanced on the city walls.

Sir Victor ordered his men to prepare for battle, but the king interjected. "No! Everyone stop! He looked Sha'koth in the eyes and attempted to settle the situation once more. "Sha'koth, please! I do not wish to fight you. There has been a great misunderstanding."

Sha'koth barked over the increasing volume of his advancing army. "You gave that Forsaken warrior the order to destroy my city. There is nothing more to discuss."

"No, I didn't! As proof of my integrity, I offer myself to you."

"Sire, you can't." Sir Victor clasped King Areth's shoulder with a gigantic hand.

The king ignored his friend's cries. "I will come outside, alone and unarmed, to talk with you. If you wish to tear me apart after you hear me out, then there will be nothing to stop you."

My life is a small price to pay for the final goal of ultimate peace.

The He'en raised an arm to the sky and hissed. "Stol ce'ease."

The Marusi army stopped advancing at once. He looked down at the relatively small King staring up at him through eyes filled with desperation and nodded.

"Very well," Ska'koth said. "We shall talk . . . but I will not hesitate to kill you and raze your city to the ground if I dislike what you say."

Sir Victor cautioned and pleaded with King Areth not to go, but he remained steadfast. Subtly tapping the kytling crest on his breastplate, he nodded at his most trusted knight.

Sir Victor loosened his grip and bowed as the king ordered the gatekeeper to raise the portcullis.

With a mighty creak, the heavy iron gate began to rise. An array of missing stones on the ground appeared where the spiked ends of the portcullis rested when shut. When it reached head height, the king stepped forward, still refusing to break eye contact with the towering Marusi. The moment he stepped through, it slammed shut to the ground behind him with a loud crack, which lingered then dissipated into silence.

The king bowed to the seething He'en.

Sha'koth pointed his gleaming Deepset Coral spear at King Areth's throat. Ready to attack, he gripped the wooden shaft tightly.

At this range, the gleam of the He'en's crown sparkled even more brilliantly as the single point rose up like a horn from his head. The He'en blinked his multiple eyelids as the silence droned on, further raising tension.

The king began, "Your Grace, tell me, in your own words, what happened with the Queen of the Forsaken?" he maintained his gaze, ignoring the threatening point of the spear aimed at his neck.

"The queen didn't make an appearance. Instead, a small Forsaken woman with black hair and darkness in her red eyes showed up... with your men. She told me you ordered them to destroy us and steal our shard."

The king's face morphed from regret to horror. *Why would Lucia betray me? She stands to gain nothing from this!* "Knas condemn her! She has lied to you. The Queen and I—"

"Are you not allies?" Sha'koth jolted his spear.

"Yes, but—"

"Then an attack by them, is an attack by you!" The He'en pressed his spear to the king's throat, indenting the skin.

Sir Victor ran to the portcullis and gripped it, knuckles drained of all colour. "Open this damned gate!"

"Listen to me, Sha'koth." King Areth lowered his voice and pleaded. "The queen was under a strict agreement to visit you herself and request that you join our alliance. We have already forged an alliance with the Wolven; we want peace between all; we want you to join us in the quest for a better Naeisus."

Sha'koth lowered his spear a little and waited.

King Areth cleared his throat. "I have no idea why she would betray not only me, but all of us. My only guess is that she is merely using us and the Wolven to gather the shards and she cares not for the alliance. That hurts me even more because…"

"Because?" hissed the He'en.

"Because I was foolish enough to begin to care for the queen and I was under the impression that she cared about the unity of Naeisus as much as I do. Her betrayal is like a knife through my heart."

"A Forsaken caring for peace, is this some kind of joke?" The Marusi leader raised his spear again. "You mock me, King Areth!"

"No, He'en Sha'koth, not at all. Queen Lucia has betrayed not only me and my people, she has betrayed you and your people, and she has made a mockery of this alliance." He sighed, wounded from this news. "I'm gravely sorry your shard was taken from you. That was neither the plan, nor the intention."

The king lifted his hand to his breastplate and slid aside the crest, the radiance of the Mys shard spilling out. He plucked it from its holder and stretched his arm out, offering it to the He'en. "Here, this is the Mys shard. It has healing powers, though it will not heal fatal wounds. I want you to have it, as proof that I had nothing to do with the destruction of your city. I know it won't repair your city, but I hope it will go some distance to making up for the shard that was stolen from you."

Sha'koth dropped his spear and gently took the shard in absolute astonishment. He scrutinised it through his large, black eyes as he rotated it between his slender, webbed fingers. He placed the shard in a small pouch on the shoulder strap of his leather battle gear and picked up his spear, placing it against his shoulder. He raised a hand and barked an order. "Stol Sparae!"

The He'en's troops obeyed and rested their spears against their shoulders in a wave that quickly made its way in both directions around Straeta.

Sir Victor breathed a heavy sigh of relief and King Areth smiled with reassurance at the He'en.

"So, what do you propose we do, King Areth?" asked the He'en, with revenge in his heart.

"It is my ambition to unify the races. I want an alliance between your people and mine."

The He'en rubbed his chin, sceptical. "Our alliance does not come so easily. How do I know I can trust you? This one shard doesn't equal my trust and complete devotion to your cause. Tell me how you plan to accomplish this impossible task, King Areth."

The king pondered, allowing the recent turn of events to sink in and his plans to adjust accordingly. "The Forsaken need to be dealt with. I must find out why they took the actions they did—they have hurt me in the deepest way and jeopardised the future of the entire land. It's very possible Ulv Nikos knows nothing about this betrayal, but we need to get word to him before they do. We can't risk the Wolven turning on us too; their allegiance is shaky at best."

"And what of the shards wielded now by the Forsaken? The two of them together will increase their power." informed the educated Marusi monarch. "They resonate in synchronicity at incredibly high frequencies, thus increasing their output."

"I see... then it is vital we get them back. The Wolven were able to infiltrate and raid their Fortress effortlessly, although the Forsaken have since reinforced their walls. Perhaps if the three of us attack together, we can take back what is ours. Let me send word to Ulv Nikos."

"No, King Areth." The He'en placed a large, webbed hand on his shoulder. "I will send word to the Ulv. For you it will take days to ride overland to the Triash Forest, whereas I can swim north from this island, directly to the western side of their home."

The king gazed with relief at Sha'koth, although he was a little perplexed at this sudden change of heart. "Are you sure? You will help us so readily?"

Sha'koth's face dropped. "Do not take this wrongly, King Areth. I am not helping you, you are helping me.

The Forsaken must pay for slaughtering my people and tearing down our home. Your knowledge of their homeland will be of great advantage. If you prove your worth and we emerge victorious, perhaps then I shall consider a more permanent alliance."

"Very well, Sha'koth. I am willing to accept these terms and will assist you in recovering your shard from the Forsaken." King Areth held his hand out to seal the deal.

The Marusi leader took the proffered hand, placing it high upon his shoulder. He then rested his own bony hand on the king's shoulder and stooped, allowing their foreheads to touch. "This is how Marusi sign a verbal contract."

King Areth smiled before gesturing at the pouch where the Mys shard now rested. "Ulv Nikos is an aggressive creature and does not take kindly to strangers in his territory. Show him that shard as proof you are working with us, along with a letter I shall pen and seal. As of now, you and your people are free to enter Straeta as you wish. I hope we can form a true alliance in the near future."

"If we take our shard back, I will be more than willing to secure an alliance," assured Sha'koth.

The king turned to the city walls. "Open the gates! The Marusi are free to enter the city!"

The gate guard stood high atop the wall began to raise the portcullis, then he stopped and pointed in the direction of Timbrol West.

"Sire! Forsaken messenger approaching!"

Sha'koth readied his spear as the Forsaken rider approached the Marusi army, slowing cautiously as he did so. A pathway through the vicious, growling warriors opened, and the rider slowed his horse to a walk, as he made his way through the sea of threatening glares. As he approached King Areth and Sha'koth, he reached into a small leather satchel at his hip and produced a scroll.

Without warning, the He'en thrust his razor-sharp spear through the helmet of the Forsaken messenger, knocking him from his horse and leaving him in a heap on the ground. Sha'koth hissed at the body. "Cursed Forsaken."

The frightened horse reared up, turned, and galloped away as the king looked on, mouth agape. He untied the scroll and read it with a furrowed brow. As his emerald eyes scanned the text, his face shifted first to anger and then to disbelief. He tossed the paper aside and locked eyes with Sha'koth once more.

"How quickly can you get the Wolven on our side?" Darkness shaded his voice.

"If all goes well, I can have them assembled here in three days. Why the urgency?"

"What if we assembled at the Undying Fortress?"

"Two days, if you can be there by then." The He'en's eyes narrowed. "Why? What has happened?"

The king's face dripped with anger. "The Forsaken have just confirmed everything you have told me—only they have blamed you."

"Why is it you believe us over them?"

"Because you are here. The letter requested our immediate back-up, due to Marusi attack. I expect they did not know you would be here so soon and they wanted me to leave my city vulnerable."

The He'en spat on the body of the Forsaken and kicked it several feet in a rage. "Those devious bastards! They try to play us for fools! No longer will they pull our strings. King Areth, I will take a handful of warriors and speak with Ulv Nikos. Will you, and all our forces, meet us on the battlefield outside the Undying Fortress?" The Marusi leader's eyes shone with hope for revenge.

"I shall lead your army as if they were my own." The king reached up and placed a hand on Sha'koth's shoulder. "Do not fail, Sha'koth. It is vital that the Forsaken's little game ends now."

"I am with you, King Areth." Sha'koth completed the Marusi handshake.

"It's settled." The king's face darkened. "We go to war at first light."

* * *

Sunrise flooded in over Timbrol East, illuminating the grand stone buildings, the towering walls, and the large army already prepared and assembled in the esplanade. King Areth rode Violetwing across the front rows of the two separated armies. One Man, one Marusi. He screamed words of encouragement and enthusiasm to both races, but as he reached the Marusi army, he halted.

"How do we know this isn't a trap?" hissed a rattled Marusi. "Sha'koth is more trusting than I, and I do not think we should follow you, Man King."

The king smiled at the headstrong warrior. "What is your name, Marusi?"

She puffed her chest out with pride and thumped it. "I am Nohalla Ma'aurite. Advisor, guard, and daughter of Sha'koth."

"What a beautiful name," said the king. "Nohalla, I do not know the fate of your father, but I assure you this is no trap. Sha'koth is a strong and wise leader and I risk losing many of my people as well as the respect of Naeisus if I were to cross him."

"How do you know the Ulv will not murder him on arrival?"

"Ulv Nikos and his kind follow strength. I have defeated him in combat and earned his respect, the Forsaken are showing incredible weakness, thus losing his respect. Your leader is also strong, and he carries with him a great power. I trust the Ulv will see our side and help us." The king's words reduced the tension, keeping the peace before the ground-shattering battle ahead.

"If you lie, and betray the honour of the Marusi, we will end you," yelled Nohalla.

Violetwing screeched with aggression, once again raising tensions. King Areth leaned around and slapped her beak, scolding her, and apologised to Nohalla. Several Marusi scowled.

King Areth cleared his throat. "Hear me now, Marusi. I am no liar. I am no traitor. The Forsaken are both of those things and they possess two shards to use against us. I do not know the fate of your He'en, but I have faith he will convince the Wolven to assist us in battle this day!

"You have a choice. You can trust my leadership, as Sha'koth has done, and ride with us to the Undying Fortress to meet your leader and fight alongside us. Or, we can fight now, lose many lives, and let the Forsaken win. For what? If we find the Wolven have betrayed us too, you have my word, as King of Man, that we will not follow their path. If you doubt my word as King, talk to that man over there." He drew his sword and pointed it at Sir Victor who stood firm.

"If you choose to fight me here and now, you are also choosing to submit to the true enemy of all our people. So, Marusi, make your choice!"

Nohalla and her people shuffled on the spot and muttered in their native tongue.

King Areth shifted his weight in his saddle, nervously waiting for a response, hoping his plans wouldn't end here and now.

After what seemed like ages, Nohalla placed a tight, blue fist on her heart. "We are with you, King Areth. As our leader has trusted you, so too shall we. But do not betray us. You have been cautioned."

With a grin, the king placed his fist over his heart as a sign of mutual respect, then rode to Sir Victor. "Are you ready, my good man?"

"As ready as I'll ever be." He gripped the reins of his large, smoky kytling and glanced over his shoulder.

Both men lowered their helmet visors and their swords pointed forward. "Onwards! May the light of Mys guide us!"

"Acaette." A strong female voice called and the Marusi army advanced alongside Man's warriors.

Two large bodies of blues, browns and silvers galloped as fast as their mounts allowed, northeast toward the Darklands. The entire force rode behind a single man, King Areth III. He led the enormous sea of battle-hardened soldiers, with Sir Victor at his side. He knew that the victory of these armies, and their alliance, all rested on Ulv Nikos showing up with Sha'koth alive.

Sir Victor erupted into a deep belly laugh and shouted over the sound of the stampede. "You'll go down in history for this, Sire!"

"Whatever do you mean, Victor?"

"If Sha'koth turns up, that'll be three Kings riding together for the first time in centuries." Sir Victor gestured to the army. "This is all your doing!"

"Nonsense, I've had the best support by my side the whole way. I could not have achieved this without you, Sir Victor . . . but we still have a long way to go, once we have the three shards secured in allied hands. We will still have three more to locate."

"Even so, for three of the five races to be allied is quite the feat. You need a nickname for the history texts!"

"King Areth III of Man suits me just fine."

"King Areth Peacebringer. Or Lifegiver. How about King Areth Pureheart III?" suggested the giant knight.

"Pureheart, eh? I like it! But you deserve another name as well. You'll be right beside me in those history texts, Sir Victor Blackrock."

A tear of pride slid down Sir Victor's face, concealed by his helmet. "Let's just see how this battle plays out. My victory at Blackrock is going to be tough to beat, but I thank you all the same, Sire."

King Areth glanced at Sir Victor, just able to make out a warm smile through the slits on his helm. The large knight broke into laughter once more and the men's chortles grew as they pushed on towards the Darklands.

Pureheart. The name spun in the king's mind. *It's brave. Just. Good. I will become the second Areth in my family to have earned a name.*

He knew if this worked, his would be a name spoken about in texts for millennia to come, alongside his great ancestor, King Areth Forsaken I.

The creation of the Forsaken by the former king was widely considered evil and unnatural. The bloodline had spent many solar cycles erasing the name from their own, and they had severed all association with the Forsaken.

As they drew closer to his goal, he felt a sense of achievement and progress, although it was greatly shadowed by the fear of the day ahead.

A certain unshakeable darkness loomed over the mission and it crawled its way into his heart like a spider hunting prey.

Chapter 10

Ferocity

The Undying Fortress stood alone in the vast, barren Darklands. Dust and rocks sprawled as far the eye could see and secluded the gigantic looming home of the Forsaken. In the centre, the grand spire twisted up to scratch the black, foreboding clouds above. At its summit, Captain Levana peered out of the large window, aimless thoughts floating through her twisted mind.

Rocks and pebbles jostled and bounced on the ground and the tower trembled, gently at first but rapidly gaining strength. The captain perked up and leaned out of the window, squinting into the distance. Through the dust, a horizon-spanning shadow emerged, growing in size.

Levana whistled in admiration. "Uh, Queenie, you might want to see this."

Queen Lucia bolted from her throne and joined her captain at the window. "Is that... is that a Marusi army? By the hand of Knas, it is! Captain, what have you done?!"

Levana spied the outlines of kytling riders becoming apparent, and grabbed the queen's shoulders, spinning her away from the window. "Me?! I told you they attacked me. Obviously they're coming to finish the job and steal our shards!"

"Send word to the Wolven and to King Areth immediately!" demanded Queen Lucia. "We need their assistance. I doubt our troops can repel an onslaught of that magnitude."

"It's too late for that, My Queen. We have to take them on alone." The captain ground her teeth. "My troops are rigorously trained and will prevail, I assure you."

"We absolutely cannot let them get their hands on either of the shards, Captain. If we must, we will use them in battle."

"We will prevail," reiterated the captain. "It's about time my blades tasted blood again…"

Queen Lucia scowled and raised a finger to her captain. "See to it that we do, or you'll be the one paying."

The captain's eyes burned a deeper scarlet than usual.

I was certain they'd be razing Straeta by now, not riding together.

The queen's voice penetrated her mind. "Captain send word to the king, anyway. We need to assemble a counter attack. The Marusi will suffer for this!"

"Very well, My Queen. I'll prepare the troops." Captain Levana began to pace out of the room, but Queen Lucia called out and stopped her in her tracks.

"Captain ensure our victory at all costs. Make them suffer."

Captain Levana grinned and bowed. Through the window, she spotted a clear division between the Marusi warriors and Man warriors. Her mind grew dizzy with the excitement of draining so many lives, so much so she'd almost forgotten about the window. She quickly beckoned for the queen to follow her. "We need to get you somewhere safe, My Queen. Head down into the tunnels and wait there for me. If I'm not back by the end of the battle, seek out His Majesty."

"No, Captain. I am fighting," insisted the queen.

Levana clenched her fists. "And what happens if they overpower us and you die? The Forsaken will be extinguished. With all due respect, Lucia, get to those tunnels." A bead of sweat worked its way down her temple.

The queen stamped her foot and huffed. "You're right. Very well, but do not fail me."

Levana in the lead, they fled the room, heading down the spiral staircase to the hidden escape tunnels beneath the Fortress. These tunnels ran for miles under the Darklands and provided four escape routes at the ends of winding labyrinths to confuse any pursuers. A small trap door beneath an oddly placed bookcase within the spire served as the only way into these tunnels.

The captain helped her queen into the tunnel and closed the trapdoor, shifting the bookcase on top of it.

With the queen safely out of earshot, Captain Levana cackled to herself. "Fool." Leaning against the doorframe to the spire, she danced one of her quick-blades around her fingers with immense skill.

She raised her voice, talking loudly. "Time to win this fight, and there's nothing wrong with a little fun along the way." She reached into her pocket and picked out the crimson and sapphire gems, rolling them around in her palm.

She clasped them and looked to the sky as the clouds darkened above her. "Let's see what you're capable of."

* * *

As King Areth led the monstrous army of Man and Marusi towards the Forsaken capital, raindrops seeped in through the slits in his kytling helmet, spraying his face.

I pray to Mys that this rain is falling naturally in this drought-blighted wasteland.

As the Undying Fortress came into view, Sir Victor bellowed orders. "Halt! Formation!" His voice roared out across the plains.

"Stol ce'ease! Fylut!" reiterated Nohalla to the Marusi.

They stopped. The thick black clouds hanging ominously overhead made it difficult to tell the time of day.

The two armies formed four equal square formations in a two-by-two grid, Marusi to one side, Man to the other. Man's cavalry led the charge, with the king and Sir Victor mounted mid-centre on their kytlings.

Nohalla scanned the horizon from the front row of her battalion, then made her way to where King Areth sat on his mount. She tapped his shoulder with her spear, scowling. "I do not see our He'en or the Wolven. They should be here—"

"Do not fret, Nohalla, they will be here."

"They had better be, or it won't just be the Forsaken meeting Knas tonight." Her gills shuddered as she walked back to her troops.

The Marusi stood tall with their spears in one hand and Deepset Coral bucklers strapped to their wrists. The armies occupied a vast section of the dusty, wet Darklands and waited for the Forsaken to make a move. Rain beat heavier and heavier, the cloth beneath their armour becoming sodden and uncomfortable.

A loud creak sounded as the heavy portcullis at the gate of the Fortress heaved upwards. The armies braced themselves. The king held a hand out signalling his army to hold their ground.

When the gate reached full height, a tiny-framed figure stepped out all alone, hands in her pockets. She strolled forward a few paces, kicking rocks as she went, and smiling at the ground.

Nohalla stirred and bared her teeth at the small Forsaken woman who stood no more than a stone's throw from her. She pointed her spear at the woman, working her troops into a frenzy. "That's her! The one that destroyed our city," she screamed.

"Hold your ground," demanded the king.

Captain Levana looked at Nohalla. Her eyes widened as did her grin. "It's you! How did you get away from my troops? Never mind, it's not important. What is important is the fact you've come all the way to me, to allow me to finish my job."

"Captain Levana, you will answer for the queen's crimes against this alliance," interjected King Areth curtly. The captain shifted her gaze, keeping her hands planted in her leather pockets.

"You got the letter? Oh, how wonderful."

Lifting his visor he shouted and water sprayed from his lips. "What are you trying to achieve? These petty power games stop now."

Levana remained silent. The rain fell heavier and she laughed harder.

The king stamped forward, drawing his sword. "Answer me!"

"Oh, I'll answer you." A sharp whistle left her lips and a rally of Forsaken archers appeared on the top of the wall, bows nocked and ready to fire.

"It doesn't have to be this way, Captain. Nobody needs to die today." Some part of him still hoped that peace was possible, yet the bigger part of him started to realise the futility of his dream of unity.

"You're right." Smugness plastered the captain's face. "Give me the Mys shard and perhaps I'll let you walk."

"Never! Not after this! Where is Lucia? She needs to answer for this. Show yourself Lucia," roared King Areth.

Captain Levana's laughter turned maniacal. "Lucia has ordered your destruction." Between fits of laughter she caught her breath, then continued, "I thought you'd have figured that out from the letter. You're supposed to be the smart one!" She calmed and smiled at the enormous army, all drawing their weapons.

A deafening ruckus of metal sliding against metal rang, trickled down the captain's spine, and wiped the grin from her smug face. She jerked her neck and scoffed, twiddling the gems in her pockets.

The rain cascaded. The army huddled together, watching in horror as the rainwater began to collect in vast, invisible containers to either side. With frightening speed, the water stacked up, towering above the warriors.

King Areth gawped at the two titanic walls of water, and in a sudden moment of terror, spluttered an order. "Quickly! Advance!"

In a frenzy, the allied army charged as the two blocks of water rose to a substantial height. Captain Levana released the Bui shard's hold on the liquid walls. A mighty surge heaved through the impossible vertical lakes and flooded the rear battalions, crushing and drowning them. The Marusi fought against the gushing waves, some clawed their way onto the sodden ground, and re-joined the charge.

King Areth's men were not so lucky.

The majority of the soaked battalion smashed and pounded against the ground and each other. Bones were broken and organs crushed with every lethal whack of the wave. Many more drowned as the surging water held them under for longer than their lungs held breath. Only a handful from the rear battalion survived; sapped of energy they panted for their lives on the battlefield.

Captain Levana laughed hysterically as the effects of her handiwork unfolded. Rainwater soaked her black hair, sticking it to her face. Forsaken archers atop the wall let loose a hail of arrows aimed at the stampeding warriors charging for their captain.

Arrows met their targets. Many bounced off bucklers, stuck into armour, or hit the ground. However, some delivered fatal blows to the eyes, throats, and hearts of the roaring soldiers. Another set of arrows was let loose and dealt more critical hits. King Areth's allied force rapidly thinned in number.

An unexpected flood of Forsaken ground troops poured out from the gates behind Captain Levana and stood ready for the assault. Forsaken warriors charged and met the army head on in a mighty clash of swords, spears, and shields.

Captain Levana used the Dion shard to manipulate lightning strikes, guessing where King Areth fought amidst the raging battle. Her arms danced, as if conducting an orchestra. She accented every stroke with a point from her slender finger and in response a bolt of lightning crashed into the ground. Arrows hailed from atop the walls, picking off friends and foes alike. Lighting crashed into groups of fighters, frying handfuls from both sides at a time.

The Marusi fought with exceptional skill. They swung their spears and thrust them into their enemies for clean kills. Their tails acted as extra limbs and gave them enhanced balance and agility. They could also be used to grab enemies and dropped weapons, which gave the warriors an edge in the fight. The battle descended into a dirty bloodbath, where honour fled and survival became the only objective. Bodies began to pile up and scatter the ground. Forsaken slowly outnumbered the king's force.

Captain Levana's eyes glowed, reflecting the chaos and slaughter before her. She grew tired of battling from afar with the shards and tucked them behind her bracer. Her curved twin blades sang as she drew them. She wanted to feel the warm splash of blood across her face, the satisfying sinking of a sharp edge into flesh, the small redemption from pain she felt, every time she saw a life slip away at her hands. With a mighty leap and a twist in the air, she catapulted herself into the midst of the fight displaying her unmatched skill with her favourite weapons. She cut and sliced her way through man after woman after Marusi, grinning as their bodies hit the ground.

The Forsaken Captain basked in the spray of warm, thick liquid as she dragged the edge of her blades across the throats of her enemies. She even cut through her own kind if they stood between her and an enemy kill. She worked her way through the rabble and hunted King Areth—for it was his blood she sought after most of all.

Nohalla ripped her spear from the skull of a Forsaken Wolven and growled at the collapsed corpse. A rapid dust cloud advanced and she raised a pointed finger. "Look!"

The fighting slowed as a low rumbling came from the West.

There, barely visible through the pounding rain, the entire Wolven army sprinted toward them on all fours at an unbelievable speed. The larger hulk of Ulv Nikos was now unmistakable as he neared with something on his back.

Nohalla's eyes widened as she made out the figure of Sha'koth. He clung to the Ulv's fur and rode the beast, his spear gripped ferociously in one hand. With He'en Sha'koth alive and ready to fight with Wolven reinforcements, the Marusi army was reinvigorated; they cheered and raised their bucklers to the sky. After blocking another barrage of arrows, they fought with more power and aggression.

Ulv Nikos howled and grunted at his army and received acknowledgments in their own language. He snarled at Sha'koth, "Jump." As they approached the walls, the Ulv leapt at the sturdy stone structure and ejected Sha'koth mid-leap.

The Marusi He'en landed spear first on the back of an unsuspecting Forsaken warrior and killed him outright. He let out a mighty battle cry and joined his people in warding off the frontal assault. His presence raised their morale beyond its previous limits.

The Wolven followed their leader, buried their claws into the stonework, and scaled the towering walls with unmatched speed and agility. The archers turned their attention to the terrifying creatures now pushing their way over the newly reinforced wall like it was child's play. The huge beasts ripped and tore their way through the panicked Forsaken troops; like the lightning that struck the battlefield, the Wolven army purged the archers until nothing but empty shells littered the ramparts.

With grunts and barks from Ulv Nikos, the Wolven leapt to the inside of the Fortress. They poured their way out through the main gate and flanked the Forsaken warriors. With one deep, long howl from the entire Wolven population, they overpowered the battle noise and demoralised the terrified Forsaken soldiers.

Surrounded by enemies and looking around in a blind panic, Captain Levana saw no way out. Her eyes shot to the empty spaces atop the walls where archers had fired their arrows mere moments ago. Thousands of Wolven reinforcements began to bite, claw, and chew their way through her seasoned soldiers. She screamed in sheer frustration and stamped her foot with a splash on the waterlogged ground. She poked her finger inside her bracer and tried to fish out the shards. She froze at a sound from behind her.

"Not on my watch, Captain Levana!" growled a breathless voice. "Your reign of destruction, and the soiling of our alliance, has gone too far."

She stopped digging for the shards and turned on her heels. A giant outline of a man materialized through the rain, wielding a greatsword with both hands and wearing heavy Eveston steel armour. His helmet coiled at the sides, resembling the horns of a ram, and his breath was a visible mist as he exhaled through the visor.

"Sir Victor Blackrock," spat Captain Levana. "It's about time I faced a worthy opponent. Your men were so unskilled, I was able to cut them down without even breaking a sweat." She chuckled at the sweet memories of taking their lives.

Sir Victor roared, "You will not find me so easy to cut down." He heaved his sword high, and with an almighty crash he slammed it into the ground where the captain had stood.

She managed to sidestep the blow and thus narrowly avoided her true death. After taking a second to adjust her stance, she readied her swords for an incoming sweep. A loud clang reverberated as she caught a downward blow on her blades, but she found herself too weak to support the knight's immense strength. Instead, she leapt backwards and let Sir Victor's sword strike the ground as she balanced herself. A third swing came in, this time from the side, and again she attempted to block it by placing her swords against her armoured mid-section. Once again she underestimated the knight's brute strength. The blow knocked her off her feet and the mighty sword came toward her with a deadly thrust. She rolled away, but the tip of the great blade snagged on her leather bracer and cut through it like butter. The two crystal shards scattered on the battlefield.

Captain Levana's eyes widened, and panic washed over her face. *For a big guy, he's amazingly fast!* Her mind raced as she scrambled to find the shards, now lying on the ground. She dove for them, but Sir Victor's giant boot stamped down and blocked her path. He roared and swung again, ignoring the Dion and Bui shards.

Captain Levana rolled away and leapt to her feet; this time she countered with speed. There was no time to calculate a precise hit, so instead she slashed wildly with one blade at his ribs. It connected with a clang then bounced off his reinforced breastplate.

Sir Victor raised his leg, kicked the Forsaken Captain in the chest with immense force, and knocked her to the ground several feet away.

Using her momentum, she rolled backwards and flipped to her feet. She dug her toes into the soft soil and charged at the knight with increasing frustration. As he swiped his sword from the side once more, Captain Levana timed her next movement to perfection and pushed off the ground. She sailed above his sword and drove her knee into his helmet, knocking it off.

The knight faced her, blood streaming from his nose and soaking his bushy beard. His face contorted in rage; with a mighty roar, this humongous man thrust his sword, aiming for his adversary's face.

Captain Levana anticipated the familiar attack and twirled to the side, dodging his thrust. The pommel of one of her quick-blades smashed into his temple and disrupted his focus. She grabbed his wrist with her other hand and held strong.

Sir Victor shook her grip and punched her hard in the face. Before she fully recovered, he brought his sword up and stepped into the strike with all his might. She attempted to block with one blade, but he smashed it away with his weapon.

Left with only one quick-blade and an impending sense of fear, Levana shook her head to refocus her vision. All that met her eyes was the great hulk of a man who stood before her, thirsting for her true death. Once again, he hoisted his heavy blade high in the air and begun to bring it down.

This time the captain ran straight for him. With a risky turn, she caught his forearms on her shoulders and utilised his momentum against him. She used one of her elbows to strike upward while her free hand yanked his wrist down to the frightening sound of a crack.

Sir Victor screamed as his elbow snapped from the captain's swift strike. His sword dropped and he swung with his fist, ignoring the splinter of bone that pierced through flesh and the cloth joint of his armour. The knight slowed as a result of the searing agony coursing its way through his arm.

The skillful Forsaken Captain now parried or evaded Sir Victor's strikes. She found her rhythm and ran circles around the agonised knight.

He grasped at any opportunity to land a fatal blow and edged the fight toward the dislodged quick-blade. He managed to grasp it with his good hand, slashing and stabbing at the air while his other arm flopped about helplessly. The spewing blood drained his energy fast.

Again, the pair locked themselves in combat, but as each second passed, Sir Victor's moves became sloppier. His vision blurred and darkened as the intense pain of his snapped arm spread like wildfire through his entire body, hazardously choking his ability. Harnessing all his energy into one last-ditch swing, Sir Victor brought the sharp blade point-first toward Captain Levana's head.

The blow parried off her bracer instead. With a quick pirouette and a calculated strike, Captain Levana leapt into the air aiming her blade carefully. Using pinpoint precision and putting all of her weight behind it, she sank her slender curved blade into the base of Sir Victor's neck and drove it down into his lung.

Everything seemed to stop.

The captain leapt off the knight's chest, taking her blade with her as blood gushed from the wound. She broke into bemused laughter as he dropped to his knees with a thud, his head now level with hers.

Sir Victor could not speak. He could not scream. He could do nothing but cough and splutter as blood filled his esophagus.

Levana gripped the shoulder of the defeated knight and pulled him close. "The Forsaken will win, Victor. We'll win because . . ." She put her lips close to his ears. ". . . I know where the last three shards are."

In one final act of bravery, Sir Victor shakily brought the blade up to her face and feebly jabbed in the direction of her blurred image. His attempt failed and his arm fell, the blade dropping to the ground. Using his last breath, the mortally wounded knight spat blood into the captain's face and slumped to the ground.

Captain Levana stood in utter awe at her surprising victory.

An agonising scream rang out and King Areth's blade grazed the captain as she instinctively fell to the side. Again, the mighty blade came in, hunting for her, but found only the curved edge of her soaked blade. Sir Victor's blood ran down the deadly weapon and dripped off, still warm and fresh.

In a rage-induced frenzy, the king swiped and slashed at the Forsaken captain who dashed, dodged, and blocked with all the speed she could muster. With his face flushed as red as the frightened eyes of his op-ponent, he kept swinging and stabbing blindly in an at-tempt to somehow avenge his fallen friend. The corpse of a slain Wolven fell on King Areth, causing him to stumble and giving the Forsaken Captain an opportunity to escape. With all the strength of his berserk state, he caught the Wolven body on his shoulders and shrugged it off with a frightening battle cry. He scanned the area, ready to continue his assault, but the elusive captain evaded him.

"Where are you, Levana?!" he screamed. "You cannot hide from me. Show yourself, coward!"

The gates were still open and King Areth made a mad dash for the entrance to the Fortress. In a frantic search for Captain Levana, he relentlessly stabbed and sliced any Forsaken warrior that stood in his way.

Sha'koth spotted his ally charging in and bellowed an order in Maurish for his troops to join the advance. The remaining Forsaken force fell into disarray without a leader and scattered, fleeing from the battle.

No effort was made to hunt the escapees, but any that happened to pass too closely to one of the allied forces was not around long enough to plead for their freedom.

King Areth scanned the abandoned streets of the Undying Fortress. The sound of the main door to the spire slamming shut caught his attention. He hurtled towards it and pulled at the brass ring handle. He heaved, gritting his teeth and screaming, but got nothing more than a few creaks from the braced entrance. Lashing out with a raging fury, he pounded and punched and slammed on the heavy oak door, demanding that the captain face him.

A large, furry claw gripped the handle alongside his. Together he and Ulv Nikos pulled with such might the lock split through the wood and the door snapped open, giving way to an empty room.

"She must be in one of the rooms upstairs," barked the king. "Find her now! I want her head."

Without question, the Ulv and a handful of his Wolven sprinted up the stone stairs to search the rest of the tower, while King Areth took his frustration out on the crude furniture lying around. A lone chair hurtled across the room, smashing against the stone wall and the bookcase in the corner suffered as many deep cuts from his sword as it took for him to exhaust himself.

Heavy scurrying came from the stairwell and the Wolven emerged with no sign of anyone else. The king looked to the Ulv with desperation in his eyes.

Ulv Nikos shook his head. "She is gone," he grunted.

"Where did she go?" bellowed the distressed King.

"We find them. We kill them. Now we go, return when stronger," growled Ulv Nikos, turning to leave the spire.

King Areth slashed the bookcase once more and panted, as it collapsed to the floor completely covering the trapdoor which had escaped his attention.

"When I find Lucia and Levana, I'm going to hand them back to Knas, even if I have to escort them myself."

King Areth clutched his chest. A burning filled his heart as he reminded himself of his fallen brother and he dashed back outside, stopping at the gates.

The fight was over.

Thousands lay dead; thousands more lay resting and wounded. The Mys shard worked overtime, healing as many of the wounded as possible.

Just outside the gates, a group of his best soldiers stood, huddled in a circle. Tears welled in his eyes and his legs began to tremble. Against the anguish, he forced himself to approach the circle.

* * *

Underground in the hidden escape tunnels, Queen Lucia stood, mouth agape.

"We have to go, my Queen. You heard what he said, he wants us dead," urged the blood-soaked captain.

The queen stuttered, unable to figure out the meaning behind the seemingly random slaughter. "But, Areth, why? Why, after everything he's been striving for? Was it all just a clever lie?"

The crudely carved tunnels split off into four directions. Captain Levana urged the queen to take the west tunnel and grabbed her wrist, tugging her.

Queen Lucia yanked her hand free and stamped her foot, glaring at the captain.

"He came here with the people that attacked us!" exclaimed the stubborn Captain. She was desperate to get Queen Lucia away from the Fortress. "He rallied the Wolven to fight us too. He overpowered us and he came to kill us both. You heard him!"

Queen Lucia stared into the empty darkness, visibly shaken. "I don't understand why."

"Lucia, snap out of it," demanded Captain Levana. "Our people need you right now. They've scattered and will more than likely meet us at the base of the mountains near the northwest exit. Let's go."

The only light source illuminating the dank escape route came from a lit torch brought down here by the queen. Captain Levana struggled to get any kind of reaction from her leader.

Suddenly, the queen's face crumpled. Her brow furrowed. Her eyes shot to the captain's, "He lied to me. He used our alliance to get the shards. He never wanted peace," bellowed Queen Lucia, now wrought with anger.

Levana took a few steps. "Now you're seeing it! Come on, we need to leave," she pressed. As she glanced over her shoulder, the seething Queen followed on.

The pair hurried down the west tunnel towards the exit at the mountain base. A strong wind blew throughout the tunnels flickering the torchlight, causing their shadows to dance along the walls.

"Why are the living so stupid?" vented Queen Lucia. "None of them have any idea what's coming for them if we don't get that completed crystal."

"Well, that's their problem. Come on, we have to get those shards back. To do that, we need to gather the remnants of our people and we need you in a capable state of mind to lead. If you are unable to perform your duties as our queen, then perhaps someone more capable should take over." A sly glint flashed across the captain's eyes.

The queen sped up, overtaking Levana. "Capable? I am more than capable, Captain. Don't worry, as soon as we regroup, we'll go after the remaining shards."

"How do you suggest we do that? I..." Levana cleared her throat. "I lost the two we had on the battlefield, when I was fighting that great oaf, Victor."

"You fought Victor?" The queen ignored the information about the lost shards.

"Yes, he came for me. It was his clear intention to murder me, so I had to fight back." She scratched her head. "That's when I lost the shards."

"That proves it, then. Victor is fiercely loyal to the king; he wouldn't attack you if he had been forbidden, even if he wanted to. Also dear, I heard you the first time—I trust you'll recover them because you are fully aware of what will happen to you if you don't."

Captain Levana gulped at Lucia's nonchalant threat, then cleared her throat. "*Was* fiercely loyal," she corrected.

"Wait, what do you mean?" The queen stopped in her tracks and turned to face her captain.

Levana laughed at the pleasurable memory of Sir Victor's life draining away. "Let's just say neither of us came out of that battle alive."

The queen's cheeks pulled tight as a grin crept its way across her face. "Good. We will make them all pay for this. The Ulv, The He'en, and especially the precious King."

The two Forsaken ambled down the tunnel giggling to themselves and plotting their next move, kicking rocks as they went.

* * *

King Areth forced his way to the centre of the huddle and froze. His eyes began to cascade and his heart pounded with a growing intensity, hurting more with every beat. Grief washed over him turning his legs to jelly. They gave out from beneath him, bringing him to his knees beside the great knight.

With tears streaming down his face, he rested a hand on the breastplate of his valiant companion and with it, complete silence fell. King Areth's heart-wrenching sobbing was the only sound.

"No... No... No, you will not take him from me!" he cried out to the heavens.

Finding new vigour in a glimmer of hope that flew through his mind, he stood. "Bring me the Mys shard, somebody. Now!"

A hand rested on his shoulder and a familiar voice soothed his ears. "It won't work, Your Majesty," a solemn, but brutally honest knight, reminded him.

The King turned to Boris, looking up at him with eyes red raw from sorrowful tears. "Shut up, you simple idiot!"

Boris didn't respond. Instead, he looked to the body of Sir Victor and back with a stern look. His voice cracked and trembled as he stood up to the devastated king. "No, Your Majesty. Victor was your best knight and, indeed, your best friend... but he was also ours. He was an exceptional commander to us all and a great man. We are all grieving for his soul right now, so don't act like you're the only one who gives a damn. The Mys shard will only heal non-fatal wounds. The best we can do for him now is give him the send-off he'd want. Please, Your Highness, let us all grieve for him."

With little more to say, King Areth simply placed a hand on the young knight's shoulder and stared him in the eyes through the flood of tears blurring his vision. "Please, Boris; you have to let me try."

Boris flashed a fake smile and nodded before retreating into the stunned crowd to attend to the injured.

For a few moments, King Areth paced around, screaming into the rain. A mixture of salty tears and rain cascaded down his despair-twisted face. His heart burned with intensifying anguish as he called out once more. "Where is my shard?"

Nohalla came sprinting to his side holding out the brilliant white gem. Before she handed it over, she reiterated Boris's words. "It's futile, King Areth. There isn't enough power in this gem to bring a soul back from Knas."

She dropped the shard into his palm.

He ignored her words and knelt. He held the shard against Sir Victor's wound, concentrating hard. Flickers of light emanated from within the gem, but nothing else happened. He tried again, this time pressing the shard in even harder, leaving a clear imprint on the knight's cold neck. Again, the shard flickered.

Tendrils of light began to seep out of it, taking hold of the knight's body. The light dove into the fatal wound and began to seal it. The king's face became a picture of hope and he focused even harder as the light shone brighter and brighter, sealing more of the gash in Sir Victor's neck.

For a few moments the light twisted and writhed around the corpse like a serpent unable to find its prey. Suddenly, the shard flickered brightly then faded and the tendrils dissipated. The gash on Sir Victor's neck partially disappeared; only a striking scar remained.

King Areth shook the knight by the shoulders, pleading with him to wake up. He slapped the face of the motionless body several times, screaming his name, begging for him to open his eyes. Finally, he pressed his fingers to Sir Victor's neck and felt nothing. Not a single beat of life flowed through his friend.

In a violent motion, the king hurled the shard out onto the esplanade, before reverting to a state of anguish. He spent a while mourning, tears searing his face and his heart sinking ever deeper into a chasm of despair. All around him heads bowed in respect of a great man, slain upon the field of battle.

Boris held out the red and blue shards in his palm. "I picked these up, Your Majesty." He glanced at his commander's body, barely holding back another flood of emotion.

The king wiped away his tears and stood. Staring rather sternly at Boris, he took the two shards and whispered 'thank you' to the knight. He paused as his troops stared at him, watery eyed, awaiting their orders. For King Areth, time seemed to stop. He looked to the shards in his hands and then to myriad troops surrounding him. He glanced once more to the body of Sir Victor and as he did, a voice echoed in his ears.

They await your leadership, my friend. Lead them.

The king's heart pounded through his chest as the voice of Sir Victor still advised him in his mind. His hand tightened around the two shards.

He inhaled deeply, his chest puffed out, and looking at his troops, he spoke. Quietly at first, but soon, his voice rang out as loud and majestic as before. "My friends, today a great man has been taken from us." He paused, fighting another surge of emotion. "His death came as a result of traitorous actions by the Forsaken. From this point on, any Forsaken spotted near our cities are to be executed. They will not claim any more of our people, any more of you. No longer are they welcome, and no longer do we fight alongside them!"

A wave of hateful grunts and spits, albeit in agreement, met his speech. He looked to Boris who quietly smiled at his leader's exceptional show of determination and muttered to him.

"Boris, arrange for his body to be returned to Straeta. He deserves a proper burial."

Boris nodded and headed off to attend to his duty.

Sha'koth and Ulv Nikos joined the circle which grew to a substantial size as the Wolven and Marusi armies now gathered around the three leaders.

"King Areth," said Sha'koth. "The power of each shard is greatly increased when another shard is adjacent to it. Please, lend me the two in your hand and I shall demonstrate." He held out his palm, displaying the Mys shard he'd retrieved.

The king nodded and dropped the Bui and Dion shards into the scaly blue hand of the He'en, showing full trust in his new ally.

The Marusi leader proceeded to grip all three shards together and punch a hole into the soft mud, burying his fist. A familiar white glow crept across the ground, dancing around the wounds of the injured soldiers with a majestic elegance. Light wisps entered their bodies and repaired the damage of battle, putting on an awe-inspiring show of light and life. It did not regrow lost limbs, nor did it bring back the dead, but it did heal the open wounds of any living creature, whether lying on the ground near to death, or suffering silently with gashes and broken bones.

After a few moments, the radiant glow faded and Sha'koth removed his fist from the ground. He opened his palm to reveal the three pristine shards showing no signs of wear or soiling, almost as if the dirt itself was repelled.

"I thought that would save you some time, King." Sha'koth smiled his pointed toothy smile. The healed troops rejoiced at their instant recovery and joined the rear of the great circle, listening for orders.

In the centre of this great gaggle of seasoned warriors stood three leaders - King Areth, Ulv Nikos and He'en Sha'koth. Courageous, powerful, and wise, they stood basking in glory from their victory, and at the same time wallowing in sorrow from their painful losses.

A discussion on where to go from here and how to best divide the shards begun with Sha'koth openly displaying the three shards in his outstretched palm. "King Areth, you have proven today that you will stand with us. On behalf of my people, I offer our services as your allies. The same offer is extended to you and your kind also, Ulv Nikos." The He'en clenched his fist around the shards and dropped his arm for comfort as the discussions continued.

"Consider us allies, my friend," responded King Areth. Ulv Nikos grunted and nodded signalling his agreement to the alliance of the three, but unable to take his eyes away from Sha'koth's fist.

"Good, then it is decided. Let this be the start of a prosperous alliance," declared Sha'koth to the masses. Rejoicing broke out on all fronts with cheers, whoops, and even handshakes between the allied armies.

When the ruckus settled, the He'en continued the discussions, holding the shards out once again for all to see. "If we may take the Bui shard to settle into our new home city, we would be most grateful. The shard's power is to control the waters; we used it to keep the lake calm during storms and flowing during winters, so it would not freeze. We would like to make use of its power again for those same reasons." He looked to the other two leaders for confirmation.

"Dion shard help Wolven," started Nikos. "Power help forest grow strong. Keep ground rich, Wolven expand Den," said the Wolven leader.

King Areth smiled at the giant creature and patted him on the arm. Surprisingly to him, the Ulv's fur felt soft and light, yet somehow thick and oily.

"Of course, my friend. I want to take the Mys shard for my people. I cannot risk losing more of my citizens so in this endeavour the healing powers of the Mys shard will greatly benefit us." The king smiled at each of the leaders in turn. They both nodded at him, and he and the Ulv took their appropriate shards from the He'en's hand.

Sha'koth placed the Bui shard in the familiar leather pouch on his shoulder strap. "Then it's settled. A shard each to secure our alliances." He raised his spear to the sky in celebration. Another grand huzzah from the surrounding forces echoed out for miles across the barren Darklands. The deafening sound of howls and growls from the Wolven, whoops and shouts from men and women, and the cheers and the clack of spears bashing against spears from the Marusi, filled the air.

Quite a long while passed before the noise died down again allowing the king to speak once more. As he spoke, he paced in circles on the spot to further project his voice. "It's far from over, my friends. There are still three shards to find before the Forsaken find them. There is a rumbling coming from the Golzhad region that threatens a devastating volcanic eruption, and another source of rumblings that we have not yet located. Ulv Nikos, He'en Sha'koth, may I suggest that you each send scouts to the far corners of Naeisus to look for shards? We cannot risk the Forsaken getting their hands on even one of the missing shards, as we do not yet know their power. Also, let us not forget the brave souls we've lost today. Keep them dear to your hearts and fresh in your memory. Know that they will be avenged soon. They did not die in vain!" He bellowed with a burning passion.

"As soon as we've settled in our new home, we will join your search, King Areth." Sha'koth also spoke loudly enough to address the masses.

"We fight as pack! Now, Wolven go home." Ulv Nikos raised his head to the sky and howled. His forces separated from the rest of the army and began to spill out to the west. A pathway cleared for the Ulv and he sprinted to the head of the pack, leading the Wolven to their home.

Sha'koth placed a hand on the king's shoulder and bumped heads with him, bidding him farewell.

Seeing no point in staying at the now desolate Undying Fortress, King Areth ordered his troops to mount up and ride for home. With a lump in his throat, he verified the careful treatment of Sir Victor's body and was reassured that he had entrusted Boris with the gentle task of returning the big knight safely.

"When we get back, we have a great funeral to organise for a great man," he yelled. With that, he leapt upon Violetwing's back and stroked her feathery neck. "Come on, Vi. We're heading home."

Chapter 11

The Aithur

"**Y**ou're lost, aren't you, my dear?"

"Lost? Of course not! I know these escape tunnels like the back of my hand," fumed Levana.

Queen Lucia let out a muffled chortle. "We have been ambling around for at least half a day."

"Look, these tunnels stretch all the way to the edge of the Darklands. It's not a quick stroll. Besides, we've had plenty of time to discuss our revenge."

The queen's entire demeanour shifted. Her face darkened, and her fists curled. "About that . . . you lost the shards, Captain."

Levana stopped in her tracks. "But I killed Victor, my Queen. You know how competent of a leader he was; the king's troops are surely in disarray."

"As are ours, if you hadn't noticed."

The captain continued to walk. "With his best friend gone and the army in chaos, now would be the perfect time to strike." A flash of menace crossed her face.

A smirk returned to the queen's face. "I think I know what you're planning, my dear. Just remember, if you fail me again, I will bring you down."

"I won't."

Just what does she have on me?

"Are you sure you know where you're going, Captain?" inquired Queen Lucia with a hint of mockery.

"Of course, I do! We made a left at the fork back there, and we need to make another left at the next one." She thrust the torch forward in an attempt to see further into the distance, but it only served to disturb the flame, causing their shadows to dance along the earthen walls. Captain Levana danced alongside them, chanting a song she'd made up about having the king's head for treachery. Queen Lucia found this rather amusing and even joined in with the lyrics as she followed the captain's lead.

In the dark underground, time dissolved for those who did not need to sleep or eat. Although they weren't aware of it, they had been ambling through these tunnels for almost four days. Suddenly, the queen cried out in anguish.

Captain Levana drew her one remaining quick-blade and turned, ready to attack an assailant. After scanning for a moment and seeing nothing, she grunted and sheathed her weapon.

"A dead end! We're stuck here, aren't we?" barked Queen Lucia

"Shh! Look," hushed the impatient captain. She walked towards the dead end and pointed the torch at the wall.

In the dim, fluttering light, two jagged edges of rocks protruded from the soil, looking out of place. Captain Levana urged the queen to stand back and handed her the torch. She proceeded to run at the wall, plunging her fist into it and dropping back, only to be showered with a sudden barrage of falling dirt and rocks. Shaking her boots off and dusting her shoulders, Captain Levana retrieved the torch from her bemused Queen and held it up once more. Queen Lucia's eyes widened, as the protruding rocks now formed part of a crude stone staircase, leading upward.

Levana puffed her chest out and thumped it. "I told you I knew the way." She pushed through some more dirt and led the way up the stairs.

The staircase didn't go on for more than a few steps, before a solid stone wall made yet another dead end. Again, the captain took charge and placed her shoulder against the wall, heaving with all her might.

"A little help," she demanded.

The queen obliged. Under their combined strength, the rock began to slide, letting in a blast of fresh, cold winter air. Snow danced into the tunnels and the sudden burst of air extinguished the torch in Captain Levana's hand, plunging the pair into darkness.

As they exited the tunnel, a gentle wash of moonlight illuminated a thin layer of snow covering the ground.

They replaced the stone slab covering the entrance and walked out of a small, secluded grove, amazed at the silhouettes surrounding them.

The dazzling glitter of stars and the two bright moons painted the land with just enough light for them to see thick grass poking through the surrounding snow. They turned around to face the grove and their mouths fell open. Behind them, in the distance and stretching up to touch the millions of stars, sat the great Triash mountain. The base of the mountain stood at least a mile from them, yet the vastness of it made it feel almost as if it were within touching distance.

Captain Levana pointed at the mountain in wonder before barking an order. "Come on, we need to get to the mountain," she enthused.

"Why's that, my dear?" enquired the perplexed Queen.

Levana attempted a grin, but her discomfort shone through. "Because, My Queen, my soldiers have a plan in case of catastrophe. They send word to Rogue who will meet us here, until we know that the Fortress is safe to occupy again."

"Why would we want to go back to the Fortress? They'd only attack us again once they knew we were back."

"But this time, we prepare," replied the smug captain. "We know how each race attacks, we know their moves, and we know what we are defending against. During that fight, I observed them closely."

Queen Lucia shot daggers at her. "Of course. This is the reason I made you my Captain. But don't forget, Levana, I am the one who gives the orders. If you dare threaten my position—"

"Apologies, My Queen. I mean no disrespect." Levana bowed, but she wore a scowl behind a curtain of thin, charcoal hair.

Queen Lucia smiled sweetly and pointed in the direction of the Triash mountain. "Onwards, then," she giggled.

The two Forsaken women walked briskly toward the base of the mountain for what seemed like an age, both remaining silent. Frozen snow crunched beneath their feet as they went, eerily mimicking the sound of bones breaking, at least to the captain's ears. Snow droplets drifting on the sharp breeze settled in their hair, mirroring the sparkling night sky, and rested for a long while before either being blown away again or melting away.

The ground began to slope upward, and Captain Levana searched along the steep incline for a moment before finding a flat section and flumping to the snow-covered ground, lying on her back. She patted the space beside her and the queen knelt with grace, easing herself into the same position as the captain.

"Why are we doing this?" asked Queen Lucia after a moment.

"What else are we going to do while we wait but stare at the stars? Damned troops should have been here before us!"

Queen Lucia returned her gaze to the amazing night sky. They lay there, silently appreciating the nature surrounding them; above them shone the two moons of Naeisus—Bo and the slightly smaller Dalon. These moons orbited one another as they circled the planet, often eclipsing each other.

Tonight, however, both moons hovered side-by-side and full, as if watching over the world. This marked the midpoint of a lunar cycle which took fifty-six Naeisan days. Six lunar cycles completed a solar cycle, a system that all the denizens of the land knew well. Swarming the rest of the sky hung millions of various sized pinpricks. Many of the larger ones glowed red while the smaller ones shone white or blue, but one stood out in particular. Just to the west of Dalon, a gem at least twice the size of the others, glittered in the sky. The edges of this star danced and vibrated with immense energy; for this reason it had earned the nickname 'The Dancing Star'.

The silence of the night loomed over the pair, broken only by the occasional rustling of leaves.

Lost deep in her memories, Levana finally broke the silence. Her voice came out meek and frail, almost cracked as a sudden sadness swept over her, "Lilith and I used to love watching the moons… "

Queen Lucia swallowed hard and tucked her hands underneath her back, concealing trembling fingers. "Lilith? Oh yes, that twin sister of yours from your living days." An air of annoyance floated about her words. "I'm surprised you still remember her. It's been many hundreds of solars since I brought you back after that Wolven attack. Isn't it time you forgot about all of that?"

Levana bolted upright and shot a nasty look at the queen. "If you were quicker, you could have saved her too."

Lucia turned her head and smiled sweetly. "We never did find her body, my dear. Most likely devoured by Wolven like your—" The queen stopped herself mid-sentence and averted her gaze to the night sky.

Levana finished the sentence for her, almost in a whisper. "Like my children, you mean." She fell backwards into the snow and resumed her stargazing.

The surrounding air became tense and thick, almost stagnant, as both Forsaken women became lost in their own minds.

Eventually, Captain Levana raised a lazy finger aiming it at Bo and Dalon, breaking the tension. "Some say those moons are the eyes of the Yultah. Some say there is a being even more powerful, one who created the Yultah, and those eyes belong to that being." She uneasily reminisced over her ground-shattering encounter with Knas.

"Nonsense, Levana. We've met Knas; her eyes look nothing like that. They are far more terrifying, I think."

"Are you sure? Do we really know what she looks like? Think hard. What did you actually see, Lucia?"

"It was so long ago. Come to think of it, I don't actually remember anything about her," she exclaimed, surprising herself.

"Exactly! The more I think about it, the less I remember. In fact, the only thing I do remember is a void and a silent voice. It was like words were being written into my mind."

"It seems you're correct, Captain, but what does this have to do with the moons?"

"We know a greater power is at work in the Yultah, we've experienced it. If there is one above them, one even more powerful, why does that one simply not give our souls to Knas now?"

Queen Lucia raised both arms amidst the drifting snowflakes and grasped at the air. "Perhaps for the same reason Knas cannot simply come and take them. All evidence points to the six being unable to interact directly with our world, but in the end it is all beyond our understanding."

"What I'm trying to say is, what if the Yultah are not divine at all?" Captain Levana's eyes sparkled with excitement. "If they are simply mortal beings on another plane of existence, what's stopping us from challenging them and ruling their world?"

"Let's focus on this world first, my dear," replied the queen with an air of darkness.

The captain grunted. She was unsatisfied with the queen's answer, but chose not to pursue the conversation any further; instead she opted to absorb the beauty of the starry canvas above her and found herself lost in the dream of conquering new worlds.

After staring listlessly into the night sky and making patterns from the stars for what seemed like ages, the restless Captain Levana declared her boredom. She sat up and shook off much of the snow that settled on her body, before leaping to her feet and dusting herself down.

Queen Lucia also sat upright, shaking some snow from her garments. "Where are you going?"

"For a walk. We could be here for days before those incompetent buffoons find us. We may as well see what's around." She swung her arms from side to side and stretched.

"I'm growing tired of lying here. I'll accompany you, my dear."

The queen stood and dusted down her regal dress, then smiled at the captain and ushered her to begin walking. Captain Levana led the way around the eastern side of the mountain until she came across a small, enticing path that snaked its way up the side of the incline, then disappeared over the top of a ledge.

The captain began to follow the path with the queen in tow. "This looks interesting. I heard there is a lake atop this mountain. Fancy a swim?"

"Yes, Lake Aithel. I've been there once, hundreds of solars ago. The water is unusually clear and calm. The living say that those waters are the most invigorating of all, however, getting to the summit of the mountain is not an easy task; one wonders if the journey is worth it."

"Invigorating, huh? Maybe a quick dip will ease this damned pain and go some way to releasing *Her* grip." The captain glanced to the night sky with contempt.

"I very much doubt that, it didn't for me that one time." sighed Queen Lucia. "But, there is little else to do until someone else gets here, I suppose."

The path grew steeper as they climbed, but it didn't stop Captain Levana from leaping, swift and agile as a gazelle, bounding higher and higher up the mountain path. Queen Lucia followed close behind, displaying a similar dexterity, as she grabbed outcroppings and heaved herself to greater heights. Eventually the path flattened out again and they peered over the edge at the ground far below them.

The grove where they had emerged from the underground tunnels was now almost invisible in the distance. Stretching out for as far as the night allowed them to see, was nothing but dazzling white snow, covering the usually luscious grassy plains. Snow that blanketed the few Triash saplings that grew on this side of the mountain; snow that blurred the edge of the Darklands in the far distance.

Following the path further around and turning a corner, revealed a landslide of rocks blocking the way ahead. The captain groaned and flopped her arms to her sides in disappointment.

"Great." Sarcasm infected the queen's response. "What now, Captain?"

"This rockslide is too large to go over or around, and I fear there is no other route to the top. However . . ." She scanned the cliff face suspiciously, her eyes flitting from rock to rock.

"Can we not dig—"

Captain Levana interrupted the queen, holding a finger out to reinforce her stance. "We'll have to turn back and check for a new route. I spotted an outcropping back there." She pointed her thumb over her shoulder.

"Or we just give up entirely and go back to the bottom," suggested the tired queen.

"We're already halfway. Why stop now? Let's humour ourselves and check for more routes," said Captain Levana with a mocking smile. "I think there's something worth looking at around here." She hopped past Queen Lucia, once again leading the charge to Lake Aithel at the summit.

Ignoring the path trailing down the mountain, Captain Levana hugged the face of the mountain, crossing an incredibly narrow ledge. She used cracks or gaps in the wall as handles to keep her balance.

A sheer drop awaited below, one that taunted and threatened them with true death if they were not careful. The captain cautiously placed her foot forward and found a larger shelf which seemed stable enough to rest on. Her other foot followed. Finding herself safe, she exhaled a sigh of relief and checked on the queen's progress.

Queen Lucia was several steps behind, also approaching the shelf. As she readied herself to step over, the ledge beneath her gave out. She slipped and shot out a hand to grab a hold of something. With incredible reflexes, her fingertips found a crevice and gripped tightly, leaving her dangling from the wall.

A glimmer of hope dashed across the captain's eyes but was quickly concealed behind a gasp.

Queen Lucia grinned as she began to swing. She remained calm and eyed the wall ahead of her, confident in her own abilities. When she built enough momentum, she let go and propelled herself towards another out-cropping which she caught with both hands. Her feet shuffled along the face of the mountain until they found the remnants of the ledge and she hastily shimmied up onto the shelf to join the silently disappointed captain.

The queen fixed her hair and grinned. "You didn't really think I was in danger, did you, my dear?"

"It's a shame, Maybe I would have finally been Queen," jested Captain Levana in a feeble attempt to cover her disappointment. Quickly, she turned and continued to follow the shelf, with Queen Lucia watching her through squinted eyes.

Following the shelf around a small bend, Captain Levana spotted something just out of reach above them.

She pointed up to a small opening in the cliff. "Up there! It looks like an entrance. A cave of some kind. Come on." She made out a clear, but risky, path to get there. She gripped the wall and began to bound effortlessly, this time keeping a closer eye on the queen, who was starting her own steady climb just behind.

Up and up they went, finding any small gap or outcrop to hold or stand on until the Forsaken captain's fingers gripped the mouth of the tiny opening. She hauled herself up and crawled inside, out of the queen's view.

As Queen Lucia neared the entrance, gasps of wonder came from within and she quickened her pace to see the cause of the fuss. Also heaving herself up and squeezing through the small gap, the hole in the mountain opened up into a giant, cavernous room. Great stalactites hung ominously from the ceiling and imposing stalagmites pierced through the ground, many of which would dwarf even the Ulv.

The cave pulsed a soothing light, illuminated by a pool of water at the centre. It radiated a gentle cyan, lighting Captain Levana's awe-struck face. She stood on the edge of the pool watching wisps of light hover and fly just above the surface, weaving amongst one another in an intricate, delicate dance. A constant, gentle dripping from the room's central stalactite caused soft ripples to swim across the magical pool.

"This looks incredible! What are these little balls of light above the water?" asked the captain.

"I have no idea; I suspect this pool has built up over the ages with water from the lake above. Perhaps the strange lights have something to do with it filtering through the rocks."

"Maybe." Levana grabbed a rather large stone. "I wonder how deep it is." She dropped the rock into the pool with a plop and watched as it sank deeper and deeper, fading from view.

"Huh." She shrugged.

Suddenly, the stone ejected itself from the pool and slammed against one of the cavern walls with a loud clap that echoed around the chamber. Queen Lucia approached the pool and glared into its endless depth. The two Forsaken women glanced at each other, mouths agape and brows furrowed in confusion.

Captain Levana made a grab at one of the drifting lights, but her hand passed through it, not even so much as disturbing the surrounding air. She picked up another rock and tossed it in hoping for a repeat performance, and sure enough, the pool spat it right out again causing another loud clap to ring around the interior of the cave.

She knelt by the edge and swirled her hand around in the water. Something was amiss—it acted and felt almost like normal water, save for the freezing temperature, or so the captain thought at first. She swirled her hand again, this time for longer, and quickly snapped it backwards. "Ouch! That burned! It is freezing cold, yet my hand feels as if it were in a torch."

Her gaze remained fixated on the water, still swishing and swirling by itself.

The swirling intensified, beginning to form peaks at several points. The swishing spread and grew, until the whole pool washed and danced with a vibrant energy.

The two Forsaken stepped back in horror as, without warning, three thick columns of water rose to the ceiling, then fell away with a splash. Despite this violent performance, not a single drop of water spilled.

Queen Lucia and Captain Levana looked up and recoiled in fright. Three hovering entities floated a few feet above the surface of the pool.

These entities took on rough humanoid shapes, seemingly as fluid as the water from which they came. They glowed the same shade of cyan as the pool, and appeared to have wings on their backs, although the nature of their liquid forms made it difficult to discern. Levana drew her blade and stepped forward, but Queen Lucia stood at ease and signalled for the captain to stand down.

The entities hung in the air, drifting from side to side but remaining quiet.

"Hello." started Queen Lucia, attempting to maintain an air of Majesty in the presence of these unknown creatures. "Who are you?"

"Who are we? But who are you to ask?! The queen of the Forsaken no less, comes to us with a task." The entities' voices almost became one with the cool breeze outside. It was unclear which of the featureless, translucent figures had spoken.

"How do you know who I am?" A task? I have no task."

"A task you have, to find the shards is your desire, and a king to kill, a king you feel a liar."

Queen Lucia's eyes lit up. "Yes, the shards! You know of the shards?" She took a step forward and pleaded. "Please, who are you and how do you know all of this?"

A childlike giggle echoed around the cavern sending chills down the spines of the women.

"Yes, yes! The shards we know! We are the Aithur and a shard we shall show!" The entities dissolved back into the pool with another giggle that lingered in the cavern for longer than was comfortable.

Queen Lucia looked over her shoulder at the angry-looking captain and shrugged. "Did you hear that? They have a shard! Did they want to show it to us?"

"Give me the order, Lucie, and I'll cut them down and take it!"

"It's hard to understand their rhymes, but it seems they did not wish to harm us. Hold yourself, Levana."

"I don't trust them," Levana grunted.

"You don't trust anyone. Let's hear them out, maybe they—"

A watery rumbling cut her short. The columns shot out of the pool once more and the three winged entities reappeared, hovering above the lake's surface. This time, however, something was different.

The blue glow darkened drastically, turning almost black, and inside one of the watery creatures floated a small ebony gem. It hovered there, darker than the night sky, reaching out with horrible dark tendrils that seemed to feel their way around the cavern.

"Bloody Knas, it is a shard! It's one of the legendary six, there's no doubt! Look at the way it calls out to us!" Captain Levana made a sudden movement forward, and the shard dropped into the pool.

Captain Levana cried out as the shard sank helplessly into the depths. "Give us that shard, or I will end you!"

An unsettling chuckle responded to her demand, which served to remove every ounce of threat. The Aithur kept their near-onyx colours as big, human-like grins now appeared on their otherwise featureless faces.

The captain rushed to the pool's edge but halted in her tracks by a warning from the Aithur, whose grins remained fixed.

"To dive in and chase you would be a fool, for there is no bottom to our mystical pool."

Captain Levana growled and sheathed her dagger, scowling at the entities.

Queen Lucia urged her to settle down, and then attempted to negotiate with these mysterious beings. "Which shard is that, and what is its power?" she asked with the utmost of respect.

"The power of Knas this shard contains, it can reduce your enemies to mere remains." The cave seemed to darken at this response, and the creepy grins on the strange entities grew wider, almost wrapping around their watery heads.

The Forsaken captain stamped her foot, pointing at the Aithur. "What exactly are you?"

"Levana, please," snapped the queen.

"A cursed being we are, and that's all you shall know. We are not your friend, but neither are we foe," whispered the Aithur.

"Let's take it by force," hissed the captain.

Ignoring her captain's statement, Queen Lucia continued the conversation with the Aithur, working to hide her inner fear of these peculiar creatures. "Aithur, tell us, is there anything you'd be willing to trade for that shard?"

"A trade we will not make, but discord is our desire. Prove you are worthy, and receive what you require."

"Discord? How? What do you want in return for the Knas shard?"

The Aithur began to swirl and twirl around each other, merging into one giant creature looming above the pool. This single Aithur filled the entire back of the cavern and peered at the tiny Forsaken women below, intimidating them with its eerie grin. A loud, gravelly whisper reverberated around the room, penetrating the souls of the Forsaken. "Solve this riddle to gain the shard, for you, oh Queen, it shouldn't be hard."

The queen backed away a few paces. "Riddle. Okay. What's the riddle?"

"Here is the riddle for you, the Queen; listen carefully to know what we mean. Royal blood flows strong in their family tree; go forth and bring the heads of three. Slay these kings and incite the wars; only then will the shard be yours."

Queen Lucia pondered for a moment, holding her hand to her delicate chin.

"What in Knas' name is this? Just give us the damn shard!" ordered Captain Levana.

"Levana, shut up," barked the queen. "If you cannot contain yourself, wait outside!"

The captain growled with fury, but held her ground.

Queen Lucia continued to ponder. "The heads of three . . . royal blood . . . you want the heads of three kings?"

"What we ask is very clear, bring us these heads, Queen Lucia, my dear."

Another eerie and unsettling giggle floated about the cavern, almost as if the Aithur amused themselves.

Queen Lucia remained outwardly unfazed and smiled. "But why do you want the heads of three with royal blood?" she asked politely.

The grin of the giant Aithur morphed into a threatening scowl as it replied in a demon-like hiss, which shook the two Forsaken to their very cores.

"Our reasons are not your concern. It is for discord that we yearn."

As suddenly as the Aithur had appeared, it melted once again into the pool of water and the room instantly returned to its previous luminosity.

The queen held her hand out to the pool and urged for them to return, but the pool didn't so much as ripple. "Consider it a deal! I'll bring you their heads," she yelled into the empty cavern.

"So it's true… " mumbled Levana to herself.

"Hm?" Lucia turned on her heels, deaf to the words of her captain.

"Lucia, how do we know we can trust these things?" asked the captain rather meekly.

"We don't, Captain. All we know is that they have the Knas shard and are willing to give it to us if we bring them the heads of three kings. I already have one in mind, don't you?"

Darkness filled the captain's red eyes. "Oh I like your thinking! Two birds with one stone! I can think of another two without putting much effort into it."

Upon leaving the Aithur's cavern, the two Forsaken shielded their eyes as they adjusted to the dawn sunlight, spilling its radiance across the land.

Levana sighed, peering down the rock face. "Come on, let's get back to the base."

"The three heads we need are those of King Areth, Ulv Nikos, and He'en Sha'koth. That much is clear," said the queen with an aggressive malice in her usually tender voice.

"We know Straeta well; we know the layout, the entrances, and exits. We even know where the king and his precious children sleep. It wouldn't take much to assassinate them as they slept, especially now that lumbering oaf, *Sir* Victor is out of the way," mocked Levana.

"I wouldn't underestimate him, my dear. He is a highly intelligent and incredibly skilled man, regardless of whether we like him or not. No. First we need to break him, and to break him we undo all that he has worked for. We take Nikos first—with their Ulv gone, the Wolven will fall into disarray, fighting and tearing chunks out of one another to prove they are strong enough to be the next Ulv. Pathetic and primitive if you ask me."

"No offence, Lucie, but how will that affect Areth?" Hunger filled the psychotic captain's eyes. "I say we just take his head as soon as we can."

"Because, you fool, Ulv Nikos is the only link to the alliance with the Wolven. The next Ulv won't uphold that. Do you think that idiotic race of wild dogs knows anything about honour? They will drop the alliance with Man in a heartbeat, and the poor, disillusioned King Areth will fall into a panic."

"I like it. So with the king too preoccupied to worry about us, the last thing he'll expect is an attack, right?"

"Right. Since you destroyed Alkra—a move which I'm only just starting to condone—the Marusi are too busy building something else. A city isn't built in just one cycle. With the Wolven out of the picture and the Marusi too busy to help, the king will be powerless. His little army won't stand up to the power of the undead, despite the losses we have suffered. Knowing him as well as I do, he'll only have the Mys shard to help him. That won't do much against a swift strike. The Mys shard cannot cure death, remember." Her mind ran wild with the idea of obtaining a new, powerful shard. Greed began to consume the Forsaken monarch once again.

"Brilliant! So that's two heads. What about the great and wise Sha'koth?" asked the captain as she shuffled further down the path.

"That's the easiest of the three. The Marusi will no longer have any allies. They are still weak and disorganised; taking them out with the power of the risen soldiers from both Wolven and Man will be simple. Obviously along the way we will have stolen the shards they all possess— we then trade the heads for the Knas shard and four of the six will belong to the Forsaken."

Captain Levana grinned from ear to ear. "Our time is coming it seems, My Queen. I'm only glad you chose me assist you through the entire plan." Her undead heart filled with the excitement of this revolutionary plan.

Queen Lucia halted and stared her captain dead in the eye, smiling from the side of her mouth. "Well of course. I trust you, Levana."

"Oh? You do?"

The queen leaned in to her captain's ear and whispered. "Even if you killed me, the Forsaken would string you up and avenge me. I've made sure of it." She pulled away and laughed almost maniacally, continuing her walk.

Captain Levana laughed nervously alongside her, curling her hands into fists.

The queen raised her arms to the sky. "Once we own four of the six, we will have the power and the army to sweep this world for the final two, and when that crystal is ours, even Knas herself will tremble before the darkness. Being dead will no longer be a burden, but a blessing. Immortality without disease, fatigue, or pain. This world will belong to us!"

As they neared the bottom of the mountain, three Forsaken riders approached through the snow leading a handful of spare horses behind them. The morning sun shone in the eyes of the queen and captain and cast the shadows of the riders far ahead.

"Finally! They took their time, useless idiots," jeered the queen.

Captain Levana remained silent as the riders drew nearer with as much haste as the horses allowed.

"My Queen," yelled the fiery-haired rider leading the recovery mission. "I'm relieved to see you safe and well."

"Why wouldn't I be safe and well?" spat the irritated monarch.

"N . . . no reason, Your Grace." She pointed in the direction of the fortress with a trembling finger. "We have located two large groups of Forsaken making their way back to the Undying Fortress as we speak. The Fortress itself is deserted; no enemies have been sighted nearby."

"Good. When we return, we have a lot of work to do. I want something fixed atop the walls to stop those damn Wolven climbing over them, I want large weapons on the front gates to stop armies from getting in, and I want more skilled troops!"

Levana giggled childishly behind the queen and piped in, "You heard the queen. From now on, I'll be running more vigorous training exercises for you bunch of amateurs!"

"Of course, Captain. But now we must hurry back, we are bordering the Wolven's home and if they find us here, there is no way we can stand up to them."

The queen pondered for a moment, looking at the Triash Forest behind her and struck upon an idea. Her face lit up as the idea hatched into a steadfast plan in her mind. "You're right; we are near the Wolven's home. Tell me, how many Wolven Forsaken do we have?"

"Not many, Your Grace. No more than two-dozen at my best guess."

"And young Wrath, how is he adjusting to being one of us?"

"He's still getting used to the pain, but he's strong."

"Strong enough to attack his own kind?"

"I don't follow, Your Grace."

The queen stepped forward to confront the soldier at an uncomfortably close proximity. "I'll make it simple for you. I want the Ulv's head. Is he capable of leading some of ours into the Triash Forest and getting it for me?"

The warrior trembled, trying her best to remain steadfast and replying as accurately as she could. "He has shown no signs of trying to escape or attack us, but he's still unhinged and capable of turning against us."

The Forsaken warrior feared for her soul at the renewed ruthlessness of her queen.

Slowly, Queen Lucia began to smile. Her whole face softened as she placed a cold hand on the warrior's scarred cheek. "That's good enough for me, dear."

The queen and her captain strolled past the three horse riders and mounted two of the spare steeds that awaited them. They nodded to the rest of the troops, reared around, and galloped off in the direction of their home, without so much as a word.

Shrugging, the others quietly followed suit. It was undeniably clear to them that Queen Lucia was in a strange mood and had reacquired some of her legendary malevolence. Once again, the Forsaken slipped into a state of dread and fear of their leader, no longer daring to question her word.

Chapter 12

Wrath

The air inside Death's Arms stank of damp and mould. Captain Levana's chair groaned as she leaned forward, gripping a tankard in one hand and staring Wrath directly in the eye. The silence was deafening as the captain swigged from her tankard and glared at her Forsaken counterpart.

Wrath slammed a giant clawed fist onto the table with a boom. "I demand to know why you have called me here, yet you sit in silence..." Wrath had done well to learn the language during the time he'd spent as a Forsaken, much to their surprise.

Captain Levana leaned back in her creaky chair and huffed, amused at the outburst.

"What is so funny?" Wrath growled at his cocky superior.

"I am your Captain, Wrath. I have hundreds of solar cycles of fighting experience. It was I who created you, it was I who slayed the great Victor Blackrock." She grinned and took another sip. "If I were you, I'd show a little more respect."

"Damn your respect, and damn you back to Knas!"

"I like you, dog."

Wrath bared his teeth and growled at the insult but allowed the captain to continue talking.

"You're strong; you are your own boss. That is why the queen has selected you to lead a special mission."

"I'm not interested." The giant creature stood to leave.

The captain shrugged. "It involves returning to your old den in the Triash Forest." She took another swig, moving nothing but her eyes to look at Wrath. His ears pricked up and she smirked.

Levana took a final swig and tossed the empty tankard onto the table. "I knew that would get your attention. We have the Knas shard in our reach; all we need is Ulv Nikos' head."

Wrath's eyes fell.

I should honour the strength of the Ulv. He still overpowered me. But by rights, I am now Forsaken and this Queen Lucia is stronger than he, should I honour her too?

The captain waited. A piercing silence fell around the empty tavern.

"Nikos killed you, we saved your soul. We gave you a name! Now is the time for your revenge, Wrath."

The Wolven Forsaken's head dropped. He sighed and gave in, returning to his seat. "What must I do?"

Captain Levana jerked forwards and slammed both her palms on the table, grinning with hunger in her eyes. "My dear Wrath, the plan is simple. I will place you in command of as many Wolven Forsaken as you need. You will go to the den, slay the Ulv, and bring us back his head. How you achieve this is up to you."

"They will smell us instantly. It is a foolish plan!"

"Then come up with a better one—just bring me that head!" Levana bolted to her feet and her chair collapsed behind her as she stormed out of the tavern.

* * *

Queen Lucia paced her throne room, playing with her fingers. She shuffled to the window once again; this time a cold smile lit up her face—a smile brought on by the sight of half a dozen Forsaken Wolven gathered together and listening to orders from an aggressive Wrath. His growls and snarls floated into her ears as she watched his aggression grow, easily distinguishing him from the others by his size and darker fur. Despite the fact he remained unchanged since turning Forsaken, he somehow seemed bigger and altogether more intimidating.

Wrath barked his orders with an authority that the other Forsaken dared not question.

"The queen wants Ulv Nikos's head," growled Wrath. "Captain Levana has told me that with it, they can access a new shard—a shard to help the Forsaken fight back against the other races."

"Captain Levana told you? Where's the proof?" argued one of the Forsaken Wolven.

"I have no proof, but I'd rather she has the Ulv's head than ours."

"You're asking us to murder our own kind!"

"We are Forsaken, now! Ulv Nikos was the one who killed me; if the Wolven laid eyes on us we'd all suffer our true deaths."

"Forget it! I'm still a Wolven in my soul," the disgruntled soldier hissed.

Wrath strode towards the warrior and bared his teeth. "We do this mission for the queen, or we meet Knas again!"

The agitated Forsaken began to walk away from the small group, but Wrath leapt upon him, pinning him to the ground. He kicked and clawed but Wrath's strength overwhelmed him, keeping him pinned.

The Forsaken screeched, struggling for his life. "Let me go! What you're asking us to do is unreasonable."

"I've told you," snarled Wrath. "It's either him or us,"

"Go to Knas, dog." He spat in Wrath's face.

In a frenzy, Wrath sank his vicious teeth into the neck of the disrespectful Forsaken and tore out his throat.

The struggling creature yelped and howled as his soul dripped out of the fatal wound. The flesh ripped away easily, leaving nothing but a gaping hole and lifeless corpse on the ground.

Wrath reared back on his hind legs and glared at the remaining four Forsaken Wolven. "Does anyone else still think this is unreasonable? Does anyone else want to question our reasons for doing this?"

Silence lingered over the group. Fear flashed across the eyes of the remaining four, all of them refusing to look at the rapidly decomposing body of their slain brother.

A slow clapping came from behind the nearby ruins of a wooden shack. A pair of boots followed the sound as Captain Levana strode from the shadows in admiration of Wrath's display of strength. "Good, very good, Wrath," she commented complacently.

Wrath glowered at her.

A demonic grin wrapped around her face. "I'm pleased you have decided to do the right thing. With your help, that shard will belong to us."

"You still haven't told me how this will gain us the shard," grumbled the reluctant warrior.

"And I don't need to. If you want the orders from the queen herself, then go and talk to her. I'm not stopping you." She gestured up to Queen Lucia stood alone in her window, grinning at the Forsaken. "So tell me, Wrath, how will you achieve this?"

All eyes now looked to Wrath to come up with a plan that would enable five Forsaken Wolven to overcome thousands, get to the strongest, fiercest Wolven of them all, kill him, and then somehow escape with the head of the vicious beast.

Captain Levana sighed and interjected the silence. "Well? We're all waiting to hear your brilliant plan." She flung her arms wide.

Wrath growled before a plan began to form, the beginnings of which leaked out of his mouth. "There is no doubt that the Wolven will be able to smell us as soon as we step foot inside the den. We are dead, blood no longer flows within us, this is not hard for a Wolven to smell. To get around this, we will need to stay downwind. I know of three entrances to the den and depending on the wind, we will enter from one of these. Once inside, we all know where the Ulv's chambers are, so we will make our way there. We must keep our eyes to the floor; if they can't distinguish us by our scent, then our eyes will surely betray us."

"Oh, a wonderful plan, Wrath! So all of you make it to Nikos, and you believe you can take him down, along with his guards?"

"We will try!" He pointed a threatening claw at his Captain. "If we fail, then it will be up to you to claim his head."

"Then don't fail, Wrath." She glanced at Wrath with menace in her eyes. "Come back with his head, or don't come back at all! That applies to the rest of you dogs, too."

"Don't call us dogs, undead scum," he barked.

Captain Levana paused. With a grin, she strolled over to Wrath, pushing her tongue into her cheek. Squaring up to Wrath, she tilted her head back and stared at his furious, snarling face. "Or what, little puppy?"

Wrath ground his teeth together, saliva now seeping through the gaps and dripping from his furrowed snout. His claws dug into his own hands as he used all of his might to not lash out and attack the captain.

"I thought so. Don't forget your place, dog." The captain turned on her heels and strode away from the group.

Wrath waited until she was safely out of earshot before muttering to himself. "When I'm done with the Ulv, it'll be your head next."

Wrath growled and snapped at his cohorts. "I don't care about any of you. I don't care about the captain. I don't even care about the queen. I care about exacting my revenge on Ulv Nikos. If any of you hinder me in any way your heads will be the ones rolling. Do any of you object?"

Not a peep came from the Forsaken Wolven. They all glared past Wrath, staring off into the distance behind him.

"Good. Follow me, keep up, and do exactly as I order," he spat.

As soon as they left the confines of the Fortress, Wrath crouched to a sprinting position and shot off towards the distant snowfall. His group followed suit, pushing their bodies to the very limit but failing to close the gap with their commander. The Forsaken Wolven covered ground with immense speed, stampeding over dust and rocks until the cold dirt ground melted away and white patches appeared.

Snow crunched under their huge paws, but soon began to disappear just as quickly as the forest grew denser. The sprawling canopy collected most of the snow at this point, the weight of it supported by the giant, thick triash leaves.

Wrath slowed as the twisting trees stood at full size, crammed tightly together. His rage faded, and his vigilance took over. Glancing over his shoulder, he confirmed the other four had entered the thicket.

Raising his snout to the treetops, Wrath felt a breeze blowing in an easterly direction and let out a series of low grumbles that alerted the others. He kept his nose to the air to catch early warning of any nearby Wolven. He had the wind on his side, however, and caught the faint scent of Wolven scouts a great distance away, too far to be a concern.

He raised his claw and grumbled again as he pointed out the hidden east entrance to the den. It lay just beyond a ridge, concealed by the winding roots of a Triash tree, burying themselves deep below.

The group shuffled along the ridge until they eased themselves down without making too much noise. The plan was to go down along the underside of the ridge to the hidden entrance. Gripping the top of the ridge,

Wrath dug his claws into the earth and let himself slowly slide until his hind claws were planted firmly on the ground below.

The other Forsaken followed suit, but as Wrath led the way to the entrance, an almighty crash and a cacophony of snapping twigs and heavy rustling of leaves ripped through the air. His head darted around and he saw one of his group picking himself up from the ground, a look of shock on his face.

Wrath growled and pricked his ears up. In the distance, he heard the sound of charging footsteps.

They're coming.

The smell of living Wolven fur intensified in his nostrils. His eyes widened and his ears flitted around in the direction of the approaching footsteps, accompanied by more snapping twigs and rustling leaves.

Wrath growled. "You fool." He hissed at the clumsy warrior behind him, trying his hardest not to raise his voice. He scanned the environment and decided the best course of action would be to make a break for the entrance a few hundred feet ahead. Moving swiftly, the group made their way toward the entrance, doing all they could to lower the risk of detection from the advancing scouts.

Wrath sniffed the air again. Three... no, four scouts—now close enough to see, if the trees weren't obstructing the view. Wrath hurried along, but before he made it to the den opening, the four scouts leapt as if from nowhere and set upon the group.

One of the Wolven landed on Wrath, knocking him to the ground and pinning him. The furthest scout howled, signalling for back-up.

Wrath kicked off his attacker and turned the tables, holding him down and clawing violently at his face. Blood and fur flicked about in multiple directions as Wrath mutilated the face of the already dead Wolven. Behind him, the other four Forsaken fought and struggled against the three scouts until one by one, they had dispatched all of them, except for one who scampered away.

"Leave him." Wrath made a dash for the entrance, claws dripping with fresh blood, leaving a trail behind him.

Without question, the others followed; their fur was soaked red with the lifeblood of the victims they left on the ground behind them.

Wrath sniffed around the base of a tree until he found a small opening with blackness beyond. He clawed away the dirt and burrowed in, falling into one of the many underground tunnels and landing gracefully on his feet. As he took a few steps forward, he heard four more thumps behind him.

The small band of Forsaken Wolven waited a moment until their eyes adjusted to the dark. The wind drifted around in the tunnels, blowing gently eastwards. Wrath's fur swayed as he took a few steps forward, reorienting himself with these once-familiar surroundings.

Sniffing the air once again, he let out another low grumble and began to head down the tunnel, attempting to stay downwind and racking his memory in search of the shortest route to the Ulv's chamber.

"What if that scout gets to the Ulv before we do?" uttered one of the soldiers.

"Then we die," Wrath snapped. "Let's make sure that doesn't happen or you'll die first." Working their way through the winding tunnels, the group hid and darted around corners and intersections. They kept their senses sharp, on the lookout for any Wolven who might bring their mission to an end.

With creeping stealth, they drew closer to the Ulv's chamber. Communicating almost exclusively with body language, and near-silent grunts and snuffles, they arrived at the grand central chamber.

Wrath and his warriors hid just outside the entrance, observing the thousands of Wolven scurrying around, doing their various duties. He looked over to the northern part of the room and nodded up at one of the hundreds of entrances, claiming with absolute certainty that it was the way to Ulv Nikos's throneroom.

"Over there? We're never going to make it without being spotted," whimpered one of the Forsaken soldiers.

"Silence! Keep your eyes down and follow my lead."

At that moment, an ear-splitting howl echoed around the room, originating from the far end of the room. Suddenly, thousands of Wolven were plunged into a frenzy, setting loose a great sense of panic in Wrath's soul.

"Quickly! Get in there and make a run for that entrance! And keep your eyes down!"

"Are you insane?" replied one of the other warriors.

"Do you want to see Knas again?" snapped Wrath, as he jumped out and led the charge towards the Ulv's chamber.

The group of five sprinted across the enormous chamber and took advantage of the chaos, blending in with the other Wolven, all scrambling to various entrances. The scout who had escaped earlier, made it to the centre and alerted the other Wolven. Thousands of them flooded the tunnels and chambers of the den in search of the enemy.

Dozens of beasts were sprinting across the chamber, but not a single one paid any mind to the Forsaken running past them; they were but five in a sea of thousands. The scents of the undead merged into the background and their red eyes remained hidden as they faced the floor.

Running for what felt like an age without stopping, the five Forsaken reached the wall below the entrance to Ulv Nikos's chamber. They dug their claws into the earthen wall and started to climb; chunks of dirt fell, as they scrambled their way higher and higher, until they reached the opening.

Wrath hauled himself up and stood face-to-face with one of the Ulv's guards. The guard sniffed and stared into the Forsaken commander's deep crimson eyes, but failed to react in time. Wrath plunged his razor-sharp claws into the belly of the beast facing him and worked his claws around the guard's insides, slicing through his innards and doing as much damage as possible. As he removed his claws, he used his free hand to rip out the throat of the guard. Blood poured from his wounds, soaking Wrath's fur.

The other Forsaken clambered into the entrance and witnessed Wrath looking over the dead guard's body with blood dripping from his fur and claws. His face contorted in rage and he made a dash down the corridor. The others couldn't keep up, even at full speed, and they kept checking behind them for more Wolven warriors and guards.

Working his way down the long, winding tunnel, Wrath emerged into the Ulv's chambers, panting and snarling.

Ulv Nikos, sitting alone, leapt from his wooden throne, now decorated with the Dion shard, and bared his teeth ready for combat. *"You! I should have killed you again when I could!"*

"This time, Ulv Nikos, it is you who shall die," Wrath threatened the Ulv, baring his own teeth. "And you won't be coming back.".

The four Forsaken Wolven emerged from the entrance to the chamber, but held back on Wrath's orders.

"Queen Lucia wants your head and now that I'm here, she'll get it. I just want you dead!" Wrath lunged for Ulv Nikos, landing a deep gash across his ribs.

The Ulv yelped and retaliated, leaping upon Wrath with all his Wolven might. The two mighty creatures became locked in vicious combat, slashing, clawing, and biting. The Forsaken warriors at the entrance snarled and barked for their commander as blood flew and splattered across the chamber. Chunks of fur and flesh tore from both combatants and the loud echoes of growling, snarling, and yelping rang out through the tunnels.

The ruckus attracted nearby Wolven who now hurtled down the tunnels toward the Ulv's chamber. The Forsaken warriors turned their backs to the fight, hunched over, and bared their claws ready for the oncoming Wolven. At this crucial moment, they placed their full trust in their leader to defeat the most powerful Wolven of them all.

Ulv Nikos pinned Wrath to floor and snapped at his throat, missing by mere inches.

Wrath strained with his entire strength, keeping his forearms across the throat of the Ulv, preventing him from getting any closer. With great difficulty, he managed to raise his hind legs and dig his claws into the thighs of the Ulv, who leapt back in pain. The two stood again, facing one another and growling furiously.

"Wrath!" barked one of the Forsaken. "The Wolven are coming."

"Hold them off! I'm not finished with Nikos yet," he snapped in an almost demonic tone.

Ulv Nikos hissed. *"Wrath? You are named? Only the Ulv has a name."*

"Then prepare to step down, Nikos. I will guide the Wolven to true greatness!"

"Kill me first!"

"I'm planning on it!"

Leaping at each other once more, the two mighty beasts continued to tear shreds out of each other. Blood poured from Ulv Nikos's wounds, slowing his movements and putting him at a clear disadvantage.

Wrath didn't lose blood or become tired, and his body no longer needed blood or oxygen to sustain itself, although one fatal strike and Wrath's soul would be released to Knas with no way back.

As the two continued to battle and slash, six Wolven reached the Forsaken guarding the chamber entrance and began their own brawl. The tunnel descended into a bloody scrap between these powerful beasts—between the living and the dead.

Dozens more Wolven guards scrambled into the corridor, joining the fray. Blood, fur, and flesh littered the soil walls, as lethal strikes and slashes dug deep into the bodies of the warriors. For every living Wolven slain, another two took their place and the corridor swelled with more bodies and more beasts. The Forsaken were forced to stepped back, fighting on their back feet. The overwhelming numbers of the living began to take a toll.

Suddenly, the fighting stopped and every creature ducked, clutching their pointed ears.

A blood-curdling screech froze every one of them as pure dread filtered down their spines. All eyes turned to the source of the screeching, just in time to witness Ulv Nikos sitting upright against a wall with Wrath standing on his shoulders, his hind claws buried into the Ulv's flesh. With his front claws sunk into the sides of the Wolven leader's neck, Wrath strained upwards with all the strength his rage brought him.

Ulv Nikos struggled and screamed as his head was being wrenched away from his body. He clawed at the Forsaken's arms in a blind panic, flailing in a desperate attempt for his life. Wrath's weight proved too much, especially with all the blood the Ulv had lost over the course of the fight.

With an almighty roar and a deafening squeal, Wrath pulled Ulv Nikos's head from his shoulders. A jet of blood erupted from the wound, soaking the surroundings and leaving every other beast dumbfounded.

Wrath leapt away from the Ulv's body, leaving the headless mass to collapse to the chamber floor. The rest of the blood drained from it, absorbed by the soil.

Holding Nikos' head by the ear and displaying it to the Wolven at the entrance, he roared once again. "Behold, the head of your wise and powerful leader. Ulv Nikos is dead, I am taking his place!"

The other Wolven snarled at the haggard Forsaken and argued against him, ceasing their attack to comprehend the event they just witnessed. One of the Wolven warriors stepped forward and spoke to Wrath in their mother tongue, hissing and growling at the victor.

Wrath growled back and then puffed his chest out, bellowing in the language of the Forsaken. "My soul is Wolven. My strength is Wolven. Do any of you want to challenge me on that?" Blood still dripped from his teeth, complementing his intimidating eyes. The Wolven whimpered and grumbled amongst themselves, conflicted. "Well?"

After a long silence, the Wolven bowed to their new leader who tossed the head of the former Ulv to his Forsaken counterparts. "My name is Ulv Wrath! Wolven, escort these Forsaken out of my den and let them go free. Then tell all the other Wolven that their new Ulv is staying right here!"

Many of the Wolven troops bowed and grumbled, but others seemed less than accepting of their new leader, and they growled before speeding off down the corridor ahead of the compliant ones. None of the living Wolven dared challenge the display of power they had just witnessed. It was in their tradition, in their blood to respect strength, and only the strongest Wolven could claim the position of Ulv.

The few remaining Wolven grumbled at the Forsaken Wolven to follow them out of the den, but one of the undead turned to Ulv Wrath. "If you are leading here, then what do we tell the queen, Ulv Wrath?"

"Bring her the head; tell her I am staying here with my people. Tell her that the Wolven no longer regard the Forsaken as enemies and tell her that this doesn't mean she can get her dirty dead hands on our shard. I was born a Wolven, I died a Wolven, and I still walk here on Naeisus as a Wolven!"

"Very well. We shall return to Queen Lucia with the head, but she will not like you staying here."

"Then she can deal with that problem herself."

The Forsaken followed the living Wolven out of the den and emerged above ground in the Triash Forest.

* * *

The Forsaken Wolven returned to the Undying Fortress under the dark shroud of night, with the head of the former Ulv Nikos. The heavy gates creaked open to let them through.

Captain Levana greeted them looking cruelly smug. "Ah! The head of Nikos." She grabbed the giant Wolven head with both hands and held it close to her face. The head still displayed an expression of pain and suffering, warming the captain's cold heart and bringing a wide smile to her face.

"Looks like his death was not quick or enjoyable! Tell me, did he suffer? Please say he suffered!"

The captain danced with the head, spinning, twirling, and humming a little tune to herself. Her shoulder-length hair swished behind her as she spun and giggled at the head. She paused her entertaining dance to glance around for Wrath. "Oh, and where's Wrath?"

"Wrath pulled Nikos's head from his body while he was still alive, then took his place as Ulv of the Wolven," replied one of the soldiers meekly.

Captain Levana halted her dancing altogether and dropped her arms, still gripping the massive Wolven head by its ear like a child gripping a teddy bear in the night. As her arms dropped, so did her face.

"He made himself Ulv? And the Wolven haven't challenged him on that?"

"His display of power was too impressive to be questioned. He said he is still a Wolven in his soul and is remaining there to rule his people. He also said that the Wolven no longer consider the Forsaken as enemies. If the queen—"

The captain raised her hand, silencing the warrior as he spoke, and stomped towards him. "Whoa whoa, hold that tongue of yours, dog. Follow me, now! Just you. You other three are free to go."

Captain Levana led the Forsaken Wolven up the steps of the central spire and into the queen's chambers.

Queen Lucia stood against the window staring longingly out at the busy night sky and the two eclipsing moons.

"My Queen, the mission was a mild success." The captain ushered the warrior to step forward.

Queen Lucia turned to see the head of Nikos sailing through the air towards her. She caught it with both hands and cheered, walking to a new, custom-built shelf above her throne and placing the head atop it. "Levana, my dear, why did you say the mission was only a *mild* success?" The queen's eyes flitted between the captain and the warrior, looking for any clues as to the bad news.

"This puppy here will tell you. Go ahead, dog; tell her what you told me."

Captain Levana shoved the Forsaken towards the queen and ordered him to talk.

"M-My Queen, Wrath is now, the Ulv of the Wolven."

"The bloody Ulv," interrupted the captain. "A Forsaken is now the leader of the entire Wolven race. And you know what else? He renounced his Forsaken identity."

The queen looked to her feet and huffed. "Such a shame. Wrath was strong."

The captain walked to the wall and plucked a mace off its display mount, fingering the spikes on the end of the heavy steel ball. The Forsaken Wolven swallowed hard at an impending sense of doom clouding the room but stared with a plea behind his eyes at the queen's smiling face.

"Don't worry; he no longer regards the Forsaken as enemies. Isn't that right, dog?"

Before the innocent Forsaken warrior had a chance to respond, Captain Levana leapt into the air and smashed the mace over the back of his head, cracking his skull and allowing his now soulless body to slump to the floor. Agitated, she turned to the queen. "So now the Wolven will know all of our weaknesses. They know our plans, they know—"

"Hush, my dear Captain. Calm yourself," said the queen with a raised finger. "This could very well work in our favour. If we keep Wrath on our side, we have the might of the Wolven with us. Wrath has single-handedly eliminated our largest threat." She wore a satisfied smile.

A wide grin flashed across Captain Levana's face. "I suppose he has."

"The Forsaken will rise once more, my dear," whispered Queen Lucia, a quiet flame burning in her blood-red eyes.

Chapter 13

Vengeance

The snow fell thick and fast over Straeta, bringing a sharp, frosty wind with it. King Areth reached out a hand and brushed snow away from Sir Victor's grand headstone. The king had him buried beside the great mound of earth that represented Tur, the Yultah of the land. Tur was also associated with strength and this fitted the valiant knight best, he thought. The mound itself had a small base and a sharp incline, forming more of a pillar than a mound, and was one of six representations of the Yultah in the cemetery.

The cemetery itself formed a large ring around the main church, with the six representations evenly spread about its interior. The closer one was buried to one of these revered symbols, the more respect that person had earned during their life.

Most of the royal family were buried around the statue of the sun on the north side representing Mys, the Yultah of light; for their reigns were often filled with joy and happiness. Opposite this statue, to the south, was a similar stone representation of the moons, Bo and Dalon, symbolising Dion, Yultah of Darkness. Evenly spread around the rest of the cemetery, were not only the mound of Tur, but also the circular fountain of Bui, Yultah of water, the giant headstone of Knas, and the young Triash tree of Gol, the Yultah responsible for life.

The king stood in a long bearskin coat to shield him from the cold, but underneath he wore his formal wear in royal purple, ready for the Small Council meeting this morning. He wore his gleaming gold crown atop his auburn hair, now falling just beyond his shoulders, and raised a hand to stroke the thick red beard that kept his face warm over the winter cycles.

"I miss you, my friend," said the king with a lump in his throat. "The cycle of Dion has passed, and I still cannot find one to fill your boots. There are none as strong or as trustworthy as you, and none I consider as close to me as you were. Part of me hates you for leaving me. Why, Sir Victor? Why now? Who will protect my children and I? Who will teach Areth how to fight and be fierce in combat?" A tear trickled down his cheek and he began to stutter his words, barely holding back the flood of emotion that tried to take over his body.

"Sir Victor Broadbeard Blackrock..." He silently chuckled at the memory of that conversation. "I promise you, I will avenge you. I will destroy the Forsaken and I will take Levana to Knas personally if I have to! I hope death is nicer than this life, I hope you're in a better place. I will see you soon, my friend, but not before I'm done with those bastards. I love you, Sir Victor, and I will never forget you."

At that moment, King Areth felt a gentle tug at his hand. He wiped away the tears in his eyes and turned his head to see young Eleanor's solemn face looking up at him.

"Father, it's okay. Don't be sad, Sir Victor is in the happy place now, just like mummy."

The king picked his daughter up and hugged her tightly, resting her on his hip. "You're smart for seven, my little one." He coughed and cleared his throat to hold back another surge of emotion.

Eleanor's perfect smile warmed his heart. He stroked her shimmering sunset-coloured hair and kissed her forehead softly. "I'm proud of you, Eleanor. I'm proud of all four of you. Come on, it's cold out here, let's go inside and warm up by the hearth."

"Don't forget your important meeting, Daddy," she reminded him with pride.

"Of course! The council meeting! Where would I be without you, my sweet?"

Eleanor giggled before King Areth carried her away from the church and up the cobbled hill to Straeta Keep, the snow crunching under his heavy boots as he went.

Once inside, the king placed Eleanor on a large armchair beside the raging hearth. The interior of the keep's library was warm and dry, and his other three children sat in their own armchairs reading a selection of books from the literature rich shelves. Areth buried his nose in a history book, Evelyn's eyes darted across pages of a fantasy story about princesses and castles, and little Anya perched on Lissy's lap, trying her best to read from a children's book that Lissy herself had written especially for the young princess.

Areth glanced at his father and turned the book to show the page he was on. A sketch of a heroic-looking figure in full battle armour stood out on the page. "Father, the book states this is King Areth I, and he looks just like you! Even his hair is the same!"

"Your fascination with Naeisan history never fails to make me smile, my boy."

The king looked over at the finely pencilled sketch, squinting a little to focus his eyes. "Ah yes, the first notable King of Mankind, and our great ancestor and namesake, no less! He was rumoured to be the only king without a beard, but I'm not sure how true that is!" He chuckled. "That isn't to say you have to have a beard to be King, of course."

"What became of him, Father? This book seems incomplete."

King Areth took a few slow strides over to where his son sat and perched himself on the thick leather arm of the chair. He leaned in and began to explain their history in his own words.

"That book was written by King Areth II, his son. The story goes that King Areth I died at the Golzhad volcano, searching for a way to defeat the Wyrms, but after a fight with Knas herself, he came back and became the very first Forsaken. After the great War of the Wyrms, when Sir Peter defeated the Great Wyrm, he and his Forsaken warriors were exiled by King Areth II because the dead made the living feel uncomfortable, and also because the Forsaken King wanted his throne back from his son. Since then, the living and the dead have never seen eye-to-eye and it's only now I can understand why. There is something corrupt about them. Their souls may still be here, but they have lost some sense of morality."

All eyes fixated on the king, the mouths of the younger ones agape. Evelyn's brow furrowed and she tilted her head to one side. "Father, the Wyrms aren't real though. How did a Wyrm kill the king if they didn't exist?"

"Well, my child, some believe the legends of the Wyrms to be true. After all, there is documentation about them from back then. However, many believe them to be a metaphor for the fires of war that consumed Naeisus—much like the current situation. There is no record of the creatures at any other point in history and, indeed, no remains have ever been found. Perhaps your great ancestor just had a very vivid imagination!"

"What do you believe, Father?" Her large jade eyes gazed expectantly into his, awaiting a reassuring response.

"It's hard to say, my sweet. With no physical evidence to go by, I would have to agree that they are likely a myth."

Evelyn grinned at the response and sank her head back into her book. Areth looked puzzled at his father's recollection of history and asked; "Father, how do you know this if the book is incomplete?"

"My son, although incomplete in places, the library's texts are still rich." He swept a hand around the room, gesturing to the shelves. "I aim to complete many of the books some day, and I'm documenting my own record of history. It's an important role of the king. Our successors will need to know what happened during our lives, to better judge the situations they are in."

"This book doesn't detail what became of King Areth II," replied the prince.

Proud of his son's thirst for knowledge, the king smiled again and gathered the attention of the room. Everyone folded their books shut and stared, anticipation gripping their curious minds. King Areth cleared his throat and looked at each of his children in turn, and then to Lissy.

"King Areth II was betrayed... usurped by the cruel King Jasper I. Our bloodline thrived, however, and eventually King Jasper's bloodline was eliminated completely, and was replaced by King Iain I. His bloodline ruled for many centuries until my father, King Iain XIV, fell in love and married a young red-headed woman by the name of Tilde—my mother, and your grandmother. Together, they had two sons, Iain, and myself.

"Sadly, Iain died of a horrible disease when he was still a boy and so the throne was passed to me. Tilde knew of her royal heritage, and so she named me. We have the blood of two royal lines, and with their joining, some say the throne has finally returned to the correct family, and name."

Areth's jaw dropped and his face became a picture of excitement. "Whoa, I never knew you had a brother, Father! What was he like?"

"I don't remember much, I was only a baby when he passed away, even younger than Anya." The king gestured towards his youngest who giggled away on Lissy's knee. "He was nearly ten solars older than me. When my parents lost him, they brought me up to rule in his place, much like I'm teaching you, son. Do you remember Grandma Tilde?"

"Only a little, I remember her white hair and how kind she was."

"She was a great woman, although after my father died, she lost all motivation and passed to Knas a few solars later, when you were very little."

The room fell silent once more. King Areth glanced out of the window at the blizzard outside and looked over to Lissy. He cleared his throat once again, getting her attention. "Shall we attend this meeting then?"

Lissy nodded and stood, placing Anya down with the book which the girl continued to read. The king whipped off his bearskin coat, hung it on a nearby coat rack, and brushed himself down before heading off with Lissy to the council meeting.

Inside the Grand Council chamber, Philos and William sat at the circular table with three empty seats remaining. King Areth took his place at the northernmost seat, and Lissy to his left. The seat to his right, however, remained vacant. He glanced at it for a moment and then his eyes dropped to the floor. He adjusted his seating and brought himself back to the people present at the table. Silence hung in the air whilst everyone waited for their King to initiate the meeting. Normally, he'd start with Sir Victor and gather military reports.

Lissy took control and started the meeting, glancing at King Areth. "The treasury is collecting well, Your Grace. The people are paying their taxes on time; the shard is still safely where you left it. I have no further details to report." She nodded reassuringly, urging him to continue.

He stuttered for a moment before finding his words. "Very good, Lissy. Thank you. Erm... William, reports on resources?" His voice carried intense sadness, which was reflected in his dulled, tired eyes.

"Yer Grace, we're fully stocked fer winter an', fanks to mining ships to Traegor, our stone deposits are now higher'n ever." William cleared his throat and shifted his weight. "If we be needin' more walls or buildin's then we need not worry about the means to build 'em. We 'ave enough food to keep the 'ole population 'ealthy through the win'er."

"Good. Philos, technology?"

Philos reached a bony hand inside his robe and from it produced a strange contraption. He placed it on the table for all to admire and reclined with a smug grin on his thin, aged face.

King Areth examined it carefully. It was a long tube, about the size of his forearm, with a curved handle at the end and another small piece of metal on which to place one's finger.

"What is it? What does it do?"

"Careful with it, Your Grace! It's still a prototype and may not function as expected. It's a Fireball propeller, but I call it a Firella for ease of speech. You hold the curved bit, rest your finger on this trigger here, aim it at your enemy, and apply pressure to the trigger. It launches a smaller version of those Fireballs I gave you at high velocity. With such power, they may actually penetrate the armour or flesh of one's enemy and explode within them." A darkness infected his speech and a strange grin wrapped around his face as the others gasped in awe.

For a moment, the rest of the council members stared in disbelief.

The king examined the Firella with intense curiosity, rotating it and eyeing it from all angles. He placed the device on the table and leaned forward, resting his elbows. "I'm impressed, Philos. How many of these can you make?"

It had better be enough to crush the Forsaken.

"I'm still working on a few issues, but I suspect I can produce up to fifty per lunar cycle, perhaps more if my funding was increased . . ."

"Fifty, eh? That's three-hundred per solar." The king's voice grew more powerful, "How much would you need to produce five hundred per solar cycle?"

Lissy lightly grasped his bicep and gave him a desperate look. She didn't say anything, but he knew what she was trying to convey. He smiled from the side of his mouth, before looking to Philos for his answer.

"Five hundred? I would estimate, say, an additional cost of five hundred gold pieces per lunar."

The king pushed the Firella towards the old man and nodded. "Done. Lissy, can you arrange for an extra five hundred gold pieces to go to Eveston each lunar cycle?"

"Sire, I'm not sure we can afford—"

"Then raise the taxes. I want my army equipped with these as soon as possible." He slammed a hand onto the table. The echo of the impact drifted around the room until it fell into silence.

Philos returned the Firella to his coat and coughed. "Sire, we really should decide on the next Master of Arms."

Everyone shuffled in their seats, their gazes listed around the room.

"No, Philos, we shouldn't. When the time is right, I will select someone personally." He silenced the room again and stood in a hurry, brushing the creases from his violet jacket. "If that is all, please excuse me." He bowed to the council.

William raised a hand, but a fierce glare from the king forced him to lower it again and shake his head, as if he never really had anything to say.

King Areth strode from the room, leaving the other three council members in an awkward silence. Philos rose from his seat and ambled out of the meeting chambers, shutting the door behind him as went.

Lissy and William looked at one another with concerned faces.

"His Majesty hasn't been well since the terrible loss of Sir Victor." William's brow furrowed as he stroked his beard. "'e needs another Master of Arms. 'is army has no effective commander and dunno what to do with 'emselves. In this state, we're all open to attack."

"Yes, you're right. Luckily, we have many good allies. Ulv Nikos isn't likely to attack us, and the He'en regards us as allies. Our only real threat is the Forsaken, but after the pounding we gave them, they are probably still licking their wounds. It's unlikely they'll mount a full-scale assault on us now." Lissy attempted to comfort herself as much as she did William.

"Even so, it unsettles me greatly. 'e needs to snap outta this grief before something truly bad 'appens. The ground tremors are worsening each day, an' we still 'aven't identified where the second set are comin' from."

"Is there another volcano to the east?" pondered Lissy aloud.

"Not that any of us are aware of. All that lies in that direction is the old ruined Korkrenus city of Taktuun, but there ain't been nothin' there fer centuries. Ever since the shatterin', both Joktuun and Taktuun have been entirely deserted, an' there 'ave been no credible sightings of a Korkrenus." William rested his full face in one of his shovel-like hands.

"Still, something is there, and something is causing these tremors." She folded her arms. "Hopefully your son and the rest of the scouts will return soon with news—they've been gone for several cycles."

"Per'aps there is somethin' further out to sea, but nobody 'as a ship capable of sailin' out that far, let alone a method of navigatin' the open ocean."

Both sat in silence for a moment, allowing their minds to wander aimlessly through the sea of thoughts that filled their heads.

Lissy placed her palms on the table and drove the conversation forward. "Still, our concern right now is the king. How do we fix this? How do we make him see that, despite his awful loss, he needs to move forward?"

"Can't you try talkin' to him? You know 'e has a soft spot for you, Lissy. 'e listens to you."

"I'll try again, but tomorrow. I think for today he should just spend time with his children; they never fail to lift his heavy heart."

"Okay, but don't leave it too long. 'is grief is beginnin' to rule over 'is good sense; he's becomin' obsessed with vengeance. It's only a matter o' time before 'e puts a dangerous plan of revenge into action and, as the King, we 'ave no right to disobey 'im." William's dull grey eyes reinforced his stern position. "We can only advise."

"You speak wise words, William. I promise I will speak with him tomorrow. Let us allow his children to lift his mood today, allow him some sleep to help him heal, and tomorrow I shall discuss the need for filling the position of Master of Arms with him. Perhaps another good friend like Sir Jacob, or Sir Markuss."

"*If* either one would wanna give up their respective posts. I know Sir Markuss takes 'is duty on the outpost very seriously. It's unlikely the king would want anyone else to watch over the land. As fer Sir Jacob, 'is life is with Timbrol and guardin' the crossin'. Per'aps Lady Sasha would want such a position though."

"She is strong and fierce, that much is true. Her skills with a sword are tough to match, but I feel that she and the king are not that close. It will be tough for him to find another friend like Victor. They practically grew up together. He has suffered a loss, like losing a brother. It will take time." Lissy fiddled with a frill on the cuff of her blouse.

William pushed his seat backwards. "Lets 'ope fer our sakes it don't take 'im too long."

"Tomorrow, dear William. Tomorrow I will try my best."

"Very good, m'lady. Please excuse me, I must be headin' back to Timbrol West to attend to the fishin' vessels."

The two remaining council members rose from their seats and strolled to the doors, opening them wide and passing through. They bowed to one another before heading in opposite directions to attend to their duties.

* * *

King Areth tucked his two youngest daughters into bed. Areth and Evelyn read quietly to themselves in their own rooms before they slept, but Eleanor and Anya still shared a bedroom and they loved for their father to tell them made up stories before they slept.

He sat at the foot of Anya's bed as she snuggled herself in cosily and then he looked across to her sister's bed. "Are you ready, my little ones?"

"Yes," they replied in sweet unison.

"What story would you like to hear tonight?" He adjusted the cotton covers over Anya's shoulders.

"Ghosts," shouted Eleanor.

"Wyrms," objected Anya. "I don't like ghosts."

Eleanor's eyes widened, and she agreed excitedly to the suggestion of Wyrms, sitting up and nodding with enthusiasm.

The king chuckled and hushed the excited girls. "Okay, Wyrms it is. I can tell you some allegedly true stories about them! Remember earlier, I told you that no remains had ever been found, and that they were likely a myth? Well, there are some who claim to know of the creatures that once terrorised the land. Some folks believe that even today, they lie sleeping underground, waiting for the right time to burst out and lay flame to land."

He clawed his hands and proceeded to tickle his youngest. She squealed with delight until he stopped and continued with the story, both girls fixated on him. The king was an exceptional storyteller. He acted out every scene, he did all the voices of the characters, and he made all the noises of the Wyrms in his story of fire. He swooped his arms this way and that way and made swooshing noises as he performed. He walked about the room and tickled his daughters with a playful roar whenever a Wyrm attacked, and they giggled and wriggled free of the monster hands that prodded at their ribs.

Eventually, the story slowed, and his voice lowered. He began to tell the ending quieter and quieter watching as his girls' eyelids became heavier and heavier, until finally, they shut. His voice trailed off into a whisper as he saw their breathing slow and they drifted into a magical sleep, filled with wonderful dreams of dragons and castles and fantasy lands.

Their faces were still smiling as he blew out the candles by their bedsides, crept out of their room, and closed the door behind him. He walked quietly down the corridor and opened the door to Evelyn's room.

"Lights out, my sweet," he told her softly.

"Yes, Father." She blew her own candle out and pulled the bed sheets up to settle in. He shut her door and followed the corridor to Areth's room at the end where he peeped around the corner to see the boy also still up with his head stuck in another history book.

"Lights out, my boy."

Areth jumped at the interruption. He had been unaware of his father's entrance, but smiled when he realised. Shutting the book, he looked at the king. "May I get a cup of water first, please Father?"

"Of course, son. But straight to bed after."

"Yes, Father." Areth stood from his bed and grabbed the candle lantern from his bedside table.

The king left his son to it and headed to his own room; as he passed the windows, he watched Dalon's shadow moving in front of Bo's crescent. It was a wonderful sight, the moons dancing around one another with each passing night, and the king often stopped to absorb the beauty of the night sky for a while before heading to bed.

Tonight, however, exhaustion set in and so he carried himself off without paying much mind to the night sky.

* * *

Lissy enjoyed watching the night sky and the billions of tiny sparkles that decorated the pitch-black backdrop. She saw the moons' interesting shapes above Straeta Keep as she leaned on her windowsill. Her long, golden hair flowed down her back and over her silk nightgown, like a gleaming waterfall running into a pool of perfectly clear water. She scanned the sky through bright blue eyes, letting her imagination run wild with thoughts of the Yultah and lost loved ones.

She pondered for a moment about whether any of those other tiny dots was home to a land similar to this one, and whether there was another person on that other land also pondering the same things.

Various glows flickered on and off in the keep as servants and workers all settled in for the night, and when Anya's bedroom light went out, Lissy smiled to herself.

Suddenly, she bolted upright at something she thought she saw.

She squinted her eyes and looked harder. A great sense of dread trickled down her spine and her heart pounded through her chest. The blood that ran through her veins turned to ice and her breathing sharpened. There, on the side of the keep, she saw two silhouettes scaling the walls. Both appeared armed with what looked like short swords.

Assassins! But who would want the king dead? Nobody can get in from the outside, the gates are always shut!

Panic set in as she scrambled around the room. The people she cared about most in the world slept in that building, and the royal guards were still in disarray.

Grabbing her coat and pulling on her heavy boots as quickly as her small arms allowed, she made for the door. She paused just long enough to pick up a small dagger and tuck it into her coat before bolting out of the house.

Lissy hurried to the keep as fast as possible, careful not to slip in the snow. Her hair flowed in the freezing wind behind her as she ran and flakes of snow soaked her as they melted upon contact. Her lips and fingers began to turn blue in the icy air, but she pressed on, fuelled by her concern for the safety of the king, his children, and their daughter.

She ran up the main path leading to the huge doors, and screamed at the top of her lungs. "Areth! Areth! Open the door!" Desperation soaked her voice.

As she approached, she lost her footing on a patch of ice and fell to the ground with a painful thud, injuring her shoulder. She lay there for a moment, attempting to absorb the pain that was rapidly spreading to her side. Her ribs began to feel unusually wet. Her eyes widened as warm liquid soaked her side in stark contrast to the cold snow.

Lissy looked down and watched her tan leather coat darken to black. She pulled the coat to one side to reveal the dagger in her coat pocket, now impaled in her side. With a mighty tug and an agonising scream, she yanked the dagger free.

Blood poured from the wound as she crawled across the icy floor, no longer able to scream through the searing pain in her lung. She dragged herself to the huge wooden doors and thumped them as hard as she could with dwindling strength.

She strained to shout. "Areth…" With one final, feeble thump, she went limp and fell unconscious. Fresh blood oozed out of the stab wound, turning the snow beneath her scarlet.

Lissy lay there motionless as snow settled over her body, blanketing her.

* * *

King Areth pulled the duvet around his shoulders. His eyes immediately fell heavy as he began to drift off into another restless sleep. Since Sir Victor's death, his sleep had grown even more disturbed and was often interrupted by dreams which revolved around losing other loved ones.

That night, they were plagued with visions of great suffering. He saw blood dripping through his cupped hands. He felt his heart wrenching away from his body, and all around him was an air of foreboding and pain. He heard distant screams that chilled his soul, screams of children that grew louder and louder, until he jolted awake. He bolted upright and heard it again—another scream that fell silent in an instant.

The colour drained from his face and his heart leapt into his throat; this time he was not dreaming. He scrambled out of bed and hurtled out of his chambers, throwing open the door and bashing his shoulder on the way out.

Upon reaching the bedroom closest to him, the bedroom of Anya and Eleanor, he barged through the door, nearly pulling it from its hinges, and yelled into the room. "Girls! Girls! Answer me!"

Frantically scanning the blackened room, the king saw the shapes of Anya and Eleanor still resting in bed, unresponsive to his bellows. In the middle of the room, outlined against a shattered window, another small figure stood facing him. He squinted. The figure reached out a hand and spoke in a broken, disturbed tone.

"Father . . . I . . . I heard them . . . they screamed, and . . ."

The voice of his sweet Evelyn echoed in his ears, struggling to get her words out. He took a step towards her before freezing at the sight of another shadow looming behind her. Time stopped. The thumping of his heart deafened him. The shadow grew taller, larger, more menacing.

He reached a hand out to the sound of tearing flesh and crunching bones.

The silhouette of a dagger protruded from the chest of his eldest daughter. His ears tormented his frozen mind with the cacophony of every last splash of blood as it hit the cold stone floor. Tears rolled down his cheeks. He strained, willing himself awake, anything to end this nightmare.

His mind screamed at him to attack, to tear the limbs off the assailant with his bare hands, but his body refused to follow. Nothing moved. His blood ran as cold as the winter air outside, refusing him even the power of speech. He watched every slow second of the dagger disappearing back through the torso of his beloved child.

Her body, now limp and lifeless, seemed to take an age to drop to the ground where she remained motionless. In her place, a dark, evil shadow still gripped the blood-soaked blade in one hand. A mocking grin wrapped around the face of the shadow, revelling in the murder of these innocent children.

King Areth's body still refused to move, his mind now screaming louder than ever to do something, to say something, but shock and paralysis had set in deep. The shadow remained still, yet somehow a cold, light hand grip his shoulder. A light brush of hair against his opposite shoulder sent further shock and despair coursing through his veins.

A delicate whisper cadenced the symphony of death and horror. "Give Victor my regards, my dear."

The force of these words pushed a barrage of tears from the king's frozen eyes as his breath stopped. Left with just enough strength to tilt his head downwards, he saw another dagger, this time protruding from his own chest. Slowly, he found the courage to raise his hands enough to cup them together and catch the flowing blood which leaked through his fingers, bathing them in warmth. He released the pool of blood in his hands and grabbed hold of the sharp edge of the blade. It ripped through his body leaving the rest of his life to seep out of the wound soaking his silk nightclothes. His legs weakened as the seconds ticked by until they gave out beneath him. As he fell, he reached out with one bloody hand, and rested it on the head of his beloved daughter, lying beside him. Two familiar, muffled chuckles swarmed his ears. A dainty boot stepped in front of his eyes.

The cold stone floor consumed the king's body as consciousness slipped away. His beloved daughter's fine, soft hair in his palm brought one final curl to his lips.

* * *

Shock and mourning choked Straeta as news of King Areth's death travelled quickly. Shops and taverns were closed, the usually bustling market street was silent. Not a single person was sighted outside that day. The sun crested the walls of the quiet city, shining through the window of William Stone's comfortably cosy house where he and Sir Jacob sat in silence. Both men, strong and wise, were reduced to tears by the devastating truth that swept across the entire race of Man.

William's wife entered the room carrying a tray of tea and set it on a small table between them. They thanked her and she nodded, wiping a tear from her own eye before leaving the room.

After several moments, Sir Jacob found his voice again, albeit still weak and fragile from the news. "Dead, William? It cannot be... how?"

"Murdered. 'e was stabbed in the back and 'is head was . . . removed. By whom we do not know," replied William in a quiet and haggard voice. "But that ain't all."

"There's more?" Sir Jacob raised a hand to cover his open mouth.

"His daugh'ers were also found dead. They 'ad all suffered fatal stab wounds. It seems . . . the Sire may 'ave . . ." William paused and looked to the floor, raising a clenched fist to his beard and inhaling deeply. "He may 'ave witnessed 'is daugh'ers die."

Further shock took over and Sir Jacob's hand dropped. Lost for words, his thoughts turned to pondering what kind of twisted individual could murder innocent children as they slept.

Mrs Stone let out a hysterical cry as she listened in from the other room.

Some more moments passed before the knight found his voice again, able to ask more questions he feared the answers to. "What... what of the boy?" He swallowed hard, bracing himself for another devastating response.

"'is body ain't been found. 'is bedroom were empty when we checked. There was a large stain o' blood in the snow outside the main entrance to the keep, but it trailed away fer a bit and then stopped altogether. Whether it be the boy's blood or someone else's, we can't be sure."

A sense of anger overcame Sir Jacob as he curled his fist and smashed it on the arm of the chair. The pain that coursed through his hand and wrist couldn't contend with the pain he felt inside his heart.

"There's somefin' else you should know, Sir Jacob." William held back, almost afraid of passing on yet more terrible information.

Sir Jacob's eyes widened, a terrified look of desperation crossed his face.

"Miss Lector is also unaccounted fer. I stopped by 'er house to give 'er the news but the door were open and I couldn't find 'er inside. The Mys shard is also gone." William ruffled his beard with a shaky hand.

Sir Jacob dragged his sore, red gaze up from the floor to meet William's. "You don't think…"

"It ain't in Miss Lector's nature to pull off such a heinous crime," assured William. "I am adamant she 'as no part to play in this."

"We cannot be too careful, William. I'm putting out an order for her arrest. If we find her, she can answer some questions. Somebody has to pay for this!"

William raised his palms. "Please, Sir Jacob, try to keep a level 'ead," urged the Master of Resources.

"I want whoever is responsible for this crime to pay! Anyone with information should come forward. If anyone withholds information, they will be arrested. Make that known, William."

William bowed his heavy head and heaved his rotund frame from his armchair. "Apologies, Sir Jacob, but if you don't mind, I 'ave to arrange an urgent meetin' with Philos. 'e is the only other member of the council remaining. Between us, we 'ave to decide the fate o' Man." William gestured to the door.

"Of course. I must gather myself and announce the news to Timbrol East and West." Sir Jacob rose from his armchair and made towards the door. "I don't envy your position, William." He opened the door and stepped out, turning to William one last time with a face filled with fire and vengeance. "Hear me now, William. The persons responsible will pay, I vow it!"

He left and slammed the door shut behind him, causing William to jump a little before letting out a hefty sigh and slumping into his armchair to think. Mrs Stone's sobs drifted through the room from the kitchen.

Chapter 14

Disruption

The next morning rolled in and the stale air of death and mourning still lingered, spreading its tragic grip to the rest of Mannis. Mounted on his grey, scruffy kytling, William Stone left the confines of Straeta and began the short journey alone to the wondrous city of Eveston.

I must call a meeting with Philos. Someone is trying to eliminate the council, but who?

He had taken precautions in the form of a large battle hammer, which he rarely used. Only two of these giant hammers existed; they had been forged from granite, especially for William and his son. The hills grew larger ahead of him and sprawled across his entire line of sight.

The kytling began to slow as he reached the foot of these hills, but William urged him to climb. "Come on lad, you can do it. I'm sorry fer pushin' ye so 'ard but we gotta gets to Eveston. I promise I'll give ye a nice hunk o' meat when we make it." Upon reaching the summit, he dismounted and allowed the kytling some respite, tilting its head and pouring some water into its mouth from his large leather waterskin. From up here, the tall twisting spires of Eveston scratched the sky. Much like Straeta, the city appeared silent and lifeless. The kytling thanked him for the water by purring softly and ruffling his feathers, but the time soon came for William to mount up and begin the treacherous ride down the other side of the hills.

"Good boy." William's bird carefully placed its talons on the ground. It outstretched its stubby, rounded wings for extra balance as it made light work of the descent.

* * *

Riding up to Eveston's main gates, William halted while waiting for the guard to open the gates. He waited and waited, but nothing.

"'ello!" he boomed from atop his kytling.

A guard, adorned with the familiar silver trim typical of Eveston soldiers, appeared above the wall. "Eveston is closed today, Sir. I am not permitted to allow any person in or out."

Furious with this inadequate response, William bellowed back. "I am William Stone, member o' the King's council!" His face flushed red with fury as he yelled. "I order you to allow me in at once! I need ta speak with Philos."

"I am under orders not to let you pass, Mister Stone," replied the guard.

"Orders? The King is dead! There is no 'igher rank than meself and Philos. Who has given you these orders?!"

"His Royal Highness, the new heir to the throne, Sir."

Fire built up in William's belly, just about ready to explode. "His Royal Highness?!"

"Yes, Sir. He demands that you attend a meeting with him in the capital."

"By 'ose orders is there now a new King? There was no meetin' ta authorise this!"

"The guards of Eveston answer only to His Majesty." The guard rested his hands atop the wall. "I am not permitted to divulge any further information."

"And this King o' yours is waitin' for me back in the capital, is 'e?" William glowered at the soldier atop the wall.

"He is, Mister Stone."

"May I at least enter fer supplies fer meself and the bird?" he asked, trying to control his rage.

"As I've said, Eveston is closed today. None may enter or leave."

"Fine! But don't pledge to this new King fer too long. Taking the throne is not 'is birth right, nor were it discussed." William reeled his kytling around and made tracks to Straeta.

* * *

Upon his return to Straeta, two well-dressed guards in full battle gear met William, both clutching a familiar handled tube holstered in a special pouch at their sides.

There was something a little odd about these guards; the trim around their breastplates shimmered silver, instead of the usual glimmering gold of Straeten guards.

"Mister Stone, please dismount your kytling and come with us," said one of the guards.

"Where are the Straeten guards?" bellowed the infuriated Master of Resources.

"Please follow us, Mister Stone. The King requests your presence."

Desperation penetrated William's voice. "The King is dead! There is no King, this is what I'm 'ere to discuss."

"The Sire will see you now, Mister Stone." One of the guards produced a smaller version of the Firella prototype Philos had displayed at the last council meeting and prodded it into William's chest. He reached for his heavy hammer but stopped immediately as the other guard pointed a Firella at his face.

"I'll take that, if you don't mind. Now follow us at once."

William begrudgingly gave up his battle-hammer, a heavy scowl decorating his livid, ruby faced. He followed one guard, while the other fell in behind him, his Firella pressed firmly in William's back.

Eveston guards flooded the city seemingly seeking something and every last one of them was armed with a Firella at their hip. As they approached the looming Straeten Keep, William kept his senses sharp and a watchful eye out for any clues.

It's barely been two days and already someone has taken over as King and seems to have the whole bloody army in their pocket. I wish Victor were still here—he'd never let this happen.

William tried to pry some information from the guards, if nothing else, to break the deafening silence of the usually bustling capital. "Who is this new King?" he demanded.

"You will meet him soon, Sir."

"Where is Philos? 'e should be 'ere, too!"

"Philos is already in the council chambers, you are the only one left to attend." The guard thrust the Firella deeper into William's heavily padded back.

"I bow to no false King! An' ease up with that thing!"

"We shall see, Sir," said the guard, in no way easing his force with the Firella.

The haste of the scurrying guards got the better of William's curiosity as he spoke up again. "Where are the Straeten guards? What are you Eveston guards looking for?"

"We are seeking those who do not accept the new King."

"What? What are you doing with these people?"

"Execution, Sir." responded the nonchalant guard.

William silenced himself, retreating into his own mind to figure things out.

I'd best keep quiet. I need to know who this new false King is and stop him somehow. If I can get word to Sir Jacob and rally the support of the Timbrol troops—

His thoughts stopped there, as the door of the keep swung open before him. A familiar dark patch remained on the ground, staining the snow. The guards escorted him down the long corridor to the council chambers at the end.

"The King wishes to see you alone, Mister Stone."

William pushed the door and stepped inside the same council chambers where he'd attended countless meetings before.

In the grand chair of King Areth III, hunched over the table grinning to himself, sat the old man, Philos. His wispy beard tickled the table and exaggerated his haggard, bony face.

William stepped forward and the door slammed behind him, causing him to check it with a start. He looked around the room for other people, but the two of them were quite alone.

Philos helped himself to his feet rather feebly and picked up the large Firella he had been hunched over.

"You?" William asked with much confusion.

"Me, what?" Philos chuckled, his voice frail and cracked.

William backed against the door. "You killed him, didn't you?" he cried.

"The King? No. No, that wasn't me, but I would shake the hand of whoever did it," he replied with glee.

William pressed his palms against the door a little as Philos began to creep around the table.

"But why? Philos—"

"King Philos I to you, Mister Stone!" Philos somehow found a powerful, deep voice, that came out of nowhere.

"Why would you want this?! King Areth was a great leader!"

"Great? That snivelling coward was giving all of our shards away with the promise of alliances. Look how that turned out! His death was a blessing to Man. The best part is that his children were killed too, so there can be no contention for the throne. Whoever did it also took out Lissy, it seems... or perhaps it was her. If it was, then she's done me another favour and taken herself out of the picture." He grinned, showing his grotesque, blackened teeth. "With Victor gone as well, it leaves just us, my friend."

"How dare you soil the King's good name! He 'ad a plan, it were working, and 'e loved his people." William stamped forward, scowling at Philos.

"He was a coward! With me in charge we will double our military forces. The people will all begin working in my workshops to produce the greatest weapons this world has ever seen. We start with these Firellas, but with time comes bigger and more powerful weapons, capable of tearing down walls and buildings. Man will be feared once again, and when all the shards belong to us, we will recreate the Yultah Crystal and eliminate all other threats to us!"

As Philos squirmed his way around the table, William held his ground, showing no fear. "Yer mad! What makes you think this'll work?"

Philos chuckled and proudly displayed his new model Firella to William, showing off its simple barrel and refined edges. He gestured to a small chamber on top of the device and tapped it gently with his bony finger.

"You see this? This is my latest and best invention. No longer do you need to re-arm after each shot. This chamber allows for multiple explosive balls to be fired from the device, one after another. Unlike the others, Mister Stone, this one is no prototype." He cackled again and stared William down from within his blackened, deep set eyes.

"But how? Who in their right mind would follow a corrupt, filthy traitor like you?"

"Fools with the promise of riches and better weapons! I've been in control of the Eveston guards for many solars, right under His Majesty's nose, and he was far too blind to even notice. Ha! Just another display of his idiocy. I was planning on waiting until he had more shards, but it seems somebody else hated him as much as I did and got there first. What a stroke of luck." He loomed ever closer to William, stopping just a few short steps from him.

"You bastard! You'll never succeed, Philos. Not as long as I 'ave breath in me body." William stepped back again and reached behind him for the door handle. As he pushed, the lock of the doors engaged. He dropped his arms to his sides, refusing to avert his gaze from the old man.

"Oh, what a pity. At least you'll be able to see your *beloved* King again," he jeered.

Philos raised his Firella with an outstretched arm and took aim at an unperturbed William.

"Go ahead, Philos. Kill me now. I will never accept you as me King, and neither will the people."

"The people won't have a choice, my friend."

Philos cackled as he squeezed the trigger. A miniature explosion in the Firella sent a pellet hurtling at William's chest. The pellet contacted William's sternum and then exploded, cracking open his ribs and tearing through his heart. He collapsed to the ground, his blood splattered throughout the council meeting room.

Upon hearing the shot, the guards outside released the lock on the door and opened it.

"Pity..." mumbled Philos as he stepped over the body of William Stone and left the council chambers. "Clean this up."

* * *

A vermillion hue hung in the air over the disrupted cities of Man. Eveston guards gathered frightened citizens, pulling them from their homes and marching them to the courtyard outside the keep. From every angle more guards surrounded the crowd with Firellas raised, threatening the masses.

Philos watched from the balcony, a manic grin painted on his face and the crown clutched in one hand. He raised his other hand and the cacophony settled.

He opened his mouth and powerful voice that surely did not belong to him emerged. "My people! It is with a heavy heart that we accept the loss of King Areth III. It is with sadness I also report the loss of his children. The other members of the King's council have unexpectedly gone missing, but it is suspected they are the ones who assassinated our great leader and have now fled, fearing the repercussions. As the only surviving member, I will be your new King," he roared in a strong and powerful voice. He stood tall with a straight back, nothing like the frail old man people were used to. "King Philos I!"

The crowd remained silent and stared blankly at Philos as he raised the crown above his head and lowered it into place before spreading his arms.

A voice cut through the silence. "Boo!"

Philos raised his arm and a nearby guard's Firella raised with it. The bang of the weapon paled in comparison to the screams of the naysayer and surrounding citizens on the receiving end.

"Do we have any further objections, my people?"

Reluctantly, the people began to clap. The clapping grew louder, but not more enthused; the people clapped out of fear for their own safety, not in acceptance of the new King Philos I.

The noise subsided, and Philos spoke his first decrees as King. "As you have all just witnessed, any disobedience under my rule will be met with execution. There will be no revolutions, there will be no resistance. If you work for me and show me respect, I will offer you the same respect. It is time for Man to rise! No longer will we be a target for the other nations. No longer will we roll over and hand our shards to others! We are a military nation!" Philos spread his arms wide, grinning at his horrified subjects. "As King, I am now recruiting as many able-bodied men, women, and children as possible. Anyone who does not wish to fight for me will be put to work researching, refining, and creating new weapons and armour for our military."

The people grimaced at him with a mixture of disgust and worry, and a ruckus began to stir. The surrounding guards raised their Firellas, and the noise subsided. The influence of the old man had been displayed and the people daren't object to him now.

He paused to scrutinise the crowd before continuing his tyrannical speech, fuelled by a lust for power. "When our weapons are truly superior, and our army is vast, we will sweep Naeisus in search of the shards and eliminate anyone that stands in our way! They are with us, or they die!"

A handful of citizens cheered at the thought of a military-based nation with greed in their eyes and began to chant King Philos I's name in support.

The new king raised his hands and grinned at the crowd as more people joined in with the chanting, his dark robe sleeves falling to his shoulders.

In one final attempt to win over the rest of the crowd, he made a closing statement. "There is a lot of work ahead, my friends, but I believe I have the strength to make the decisions that our beloved King Areth III couldn't. Once the Yultah Crystal is ours, we will all have a say in creating utopia for every last citizen. No longer will we need to fear anything... not even death!"

Within moments, almost the entire crowd erupted into claps and cheers. A minority still were not willing to participate, but for the sake of their own safety, they remained quiet. King Philos I began to cheer along with the supportive crowd before heading inside the keep attending to his first order of business.

He made his way to the throne room and carefully sat upon the royal throne, absorbing the grandeur of the situation. He called in a guard to discuss further matters. The guard strode in with more confidence than his stocky frame could contain. Despite his diminutive height, this guard had clearly seen battle, as revealed by the large scar running from the corner of his eye to his jawline, like a tear streaming down his strong, stubbly face.

"You there, what is your name?"

"Ralph, Your Majesty," replied the guard in a deeper voice than one would expect from a man of his stature.

"*Sir* Ralph now. Consider yourself my right hand."

The young knight's mouth fell open. He ran his hand over his close-cut hair and bowed humbly. "I . . . I'm honoured, Your Grace," he managed to utter.

"From now on, you will report to me all the actions of the populace, and in return I will pay you handsomely. Got it?"

Sir Ralph smiled, graciously accepting the offer of more riches and a position of command over his fellow soldiers. "Sire," he said, "what of the council?"

King Philos I stared from deep within his skull. "There will be no council, my friend. I will run everything, and where assistance is needed, I will call on you."

"Very good, Your Grace!"

"Sir Ralph, your first order is to write to the races of Forsaken, Wolven, and Marusi informing them of the *tragic* death of King Areth III and my rise to power. Further inform the Marusi and the Wolven that our alliances are still intact. We don't want any unexpected attacks now, do we?"

"At once, Your Majesty," responded the Knight about to leave.

"Oh, and Sir Ralph?"

Sir Ralph turned on his heels. "Yes, Your Majesty?"

"Did anyone ever find that awful bird belonging to the old king?" hissed King Philos I.

"No, Sire. It is thought the bird was either stolen or killed during the assassination."

"Good. I hated that thing. I would have killed it myself if it was still here." The king spoke with contempt as he waved Sir Ralph out of the throne room to attend to his first order.

Sir Ralph left in a hurry to carry out his orders while the new king sat and began to write some messages of his own. He grabbed a quill and a piece of parchment and began to write compulsory working orders for the people to be enforced by his military. In these orders, he wrote that all able-bodied individuals must choose a line of work. They may join the military, construct weapons, farm food for the populace, or mine resources for the construction of weapons. Any individual not working will be forcibly put to work for the benefit of Man, or executed where they stand if they refuse.

With an insatiable lust for power in his cold heart, he began to chuckle maniacally and muttered to himself after drafting these first orders. "Soon, we will have enough Firellas for the ten thousand soldiers who will be forced to fight for me. Under my rule, we will advance!"

* * *

Sha'koth stood and admired his new city in the gigantic Lake Rutra. This lake sat further west than their original home, and took up the majority of the

Turasis region. Although it was still a work in progress, he was pleased to find that enough Deepset coral existed at the bottom of this lake to construct Flurka, and give a home to his growing population.

Much like Alkra, this city hung like a gigantic bunch of grapes into the water, however, this time it nestled in a quiet cove shielded from manipulated weather conditions. The He'en again used the Bui shard to keep the waters of the lake settled, even when the natural weather turned sour.

Flurka gleamed with the same impressive radiance as Alkra once did, and Sha'koth proudly watched his people continue to heat and temper more titanic plates of Deepset coral to add to the impressive city. He scanned the surrounding land, taking in the wondrous vista of the Marusi's new home.

Unlike the Shu'ung lake, lake Rutra was not surrounded by mountains. Instead, almost the entirety of the land surrounding was flat, save for the cliffs to the southeast where Flurka sat. Vast hills and grassy plains engulfed the horizons for as far as the eye could see, and as Sha'koth continued to scan, he noticed a small shape approaching from the north.

As the shape got closer, the gleaming armour revealed a solitary soldier from Mannis, fast approaching on horseback. The He'en welcomed the soldier as he got nearer to the city, but the same nicety was not reciprocated.

Greeting one of the Marusi's allies with offers of food and drink did not seem to lighten this stern soldier's mood, as he simply pulled a scroll out of a pouch and thrust it at Sha'koth. "Message for He'en Sha'koth, from his Royal Highness, King Philos I."

Sha'koth scratched his pointed chin. "King Philos I?"

The rider didn't so much as acknowledge the He'en's question, instead, he sealed his satchel, reared his horse around, and rode away with an urgent haste.

Sha'koth broke the wax seal on the scroll and gently unfurled it to read the message contained within. As he read, his black eyes widened, and his gills shuddered. He dropped the scroll on the ground and sprinted to the lake's edge, calling all Marusi in earshot to the great central dome, before diving into the lake and entering his new city from underwater.

As he swam around the complex system of the city, he let out many shrill cries that cut through the water and alerted all Marusi that heard it to gather. The He'en's calling carried a great sense of urgency with it and his people gathered with an equal sense of haste to the biggest dome in the city.

Sha'koth climbed out of the water and entered the great dome, as thousands of Marusi flooded in. He made his way to a raised platform at one edge of the spherical enclosure and stood upon it, bringing silence to the masses. After a few moments, it seemed as though almost the entire population of Marusi stood comfortably in this titanic room.

Sha'koth began his speech in Maurish with a deep sense of despair floating through his voice, as it carried across the crowd.

"Men borthir . . . King Areth III til Man droth mil dorer . . ." A unified gasp carried across the room as the He'en broke the news of King Areth III's murder. He continued to inform his people about the promises made by King Philos I to honour the alliance, but his tone of voice made it clear he did not trust this new leader.

The room divided. Those who believed in the dreams of the deceased King sobbed and grieved, and those who did not shrugged at the news of his death. Mumbles and discussion filled the empty space, and Sha'koth raised his hands to settle the room once more.

He spoke louder, continuing his speech with a heavy heart and a lump in his throat. *"In addition to this grave news, I must remind you all that my time as He'en is nearly over. It's been ten solars since the last election and the elections for the new He'en are fast approaching. My final duty as He'en is to honour the great King Areth III—the Man who aided us in exacting revenge on the Forsaken and establishing our new home. Without him, we would be ruined, shardless and homeless."* He pounded his chest and a mighty humph rang throughout the room. He pounded again, the rest of his people joining him.

A chorus of thumps and humphs in honour of the fallen king filled the city.

Sha'koth finished his speech and left the stage. Every Marusi in the room disbanded to resume their usual business. The He'en retired to his throne room to think over what the future held for his people now that Naeisus' best hope for peace had been slaughtered in cold blood.

* * *

A disastrous rift had torn through the Wolven, with many refusing to accept a Forsaken as their new Ulv. Many attempts to challenge him were settled with a death, and as Ulv Wrath still sat on the wooden throne of the Wolven, none had been his. His displays of raw power and aggression during these contests of his leadership further secured his respect with the Wolven people. An Ulv without respect is no true Ulv, and Wrath had a harder time earning respect from his people than had any other Ulv before him.

He had managed to convince at least half of the pack of his dedication to being Wolven; however, the other half fled north to a second den that had been started by Ulv Nikos, and there they formed a rival pack. This rival pack had a new leader known as Ulv Rakos, and he had sworn to bring down the false Ulv.

As Wrath sat pondering the future of his people, one of his guards entered the room leading a small soldier adorned in Eveston steel armour into the chamber.

The Wolven guard growled and snorted at his leader, introducing him to the arrival of an Eveston soldier.

Ulv Wrath snarled, ordering the guard to leave as he received the message from Man.

"I have been ordered to give a message to Ulv Nikos," announced the soldier.

Despite his calm demeanour, the Ulv smelled the fear seeping from every inch of this tiny person. "Nikos is dead, I am the Ulv now. Any messages are to be given to me," he barked, snarling.

"Very well. King Areth III and his offspring have been murdered by an unknown assailant. In light of this tragedy, the people have elected King Philos I to the throne. King Philos I promises to uphold any alliances that his predecessor forged and hopes that a bright future can be shared by all." The soldier bowed as a mark of respect.

"I am not concerned by this news. Go and tell your new King that Ulv Wrath answers to nobody," he hissed.

The soldier remained silent and still.

Ulv Wrath roared at him to leave the den.

The soldier, while trying to maintain a fierce look of bravery, fled the room as fast as his legs allowed, tripping over roots as he went and picking himself up in a panic to continue his escape.

I care not about their little plights. For now, my only concern is unifying the Wolven. I must find a way to get the northern pack to reject Rakos and see me as a true Wolven. Killing him would serve to prove nothing, another would merely take his place. I must prove that I am still a true Wolven, something beyond renouncing my Forsaken identity. I am certain the strength of the Wolven pack will be restored if I prove myself.

* * *

Queen Lucia took a large draught of wine from an expensive goblet. "It looks like all of our plans are coming together, Captain," she chuckled.

Captain Levana raised her goblet. "I'll drink to that! Seems the Aithur's little deal is the push we needed."

The door crashed open to reveal a Forsaken soldier clutching a scroll. "Apologies for the interruption, my Queen, Captain," blurted the soldier.

"This had better be good..." scowled Levana.

"Now, now, my dear, let the man speak." The queen placed her goblet on the side table, folded her arms, and perched beside it.

"Thank you, my Queen. A messenger from Eveston came with this; he asked me to give it to you as a matter of urgency." He held the scroll out.

The queen walked over to the guard and slipped the scroll from his hand, not breaking eye contact with him, then lightly stroked his chin and dismissed him from the room. "That will be all, my dear. Run along now."

Captain Levana's face changed frightfully quickly from a joyous one to a dark and calculating scowl. "You think it's a declaration of war? They must know it was us."

Queen Lucia looked at King Areth III's head on the shelf, dwarfed by the giant head of Ulv Nikos beside it and laughed.

"I don't think he's going to tell anyone, do you, dear?"

"But what about the boy? We never found him—he is still alive, Lucia."

"Relax, Levana. If the boy ran, he wouldn't have survived the night. It's too cold; he would have frozen to death. Besides, if they knew it was us don't you think we'd have an army on our doorstep right about now?" She gestured out of the window at the barren wasteland.

"Just open the damn scroll, I'm itching for some more blood," demanded the captain with widening eyes.

The queen unfurled the scroll and read it to herself. She began to giggle, silently at first, but growing louder and louder until she laughed hysterically.

"What? What's so funny?" asked the impatient captain, attempting to look over the top of the scroll to catch the message.

"It says that King Areth III and all of his offspring have been murdered by an unknown assailant," read the queen aloud. She raised her eyes above the scroll to look at her captain. "See? That includes the boy."

"But we didn't—" interrupted Captain Levana, before silencing herself at the queen's scowl.

"I know, Levana, but listen to this. The people have elected King Philos I as their new king!"

"Wasn't Philos that creepy old guy on the council?" asked the captain.

"Apparently so. It also goes on to say that all matters are to be directed to King Philos himself, and that he will still honour any alliances that his predecessor forged." The queen scoffed at this letter. "It reeks of falsehood. I've been on Naeisus long enough to recognise it."

"So they have no idea it was us," exclaimed the excited captain.

"Assailant unknown, Levana. It seems not! It's funny though . . ."

"What is?"

"How they didn't mention *that*." said the queen, pointing at the Mys shard, resting gracefully in a dedicated slot in the throne. It shone by itself, showering the room with a soft, white glow.

"My guess is that they know whoever murdered the king has it, and since they don't know who murdered him, they want to play it safe. I bet the other leaders all got the same message. If they told everyone the shard was missing, it would leave them vulnerable." Queen Lucia smirked and tossed the letter out of the window. "It seems we have the upper hand, my dear."

The captain nodded to the head on the shelf. "My only worry is *him* coming back... He has the blood of the first, so we know he's capable."

"He's with his beloved children and the mighty Sir Victor; do you really think he's going to give them up, just to give us a telling off? Besides, his head is still here and the window of opportunity is fast closing."

"You're right, Lucie. In any case, I'm going to conduct some training for those pathetic troops."

The queen nodded, and the captain leapt out of her seat, marching out of the room with bloodlust in her eyes. Only the Forsaken knew of Man's vulnerability, and Captain Levana was more than prepared to exploit it.

Queen Lucia placed herself upon her throne and smiled, pondering the future of the Forsaken and dreaming of their rise to power. She was now just one head away from the Knas shard, which contained a power unknown to her.

* * *

As each leader lost themselves in deep thought about the future of their own people, the rumblings from the Golzhad volcano grew in power and frequency. The mysterious rumblings to the east also intensified and were now felt and monitored by more than just Outpost Sasha.

The dwindling populations of each race left each of them as vulnerable as the others, all caught in a delicate act of defending themselves, fighting for the shards of power, and growing in numbers. In a wicked twist of fate, it appeared the hope for peace and unity of Naeisus had died with the good King Areth III, and all of his work was left to unravel.

Unbeknownst to them all, another figure sat pondering the future of the land, and the entire fate of Naeisus hung in the balance. The tiniest bit of pressure applied to either side would tip the scales, causing a landslide of events that would forever change the world.

The figure sat poised, watching the land through scrutinous eyes, ready to apply that pressure.

Acknowledgements

*T*here are some people I'd like to express my gratitude to. Without them, Naeisus wouldn't be what it is today.

Mandy, Emma, and Dusty - Team Rhetoric Askew! The team who took me with immense enthusiasm. Thank you for believing in me and my story, and thank you a thousand times over for turning it into a reality. You are all amazing!

Miss Mumford, my old English teacher. It was because of your inspiring teaching and astounding praise for my GCSE schoolwork that I took up writing as an enjoyable hobby and eventually dreamed up and developed the world of Naeisus.

Ania, who stood by me and showed nothing but support and encouragement for my writing, even taking time away from writing your own Master's Thesis to beta read for me. Thank you.

Sammii, for being another like-minded fantasy enthusiast. Many of our conversations involve bouncing ideas back and forth, allowing me to unleash my creativity and explore avenues that hadn't occurred to me.

Steve, the guy who "doesn't read" yet smashed through the first draft in five days. The excitement this man holds for things he feels passionate about is unmatched. For weeks after your reading, you were unable to contain yourself and you spread the word about Naeisus far and wide.

Phil and James, the lads. Thank you both for being beta readers and supporting my journey, not only in my writing, but in life. You boys are always there.

The Asylum, the one group of people who are my chosen family. No blood is shared between us, but instead a supportive bond that would surpass that of even blood.

Every single other person who has ever shown support, encouragement, or even just a smile. Family, friends, Twitter family, social media supporters old and new, every single one played a part in making this a reality.

Thomas Anthony Lay

*T*homas grew up in a village called Street in Somerset, UK. At the age of just 3, he decided he wanted to live with his father, Anthony 'Tony' Lay, which proved to be the foundation of his ambitious, full-of-life personality. His father was diagnosed with pancreatic cancer at the age of 47 and passed away just two months later, when Thomas was only 14. Although this loss weighed extremely heavily on Thomas, his determined mindset pushed him forwards, now propelled by a further desire to make his father proud.

After his father's death, he lived with his grandmother, and at the age of 15, he discovered his talent for writing—through school assignments that impressed his teacher and classmates. He pursued a career in IT and subsequently landed a full-time IT support job at the age of 18. It was during the slow, boring days at this job that Thomas realised that his talent was also his passion. It was also here that the world of Naeisus formed in his mind.

At the age of 23, Thomas found work as an IT Technician at his old school, where he found the freedom and happiness to continue writing. It is here he found more motivation, inspiring the students to realise their own talents, and subsequently finished his first book in the Naeisus universe. At 24 he bought his own house in Glastonbury, UK, and continues to write for fun.

Aside from writing, Thomas is an old school nerd and loves to play video games. His other hobbies include playing the guitar and cooking.

Find Thomas Online

FACEBOOK
WWW.FACEBOOK.COM/ThomasAnthonyLay

TWITTER
WWW.TWITTER.COM/TAnthonyLay

INSTAGRAM
WWW.INSTAGRAM.COM/Naeisus

WEB
WWW.NAEISUS.COM

EMAIL
THOMASANTHONYLAY@GMAIL.COM

WWW.RHETASKEWPUBLISHING.COM